4.50 from Paddington

AGATHA CHRISTIE

Published for

THE CRIME CLUB

by COLLINS, ST JAMES'S PLACE LONDON

HarperCollins*Publishers*
77–85 Fulham Palace Road,
Hammersmith, London W6 8JB
www.harpercollins.co.uk

This edition published exclusively for *The Times*
by HarperCollins*Publishers* 2009

First published in Great Britain by
Collins, The Crime Club 1957

Copyright © 1957 Agatha Christie Limited,
a Chorion company. All rights reserved.
www.agathachristie.com
Cover art and design © HarperCollins*Publishers* 1957, 2009

ISBN 978-0-00-785336-6

Printed and bound in Great Britain by
Clays Ltd, St Ives plc

CHAPTER I

Mrs. McGillicuddy panted along the platform in the wake of the porter carrying her suitcase. Mrs. McGillicuddy was short and stout, the porter was tall and free-striding. In addition, Mrs. McGillicuddy was burdened with a large quantity of parcels; the result of a day's Christmas shopping. The race was, therefore, an uneven one, and the porter turned the corner at the end of the platform whilst Mrs. McGillicuddy was still coming up the straight.

No. 1 Platform was not at the moment unduly crowded, since a train had just gone out, but in the no-man's-land beyond, a milling crowd was rushing in several directions at once, to and from undergrounds, left-luggage offices, tea-rooms, inquiry offices, indicator boards, and the two outlets, Arrival and Departure, to the outside world.

Mrs. McGillicuddy and her parcels were buffeted to and fro, but she arrived eventually at the entrance to No. 3 platform, and deposited one parcel at her feet whilst she searched her bag for the ticket that would enable her to pass the stern uniformed guardian at the gate.

At that moment, a Voice, raucous yet refined, burst into speech over her head.

"The train standing at Platform 3," the Voice told her, "is the 4.50 for Brackhampton, Milchester, Waverton, Carvil Junction, Roxeter and stations to Chadmouth.

5

Passengers for Brackhampton and Milchester travel at the rear of the train. Passengers for Vanequay change at Roxeter." The Voice shut itself off with a click, and then reopened conversation by announcing the arrival at Platform 9 of the 4.35 from Birmingham and Wolverhampton.

Mrs. McGillicuddy found her ticket and presented it. The man clipped it, murmured: "On the right—rear portion."

Mrs. McGillicuddy padded up the platform and found her porter, looking bored and staring into space, outside the door of a third-class carriage.

"Here you are, lady."

"I'm travelling first-class," said Mrs. McGillicuddy.

"You didn't say so," grumbled the porter. His eye swept her masculine-looking pepper-and-salt tweed coat disparagingly.

Mrs. McGillicuddy, who *had* said so, did not argue the point. She was sadly out of breath.

The porter retrieved the suitcase and marched with it to the adjoining coach where Mrs. McGillicuddy was installed in solitary splendour. The 4.50 was not much patronised, the first-class clientele preferring either the faster morning express, or the 6.40 with dining-car. Mrs. McGillicuddy handed the porter his tip which he received with disappointment, clearly considering it more applicable to third-class than to first-class travel. Mrs. McGillicuddy, though prepared to spend money on comfortable travel after a night journey from the North and a day's feverish shopping, was at no time an extravagant tipper.

She settled herself back on the plush cushions with a sigh and opened a magazine. Five minutes later, whistles blew, and the train started. The magazine slipped from

Mrs. McGillicuddy's hand, her head dropped sideways, three minutes later she was asleep. She slept for thirty-five minutes and awoke refreshed. Resettling her hat which had slipped askew, she sat up and looked out of the window at what she could see of the flying countryside. It was quite dark now, a dreary misty December day—Christmas was only five days ahead. London had been dark and dreary; the country was no less so, though occasionally rendered cheerful with its constant clusters of lights as the train flashed through towns and stations.

"Serving last tea now," said an attendant, whisking open the corridor door like a jinn. Mrs. McGillicuddy had already partaken of tea at a large department store. She was for the moment amply nourished. The attendant went on down the corridor uttering his monotonous cry. Mrs. McGillicuddy looked up at the rack where her various parcels reposed, with a pleased expression. The face towels had been excellent value and just what Margaret wanted, the space gun for Robby and the rabbit for Jean were highly satisfactory, and that evening coatee was just the thing she herself needed, warm but dressy. The pullover for Hector, too . . . her mind dwelt with approval on the soundness of her purchases.

Her satisfied gaze returned to the window, a train travelling in the opposite direction rushed by with a screech, making the windows rattle and causing her to start. The train clattered over points and passed through a station.

Then it began suddenly to slow down, presumably in obedience to a signal. For some minutes it crawled along, then stopped, presently it began to move forward again. Another up-train passed them, though with less vehemence than the first one. The train gathered speed again. At that moment another train, also on a down-line, swerved

7

inwards towards them, for a moment with almost alarming effect. For a time the two trains ran parallel, now one gaining a little, now the other. Mrs. McGillicuddy looked from her window through the windows of the parallel carriages. Most of the blinds were down, but occasionally the occupants of the carriages were visible. The other train was not very full and there were many empty carriages.

At the moment when the two trains gave the illusion of being stationary, a blind in one of the carriages flew up with a snap. Mrs. McGillicuddy looked into the lighted first-class carriage that was only a few feet away.

Then she drew her breath in with a gasp and half-rose to her feet.

Standing with his back to the window and to her was a man. His hands were round the throat of a woman who faced him, and he was slowly, remorselessly, strangling her. Her eyes were starting from their sockets, her face was purple and congested. As Mrs. McGillicuddy watched, fascinated, the end came; the body went limp and crumpled in the man's hands.

At the same moment, Mrs. McGillicuddy's train slowed down again and the other began to gain speed. It passed forward and a moment or two later it had vanished from sight.

Almost automatically Mrs. McGillicuddy's hand went up to the communication cord, then paused, irresolute. After all, what use would it be ringing the cord of the train in which *she* was travelling? The horror of what she had seen at such close quarters, and the unusual circumstances, made her feel paralysed. *Some* immediate action was necessary—but what?

The door of her compartment was drawn back and a ticket collector said, "Ticket, please."

8

Mrs. McGillicuddy turned to him with vehemence.

"A woman has been strangled," she said. "In a train that has just passed. I saw it."

The ticket collector looked at her doubtfully.

"I beg your pardon, madam?"

"A man strangled a woman! In a train. I saw it—through there." She pointed to the window.

The ticket collector looked extremely doubtful.

"Strangled?" he said disbelievingly.

"Yes, *strangled*! I saw it, I tell you. You must *do* something at once!"

The ticket collector coughed apologetically.

"You don't think, madam, that you may have had a little nap and—er——" he broke off tactfully.

"I have had a nap, but if you think this was a dream, you're quite wrong. I *saw* it, I tell you."

The ticket collector's eyes dropped to the open magazine lying on the seat. On the exposed page was a girl being strangled whilst a man with a revolver threatened the pair from an open doorway.

He said persuasively: "Now don't you think, madam, that you'd been reading an exciting story, and that you just dropped off, and awaking a little confused——"

Mrs. McGillicuddy interrupted him.

"*I saw it*," she said. "I was as wide awake as you are. And I looked out of the window into the window of the train alongside, and a man was strangling a woman. And what I want to know is, what are you going to do about it?"

"Well—madam——"

"You're going to do *something*, I suppose?"

The ticket collector sighed reluctantly and glanced at his watch.

"We shall be in Brackhampton in exactly seven minutes.

I'll report what you've told me. In what direction was the train you mention going?"

"This direction, of course. You don't suppose I'd have been able to see all this if a train had flashed past going in the other direction?"

The ticket collector looked as though he thought Mrs. McGillicuddy was quite capable of seeing anything anywhere as the fancy took her. But he remained polite.

"You can rely on me, madam," he said. "I will report your statement. Perhaps I might have your name and address—just in case . . ."

Mrs. McGillicuddy gave him the address where she would be staying for the next few days and her permanent address in Scotland, and he wrote them down. Then he withdrew with the air of a man who has done his duty and dealt successfully with a tiresome member of the travelling public.

Mrs. McGillicuddy remained frowning and vaguely unsatisfied. Would the ticket collector really report her statement? Or had he just been soothing her down? There were, she supposed vaguely, a lot of elderly women travelling around, fully convinced that they had unmasked communist plots, were in danger of being murdered, saw flying saucers and secret space ships, and reported murders that had never taken place. If the man dismissed her as one of those . . .

The train was slowing down now, passing over points, and running through the bright lights of a large town.

Mrs. McGillicuddy opened her handbag, pulled out a receipted bill which was all she could find, wrote a rapid note on the back of it with her ball-point pen, put it into a spare envelope that she fortunately happened to have, stuck the envelope down and wrote on it.

The train drew slowly into a crowded platform. The usual ubiquitous Voice was intoning:

"The train now arriving at Platform 1 is the 5.38 for Milchester, Waverton, Roxeter, and stations to Chadmouth. Passengers for Market Basing take the train now waiting at No. 3 platform. No. 1 bay for stopping train to Carbury."

Mrs. McGillicuddy looked anxiously along the platform. So many passengers and so few porters. Ah, there was one! She hailed him authoritatively.

"Porter! Please take this at once to the Stationmaster's office."

She handed him the envelope, and with it a shilling.

Then, with a sigh, she leaned back. Well, she had done what she could. Her mind lingered with an instant's regret on the shilling. . . . Sixpence would really have been enough. . . .

Her mind went back to the scene she had witnessed. Horrible, quite horrible. . . . She was a strong-nerved woman, but she shivered. What a strange—what a fantastic thing to happen to her, Elspeth McGillicuddy! If the blind of the carriage had not happened to fly up . . . But that, of course, was Providence.

Providence had willed that she, Elspeth McGillicuddy, should be a witness of the crime. Her lips set grimly.

Voices shouted, whistles blew, doors were banged shut. The 5.38 drew slowly out of Brackhampton station. An hour and five minutes later it stopped at Milchester.

Mrs. McGillicuddy collected her parcels and her suitcase and got out. She peered up and down the platform. Her mind reiterated its former judgment: not enough porters. Such porters as there were seemed to be engaged with mail bags and luggage vans. Passengers nowadays seemed always expected to carry their own cases. Well, she couldn't carry her suitcase and her umbrella and all her parcels. She would have to wait. In due course she secured a porter.

"Taxi?"

"There will be something to meet me, I expect."

Outside Milchester station, a taxi-driver who had been watching the exit came forward. He spoke in a soft local voice.

"Is it Mrs. McGillicuddy? For St. Mary Mead?"

Mrs. Gillicuddy acknowledged her identity. The porter was recompensed, adequately if not handsomely. The car, with Mrs. McGillicuddy, her suitcase, and her parcels drove off into the night. It was a nine-mile drive. Sitting bolt upright in the car, Mrs. McGillicuddy was unable to relax. Her feelings yearned for expression. At last the taxi drove along the familiar village street and finally drew up at its destination; Mrs. McGillicuddy got out and walked up the brick path to the door. The driver deposited the cases inside as the door was opened by an elderly maid. Mrs. McGillicuddy passed straight through the hall to where, at the open sitting-room door, her hostess awaited her; an elderly frail old lady.

"Elspeth!"

"Jane!"

They kissed and, without preamble or circumlocution, Mrs. McGillicuddy burst into speech.

"Oh, Jane!" she wailed. "I've just seen a *murder*!"

CHAPTER II

TRUE TO the precepts handed down to her by her mother and grandmother—to wit: that a true lady can neither be shocked nor surprised—Miss Marple merely raised her eyebrows and shook her head, as she said:

"*Most* distressing for you, Elspeth, and surely *most* unusual. I think you had better tell me about it *at once.*"

That was exactly what Mrs. McGillicuddy wanted to do. Allowing her hostess to draw her nearer to the fire, she sat down, pulled off her gloves and plunged into a vivid narrative.

Miss Marple listened with close attention. When Mrs. McGillicuddy at last paused for breath, Miss Marple spoke with decision.

"The best thing, I think, my dear, is for you to go upstairs and take off your hat and have a wash. Then we will have supper—during which we will not discuss this *at all.* After supper we can go into the matter thoroughly and discuss it from every aspect."

Mrs. McGillicuddy concurred with this suggestion. The two ladies had supper, discussing, as they ate, various aspects of life as lived in the village of St. Mary Mead. Miss Marple commented on the general distrust of the new organist, related the recent scandal about the chemist's wife, and touched on the hostility between the schoolmistress and the village institute. They then discussed Miss Marple's and Mrs. McGillicuddy's gardens.

"Paeonies," said Miss Marple as she rose from table, "are most unaccountable. Either they do—or they don't do. But if they *do* establish themselves, they are with you for life, so to speak, and really most beautiful varieties nowadays."

They settled themselves by the fire again, and Miss Marple brought out two old Waterford glasses from a corner cupboard, and from another cupboard produced a bottle.

"No coffee to-night for you, Elspeth," she said. "You are already over-excited (and no wonder!) and probably would not sleep. I prescribe a glass of my cowslip wine, and later, perhaps, a cup of camomile tea."

Mrs. McGillicuddy acquiescing in these arrangements, Miss Marple poured out the wine.

"Jane," said Mrs. McGillicuddy, as she took an appreciative sip, "*you* don't think, do you, that I dreamt it, or imagined it?"

"Certainly not," said Miss Marple with warmth.

Mrs. McGillicuddy heaved a sigh of relief.

"That ticket collector," she said, "*he* thought so. Quite polite, but all the same——"

"I think, Elspeth, that that was quite natural under the circumstances. It sounded—and indeed was—a most unlikely story. And you were a complete stranger to him. No, I have no doubt at all that you saw what you've told me you saw. It's very extraordinary—but not at all impossible. I recollect myself being interested when a train ran parallel to one in which I was travelling, to notice what a vivid and intimate picture one got of what was going on in one or two of the carriages. A little girl, I remember once, playing with a teddy bear, and suddenly she threw it deliberately at a fat man who was asleep in the corner and he bounced up and looked most indignant, and the other passenger looked *so* amused. I saw them all quite vividly. I could have described afterwards exactly what they looked like and what they had on."

Mrs. McGillicuddy nodded gratefully.

" That's just how it was."

"The man had his back to you, you say. So you didn't see his face?"

"No."

"And the woman, you can describe her? Young, old?"

"Youngish. Between thirty and thirty-five, I should think. I couldn't say closer than that."

"Good-looking?"

"That again, I couldn't say. Her face, you see, was all contorted and——"

Miss Marple said quickly:

"Yes, yes, I quite understand. How was she dressed?"

"She had on a fur coat of some kind, a palish fur. No hat. Her hair was blond."

"And there was nothing distinctive that you can remember about the man?"

Mrs. McGillicuddy took a little time to think carefully before she replied.

"He was tallish—and dark, I think. He had a heavy coat on so that I couldn't judge his build very well." She added despondently, "It's not really very much to go on."

"It's something," said Miss Marple. She paused before saying: "You feel quite sure, in your own mind, that the girl *was*—dead?"

"She was dead, I'm sure of it. Her tongue came out and —I'd rather not talk about it. . . ."

"Of course not. Of course not," said Miss Marple quickly. "We shall know more, I expect, in the morning."

"In the morning?"

"I should imagine it will be in the morning papers.

After this man had attacked and killed her, he would have a body on his hands. What would he do? Presumably he would leave the train quickly at the first station—by the way, can you remember if it was a corridor carriage?"

"No, it was not."

"That seems to point to a train that was not going far afield. It would almost certainly stop at Brackhampton. Let us say he leaves the train at Brackhampton, perhaps arranging the body in a corner seat, with the face hidden by the fur collar to delay discovery. Yes—I think that that is what he would do. But of course it will be discovered before very long—and I should imagine that the news of a murdered woman discovered on a train would be almost certain to be in the morning papers—we shall see."

II

But it was not in the morning papers.

Miss Marple and Mrs. McGillicuddy, after making sure of this, finished their breakfast in silence. Both were reflecting.

After breakfast, they took a turn round the garden. But this, usually an absorbing pastime, was to-day somewhat half-hearted. Miss Marple did indeed call attention to some new and rare species she had acquired for her rock-garden but did so in an almost absentminded manner. And Mrs. McGillicuddy did not, as was customary, counter-attack with a list of her own recent acquisitions.

"The garden is not looking at all as it should," said Miss Marple, but still speaking absentmindedly. "Doctor Haydock has absolutely forbidden me to do any stooping or kneeling—and really, what can you do if you *don't* stoop or kneel? There's old Edwards, of course—but *so* opinionated. And all this jobbing gets them into bad habits, lots of cups of tea and so much pottering—not any real *work*."

"Oh, I know," said Mrs. McGillicuddy. "Of course there's no question of my being *forbidden* to stoop, but really, especially after meals—and having put on weight"—she looked down at her ample proportions—"it does bring on heartburn."

There was a silence and then Mrs. McGillicuddy planted her feet sturdily, stood still, and turned on her friend.

" *Well?* " she said.

It was a small insignificant word, but it acquired full significance from Mrs. McGillicuddy's tone, and Miss Marple understood its meaning perfectly.

"I know," she said.

The two ladies looked at each other.

"I think," said Miss Marple, "we might walk down to the police station and talk to Sergeant Cornish. He's intelligent and patient, and I know him very well, and he knows me. I think he'll listen—and pass the information on to the proper quarter."

Accordingly, some three-quarters of an hour later, Miss Marple and Mrs. McGillicuddy were talking to a fresh-faced grave man between thirty and forty who listened attentively to what they had to say.

Frank Cornish received Miss Marple with cordiality and even deference. He set chairs for the two ladies, and said: "Now what can we do for you, Miss Marple?"

Miss Marple said: "I would like you, please, to listen to my friend Mrs. McGillicuddy's story."

And Sergeant Cornish had listened. At the close of the recital he remained silent for a moment or two.

Then he said:

"That's a very extraordinary story." His eyes, without seeming to do so, had sized Mrs. McGillicuddy up whilst she was telling it.

On the whole, he was favourably impressed. A sensible woman, able to tell a story clearly; not, so far as he could judge, an over-imaginative or a hysterical woman. Moreover, Miss Marple, so it seemed, believed in the accuracy of her friend's story and he knew all about Miss Marple. Everybody in St. Mary Mead knew Miss Marple; fluffy and dithery in appearance, but inwardly as sharp and as shrewd as they make them.

He cleared his throat and spoke.

"Of course," he said, "you may have been mistaken— I'm not saying you *were*, mind—but you *may* have been. There's a lot of horse-play goes on—it mayn't have been serious or fatal."

"I know what I saw," said Mrs. McGillicuddy grimly.

"And you won't budge from it," thought Frank Cornish, "and I'd say that, likely or unlikely, you may be right."

Aloud he said: "You reported it to the railway officials, and you've come and reported it to me. That's the proper procedure and you may rely on me to have inquiries instituted."

He stopped. Miss Marple nodded her head gently, satisfied. Mrs. McGillicuddy was not quite so satisfied, but she did not say anything. Sergeant Cornish addressed Miss Marple, not so much because he wanted her ideas, as because he wanted to hear what she would say.

"Granted the facts are as reported," he said, "what do you think has happened to the body?"

"There seem to be only two possibilities," said Miss Marple without hesitation. "The most *likely* one, of course, is that the body was left in the train, but that seems improbable now, for it would have been found some time last night, by another traveller, or by the railway staff at the train's ultimate destination."

Frank Cornish nodded.

"The only other course open to the murderer would be to push the body out of the train on to the line. It must, I suppose, be still on the track somewhere as yet undiscovered—though that does seem a little unlikely. But there would be, as far as I can see, no other way of dealing with it."

"You read about bodies being put in trunks," said Mrs. McGillicuddy, "but no one travels with trunks nowadays, only suitcases, and you couldn't get a body into a suitcase."

"Yes," said Cornish. "I agree with you both. The body, if there is a body, ought to have been discovered by now, or will be very soon. I'll let you know any developments there are—though I dare say you'll read about them in the papers. There's the possibility, of course, that the woman, though savagely attacked, was not actually dead. She may have been able to leave the train on her own feet."

"Hardly without assistance," said Miss Marple. "And if so, it will have been noticed. A man, supporting a woman whom he says is ill."

"Yes, it will have been noticed," said Cornish. "Or if a woman was found unconscious or ill in a carriage and was removed to hospital, that, too, will be on record. I think you may rest assured that you'll hear about it all in a very short time."

But that day passed and the next day. On that evening Miss Marple received a note from Sergeant Cornish.

In regard to the matter on which you consulted me, full inquiries have been made, with no result. No woman's body has been found. No hospital has administered treatment to a woman such as you describe, and no case of a woman suffering from shock or taken ill, or leaving a station supported by a man has been observed. You may take it that the fullest inquiries have been made. I suggest that your friend may have witnessed a scene such as she described but that it was much less serious than she supposed.

CHAPTER III

"LESS SERIOUS? Fiddlesticks!" said Mrs. McGillicuddy. "It was murder!"

She looked defiantly at Miss Marple and Miss Marple looked back at her.

"Go on, Jane," said Mrs. McGillicuddy. "Say it was all a mistake! Say I imagined the whole thing! That's what you think now, isn't it?"

"Anyone *can* be mistaken," Miss Marple pointed out gently. "Anybody, Elspeth—even you. I think we must bear that in mind. But I still think, you know, that you were most probably *not* mistaken. . . . You use glasses for reading, but you've got very good far sight—and what you saw impressed you very powerfully. You were definitely suffering from shock when you arrived here."

"It's a thing I shall never forget," said Mrs. McGillicuddy with a shudder. "The trouble is, I don't see what I can do about it!"

"I don't think," said Miss Marple thoughtfully, "that there's anything more you can do about it." (If Mrs. McGillicuddy had been alert to the tones of her friend's voice, she might have noticed a very faint stress laid on the *you*.) "You've reported what you saw—to the railway people and to the police. No, there's nothing more you can do."

"That's a relief, in a way," said Mrs. McGillicuddy, "because as you know, I'm going out to Ceylon immediately after Christmas—to stay with Roderick, and I certainly do not want to put that visit off—I've been looking forward to it so much. Though of course I *would* put it off if I thought it was my duty," she added conscientiously.

"I'm sure you would, Elspeth, but as I say, I consider you've done everything you possibly could do."

"It's up to the police," said Mrs. McGillicuddy. "And if the police choose to be stupid——"

Miss Marple shook her head decisively.

"Oh, no," she said, "the police aren't stupid. And that makes it interesting, doesn't it?"

Mrs. McGillicuddy looked at her without comprehension and Miss Marple reaffirmed her judgment of her friend as a woman of excellent principles and no imagination.

"One wants to know," said Miss Marple, "what really happened."

"She was killed."

"Yes, but *who* killed her, and *why*, and what happened to her body? Where is it now?"

"That's the business of the police to find out."

"Exactly—and they *haven't* found out. That means, doesn't it, that the man was clever—very clever. I can't imagine, you know," said Miss Marple, knitting her brows, "*how* he disposed of it. . . . You kill a woman in a fit of passion—it must have been unpremeditated, you'd never choose to kill a woman in such circumstances just a few minutes before running into a big station. No, it must have been a quarrel—jealousy—something of that kind. You strangle her—and there you are, as I say, with a dead body on your hands and on the point of running into a station. What *could* you do except as I said at first, prop the body up in a corner as though asleep, hiding the face, and then yourself leave the train as quickly as possible. I don't see any other possibility—and yet there must have been one. . . ."

Miss Marple lost herself in thought.

Mrs. McGillicuddy spoke to her twice before Miss Marple answered.

"You're getting deaf, Jane."

"Just a little, perhaps. People do not seem to me to enunciate their words as clearly as they used to do. But it wasn't that I didn't hear you. I'm afraid I wasn't paying attention."

"I just asked about the trains to London to-morrow. Would the afternoon be all right? I'm going to Margaret's and she isn't expecting me before teatime."

"I wonder, Elspeth, if you would mind going up by the 12.15? We could have an early lunch."

"Of course and——" Miss Marple went on, drowning her friend's words:

"And I wonder, too, if Margaret would mind if you didn't arrive for tea—if you arrived about seven, perhaps?"

Mrs. McGillicuddy ignored the financial aspect.

Mrs. McGillicuddy looked at her friend curiously.

"What's on your mind, Jane?"

"I suggest, Elspeth, that I should travel up to London with you, and that we should travel down again as far as Brackhampton in the train you travelled by the other day. You would then return to London from Brackhampton and I would come on here as you did. *I*, of course, would pay the *fares*," Miss Marple stressed this point firmly.

"What on earth do you expect, Jane?" she asked. "Another murder?"

"Certainly not," said Miss Marple shocked. "But I confess I should like to see for myself, under your guidance, the—the—really it is most difficult to find the correct term—the *terrain* of the crime."

So accordingly on the following day Miss Marple and Mrs. McGillicuddy found themselves in two opposite corners of a first-class carriage speeding out of London by the 4.50 from Paddington. Paddington had been even more crowded than on the preceding Friday—as there were now only two days to go before Christmas, but the 4.50 was comparatively peaceful—at any rate, in the rear portion.

On this occasion no train drew level with them, or they with another train. At intervals trains flashed past them towards London. On two occasions trains flashed past them the other way going at high speed. At intervals Mrs. McGillicuddy consulted her watch doubtfully.

"It's hard to tell just when—we'd passed through a station I know . . ." But they were continually passing through stations.

"We're due in Brackhampton in five minutes," said Miss Marple.

A ticket collector appeared in the doorway. Miss Marple raised her eyes interrogatively. Mrs. McGillicuddy shook her head. It was not the same ticket collector. He clipped their tickets, and passed on staggering just a little as the train swung round a long curve. It slackened speed as it did so.

"I expect we're coming into Brackhampton," said Mrs. McGillicuddy.

"We're getting into the outskirts, I think," said Miss Marple.

There were lights flashing past outside, buildings, an occasional glimpse of streets and trams. Their speed slackened further. They began crossing points.

"We'll be there in a minute," said Mrs. McGillicuddy, "and I can't really see this journey has been any good *at all*. Has it suggested anything to you, Jane?"

"I'm afraid not," said Miss Marple in a rather doubtful voice.

"A sad waste of good money," said Mrs. McGillicuddy, but with less disapproval than she would have used had she been paying for herself. Miss Marple had been quite adamant on that point.

"All the same," said Miss Marple, "one likes to see with one's own eyes where a thing happened. This train's just a few minutes late. Was yours on time on Friday?"

"I think so. I didn't really notice."

The train drew slowly into the busy length of Brackhampton station. The loudspeaker announced hoarsely, doors opened and shut, people got in and out, milled up and down the platform. It was a busy crowded scene.

Easy, thought Miss Marple, for a murderer to merge into that crowd, to leave the station in the midst of that pressing mass of people, or even to select another carriage and go on in the train to wherever its ultimate destination might be. Easy to be one male passenger amongst many. But not so easy to make a body vanish into thin air. That body must be *somewhere*.

Mrs. McGillicuddy had descended. She spoke now from the platform, through the open window.

"Now take care of yourself, Jane," she said. "Don't catch a chill. It's a nasty treacherous time of year, and you're not so young as you were."

"I know," said Miss Marple.

"And don't let's worry ourselves any more over all this. We've done what we could."

Miss Marple nodded, and said:

"Don't stand about in the cold, Elspeth. Or you'll be the one to catch a chill. Go and get yourself a good hot cup of tea in the Refreshment Room. You've got time, twelve minutes before your train back to town."

"I think perhaps I will. Good-bye, Jane."

"Good-bye, Elspeth. A happy Christmas to you. I hope you find Margaret well. Enjoy yourself in Ceylon, and give my love to dear Roderick—if he remembers me at all, which I doubt."

"Of course he remembers you—very well. You helped him in some way when he was at school—something to do with money that was disappearing from a locker—he's never forgotten it."

"Oh, *that*!" said Miss Marple.

Mrs. McGillicuddy turned away, a whistle blew, the train began to move. Miss Marple watched the sturdy thickset body of her friend recede. Elspeth could go to Ceylon with a clear conscience—she had done her duty and was freed from further obligation.

Miss Marple did not lean back as the train gathered speed. Instead she sat upright and devoted herself seriously to thought. Though in speech Miss Marple was woolly and diffuse, in mind she was clear and sharp. She had a problem to solve, the problem of her own future conduct; and, perhaps strangely, it presented itself to her as it had to Mrs. McGillicuddy, as a question of duty.

Mrs. McGillicuddy had said that they had both done all that they could do. It was true of Mrs. McGillicuddy but about herself Miss Marple did not feel so sure.

It was a question, sometimes, of using one's special gifts. . . . But perhaps that was conceited. . . . After all,

What *could* she do? Her friend's words came back to her, " You're not so young as you were. . . ."

Dispassionately, like a general planning a campaign, or an accountant assessing a business, Miss Marple weighed up and set down in her mind the facts for and against further enterprise. On the credit side were the following:

1. *My long experience of life and human nature.*

2. *Sir Henry Clithering and his godson (now at Scotland Yard, I believe), who was so very nice in the Little Paddocks case.*

3. *My nephew Raymond's second boy, David, who is, I am almost sure, in British Railways.*

4. *Griselda's boy Leonard who is so very knowledgeable about maps.*

Miss Marple reviewed these assets and approved them. They were all very necessary, to reinforce the weaknesses on the debit side—in particular her own bodily weakness.

"It's not," thought Miss Marple, "as though I could go here, there and everywhere, making inquiries and finding out things."

Yes, that was the chief objection, her own age and weakness. Although, for her age, her health was good, yet she *was* old. And if Dr. Haydock had strictly forbidden her to do practical gardening he would hardly approve of her starting out to track down a murderer. For that, in effect, was what she was planning to do—and it was there that her loophole lay. For if heretofore murder had, so to speak, been forced upon her, in this case it would be that she herself set out deliberately to seek it. And she was not sure that she wanted to do so. . . . She was old—old and tired. She felt at this moment, at the end of a tiring day, a great reluctance to enter upon any project at all.

She wanted nothing at all but to reach home and sit by the fire with a nice tray of supper, and go to bed, and potter about the next day just snipping off a few things in the garden, tidying up in a very mild way, without stooping, without exerting herself. . . .

"I'm too old for any more adventures," said Miss Marple to herself, watching absently out of the window the curving line of an embankment. . . .

A curve. . . .

Very faintly something stirred in her mind. . . . Just after the ticket collector had clipped their tickets . . .

It suggested an idea. Only an idea. An entirely different idea. . . .

A little pink flush came into Miss Marple's face. Suddenly she did not feel tired at all!

"I'll write to David to-morrow morning," she said to herself.

And at the same time another valuable asset flashed through her mind.

"Of course. My faithful Florence!"

II

Miss Marple set about her plan of campaign methodically and making due allowance for the Christmas season which was a definitely retarding factor.

She wrote to her great-nephew, David West, combining Christmas wishes with an urgent request for information.

Fortunately she was invited, as on previous years, to the vicarage for Christmas dinner, and here she was able to tackle young Leonard, home for the Christmas season, about maps.

Maps of all kinds were Leonard's passion. The reason

for the old lady's inquiry about a large-scale map of a particular area did not rouse his curiosity. He discoursed on maps generally with fluency, and wrote down for her exactly what would suit her purpose best. In fact, he did better. He actually found that he had such a map amongst his collection and he lent it to her, Miss Marple promising to take great care of it and return it in due course.

III

"Maps," said his mother, Griselda, who still, although she had a grown-up son, looked strangely young and blooming to be inhabiting the shabby old vicarage. "What does she want with maps? I mean, what does she want them *for*?"

"I don't know," said young Leonard, "I don't think she said exactly."

"I wonder now . . ." said Griselda. "It seems very fishy to me. . . . At her age the old pet ought to give up that sort of thing."

Leonard asked what sort of thing, and Griselda said elusively:

"Oh, poking her nose into things. Why *maps*, I wonder?"

In due course Miss Marple received a letter from her great-nephew David West. It ran affectionately:

"DEAR AUNT JANE,—Now what are you up to? I've got the information you wanted. There are only two trains that can possibly apply—the 4.33 and the 5 o'clock. The former is a slow train and stops at Haling Broadway, Barwell Heath, Brackhampton and then stations to Market Basing. The 5 o'clock is the Welsh express for

Cardiff, Newport and Swansea. The former might be overtaken somewhere by the 4.50, although it is due in Brackhampton five minutes earlier and the latter passes the 4.50 just before Brackhampton.

In all this do I smell some village scandal of a fruity character? Did you, returning from a shopping spree in town by the 4.50, observe in a passing train the Mayor's wife being embraced by the Sanitary Inspector? But why does it matter which train it was? A week-end at Porthcawl, perhaps? Thank you for the pullover. Just what I wanted.

How's the garden? Not very active this time of year, I should imagine.

Yours ever,

DAVID "

Miss Marple smiled a little, then considered the information thus presented to her. Mrs. McGillicuddy had said definitely that the carriage had not been a corridor one. Therefore—not the Swansea express. The 4.33 was indicated.

Also some more travelling seemed unavoidable. Miss Marple sighed, but made her plans.

She went up to London as before on the 12.15, but this time returned not by the 4.50, but by the 4.33 as far as Brackhampton. The journey was uneventful, but she registered certain details. The train was not crowded—4.33 was before the evening rush hour. Of the first-class carriages only one had an occupant—a very old gentleman reading the *New Statesman*. Miss Marple travelled in an empty compartment and at the two stops, Haling Broadway and Barwell Heath, leaned out of the window to observe passengers entering and leaving the train. A small number of third-class passengers got in at Haling

Broadway. At Barwell Heath several third-class passengers got out. Nobody entered or left a first-class carriage except the old gentleman carrying his *New Statesman*.

As the train neared Brackhampton, sweeping around a curve of line, Miss Marple rose to her feet and stood experimentally with her back to the window over which she had drawn down the blind.

Yes, she decided, the impetus of the sudden curving of the line and the slackening of speed did throw one off one's balance back against the window and the blind might, in consequence, very easily fly up. She peered out into the night. It was lighter than it had been when Mrs. McGillicuddy had made the same journey—only just dark, but there was little to see. For observation she must make a daylight journey.

On the next day she went up by the early morning train, purchased four linen pillow-cases (tut-tutting at the price!) so as to combine investigation with the provision of household necessities, and returned by a train leaving Paddington at twelve-fifteen. Again she was alone in a first-class carriage. "This taxation," thought Miss Marple, "that's what it is. No one can afford to travel first class except business men in the rush hours. I suppose because they can charge it to expenses."

About a quarter of an hour before the train was due at Brackhampton, Miss Marple got out the map with which Leonard had supplied her and began to observe the countryside. She had studied the map very carefully beforehand, and after noting the name of a station they passed through, she was soon able to identify where she was just as the train began to slacken for a curve. It was a very considerable curve indeed. Miss Marple, her nose glued to the window, studied the ground beneath her (the train was running on a fairly high embankment) with close attention. She divided her attention between the country outside and her map until the train finally ran into Brackhampton.

That night she wrote and posted a letter addressed to Miss Florence Hill, 4 Madison Road, Brackhampton. . . . On the following morning, going to the County library, she studied a Brackhampton directory and gazetteer, and a County history.

Nothing so far had contradicted the very faint and sketchy idea that had come to her. What she had imagined was possible. She would go no further than that.

But the next step involved action—a good deal of action —the kind of action for which she, herself, was physically unfit. If her theory were to be definitely proved or disproved, she must at this point have help from some other person. The question was—who? Miss Marple reviewed various names and possibilities rejecting them all with a vexed shake of the head. The intelligent people on whose intelligence she could rely were all far too busy. Not only had they all got jobs of varying importance, their leisure hours were usually apportioned long beforehand. The unintelligent who had time on their hands were simply, Miss Marple decided, no good.

She pondered in growing vexation and perplexity.

Then suddenly her forehead cleared. She ejaculated aloud a name.

"Of course!" said Miss Marple. "*Lucy Eyelesbarrow!*"

CHAPTER IV

THE NAME of Lucy Eyelesbarrow had already made itself felt in certain circles.

Lucy Eyelesbarrow was thirty-two. She had taken a First in Mathematics at Oxford, was acknowledged to have a brilliant mind and was confidently expected to take up a distinguished academic career.

But Lucy Eyelesbarrow, in addition to scholarly brilliance, had a core of good sound common sense. She could not fail to observe that a life of academic distinction was singularly ill rewarded. She had no desire whatever to teach and she took pleasure in contacts with minds much less brilliant than her own. In short, she had a taste for people, all sorts of people—and not the same people the whole time. She also, quite frankly, liked money. To gain money one must exploit shortage.

Lucy Eyelesbarrow hit at once upon a very serious shortage—the shortage of any kind of skilled domestic labour. To the amazement of her friends and fellow-scholars, Lucy Eyelesbarrow entered the field of domestic labour.

Her success was immediate and assured. By now, after a lapse of some years, she was known all over the British Isles. It was quite customary for wives to say joyfully to husbands, "It will be all right. I *can* go with you to the States. *I've got Lucy Eyelesbarrow!*" The point of Lucy

Eyelesbarrow was that once she came into a house, all worry, anxiety and hard work went out of it. Lucy Eyelesbarrow did everything, saw to everything, arranged everything. She was unbelievably competent in every conceivable sphere. She looked after elderly parents, accepted the care of young children, nursed the sickly, cooked divinely, got on well with any old crusted servants there might happen to be (there usually weren't), was tactful with impossible people, soothed habitual drunkards, was wonderful with dogs. Best of all she never minded *what* she did. She scrubbed the kitchen floor, dug in the garden, cleaned up dog messes, and carried coals!

One of her rules was never to accept an engagement for any long length of time. A fortnight was her usual period—a month at most under exceptional circumstances. For that fortnight you had to pay the earth! *But*, during that fortnight, your life was heaven. You could relax completely, go abroad, stay at home, do as you pleased, secure that all was going well on the home front in Lucy Eyelesbarrow's capable hands.

Naturally the demand for her services was enormous. She could have booked herself up if she chose for about three years ahead. She had been offered enormous sums to go as a permanency. But Lucy had no intention of being a permanency, nor would she book herself for more than six months ahead. And within that period, unknown to her clamouring clients, she always kept certain free periods which enabled her either to take a short luxurious holiday (since she spent nothing otherwise and was handsomely paid and kept) or to accept any position at short notice that happened to take her fancy, either by reason of its character, or because she "liked the people". Since she was now at liberty to pick and choose amongst the vociferous claimants for her services, she went very largely by personal liking. Mere riches would not buy you the services of Lucy Eyelesbarrow. She could pick and choose and she did pick and choose. She enjoyed her life very much and found in it a continual source of entertainment.

Lucy Eyelesbarrow read and re-read the letter from Miss Marple. She had made Miss Marple's acquaintance two years ago when her services had been retained by Raymond West, the novelist, to go and look after his old aunt who was recovering from pneumonia. Lucy had accepted the job and had gone down to St. Mary Mead. She had liked Miss Marple very much. As for Miss Marple, once she had caught a glimpse out of her bedroom window of Lucy Eyelesbarrow really trenching for sweet peas in the proper way, she had leaned back on her pillows with a sigh of relief, eaten the tempting little meals that Lucy Eyelesbarrow brought to her, and listened, agreeably surprised, to the tales told by her elderly irascible maid-servant of how "I taught that Miss Eyelesbarrow a crochet pattern what she'd never heard of! Proper grateful, she was." And had surprised her doctor by the rapidity of her convalescence.

Miss Marple wrote asking if Miss Eyelesbarrow could undertake a certain task for her—rather an unusual one. Perhaps Miss Eyelesbarrow could arrange a meeting at which they could discuss the matter.

Lucy Eyelesbarrow frowned for a moment or two as she considered. She was in reality fully booked up. But the word *unusual*, and her recollection of Miss Marple's personality, carried the day and she rang up Miss Marple straight away explaining that she could not come down to St. Mary Mead as she was at the moment working, but that she was free from 2 to 4 on the following afternoon and could meet Miss Marple anywhere in London. She suggested her own club, a rather nondescript establishment which had the advantage of having several small dark writing-rooms which were usually empty.

Miss Marple accepted the suggestion and on the following day the meeting took place.

Greetings were exchanged; Lucy Eyelesbarrow led her guest to the gloomiest of the writing-rooms, and said: "I'm afraid I'm rather booked up just at present, but perhaps you'll tell me what it is you want me to undertake?"

"It's very simple, really," said Miss Marple. "Unusual, but simple. I want you to find a body."

For a moment the suspicion crossed Lucy's mind that Miss Marple was mentally unhinged, but she rejected the idea. Miss Marple was eminently sane. She meant exactly what she had said.

"What kind of a body?" asked Lucy Eyelesbarrow with admirable composure.

"A woman's body," said Miss Marple. "The body of a woman who was murdered—strangled actually—in a train."

Lucy's eyebrows rose slightly.

"Well, that's certainly unusual. Tell me about it."

Miss Marple told her. Lucy Eyelesbarrow listened attentively, without interrupting. At the end she said:

"It all depends on what your friend saw—or thought she saw——?"

She left the sentence unfinished with a question in it.

"Elspeth McGillicuddy doesn't imagine things," said Miss Marple. "That's why I'm relying on what she said. If it had been Dorothy Cartwright, now—it would have been *quite* a different matter. Dorothy always has a good story, and quite often believes it herself, and there is usually a kind of *basis* of truth but certainly no more. But Elspeth is the kind of woman who finds it very hard to make herself believe that anything at all extraordinary or out of the way *could* happen. She's most unsuggestible, rather like granite."

"I see," said Lucy thoughtfully. "Well, let's accept it all. Where do I come in?"

"I was very much impressed by you," said Miss Marple, "and you see, I haven't got the physical strength nowadays to get about and do things."

"You want me to make inquiries? That sort of thing? But won't the police have done all that? Or do you think they have been just slack.?"

"Oh, no," said Miss Marple. "They haven't been slack. It's just that I've got a theory about the woman's body. It's got to be *somewhere*. If it wasn't found in the train, then it must have been pushed or thrown out of the train —but it hasn't been discovered anywhere on the line. So I travelled down the same way to see if there was anywhere where the body could have been thrown off the train and yet wouldn't have been found on the line—and there was. The railway line makes a big curve before getting into Brackhampton, on the edge of a high embankment. If a body were thrown out there, when the train was leaning at an angle, I *think* it would pitch right down the embankment."

"But surely it would still be found—even there?"

"Oh, yes. It would have to be taken away. . . . But we'll come to that presently. Here's the place—on this map."

Lucy bent to study where Miss Marple's finger pointed.

"It is right in the outskirts of Brackhampton now," said Miss Marple, "but originally it was a country house with extensive park and grounds and it's still there, untouched—ringed round now with building estates and small suburban houses. It's called Rutherford Hall. It was built by a man called Crackenthorpe, a very rich manufacturer in 1884. The original Crackenthorpe's son, an elderly man, is living there still with, I understand, a daughter. The railway encircles quite half of the property."

"And you want me to do—what?"

Miss Marple replied promptly.

"I want you to get a post there. Everyone is crying out for efficient domestic help—I should not imagine it would be difficult."

"No, I don't suppose it would be difficult."

"I understand that Mr. Crackenthorpe is said locally to be somewhat of a miser. If you accept a low salary, I will make it up to the proper figure which should, I think, be rather more than the current rate."

"Because of the difficulty?"

"Not the difficulty so much as the danger. It might, you know, be *dangerous*. It's only right to warn you of that."

"I don't know," said Lucy pensively, "that the idea of danger would deter me."

"I didn't think it would," said Miss Marple. "You're not that kind of person."

"I dare say you thought it might even attract me? I've encountered very little danger in my life. But do you really believe it might be dangerous?"

"Somebody," Miss Marple pointed out, "has committed a very successful crime. There has been no hue-and-cry, no real suspicion. Two elderly ladies have told a rather improbable story, the police have investigated it and found nothing in it. So everything is nice and quiet. I don't think that this somebody, whoever he may be, will care about the matter being raked up—especially if you are successful."

"What do I look for exactly?"

"Any signs along the embankment, a scrap of clothing, broken bushes—that kind of thing."

Lucy nodded.

"And then?"

"I shall be quite close at hand," said Miss Marple. "An old maidservant of mine, my faithful Florence, lives in Brackhampton. She has looked after her old parents for years. They are now both dead, and she takes in lodgers— all most respectable people. She has arranged for me to have rooms with her. She will look after me most devotedly, and I feel I should like to be close at hand. I would suggest that you mention you have an elderly aunt living in the neighbourhood, and that you want a post within easy distance of her, and also that you stipulate for a reasonable amount of spare time so that you can go and see her often."

Again Lucy nodded.

"I *was* going to Taormina the day after to-morrow," she said. "The holiday can wait. But I can only promise three weeks. After that, I am booked up."

"Three weeks should be ample," said Miss Marple. "If we can't find out anything in three weeks, we might as well give up the whole thing as a mare's nest."

Miss Marple departed, and Lucy, after a moment's reflection, rang up a Registry Office in Brackhampton, the manageress of which she knew very well. She explained her desire for a post in the neighbourhood so as to be near her "aunt." After turning down, with a little difficulty and a good deal of ingenuity, several more desirable places, Rutherford Hall was mentioned.

"That sounds exactly what I want," said Lucy firmly.

The Registry Office rang up Miss Crackenthorpe, Miss Crackenthorpe rang up Lucy.

Two days later Lucy left London en route for Rutherford Hall.

II

Driving her own small car, Lucy Eyelesbarrow drove through an imposing pair of vast iron gates. Just inside them was what had originally been a small lodge which now seemed completely derelict, whether through war damage, or merely through neglect, it was difficult to be sure. A long winding drive led through large gloomy clumps of rhododendrons up to the house. Lucy caught her breath in a slight gasp when she saw the house which was a kind of miniature Windsor Castle. The stone steps in front of the door could have done with attention and the gravel sweep was green with neglected weeds.

She pulled an old-fashioned wrought-iron bell, and its clamour sounded echoing away inside. A slatternly woman, wiping her hands on her apron, opened the door and looked at her suspiciously.

"Expected, aren't you?" she said. "Miss Something-barrow, she told me."

"Quite right," said Lucy.

The house was desperately cold inside. Her guide led her along a dark hall and opened a door on the right. Rather to Lucy's surprise, it was quite a pleasant sitting-room, with books and chintz-covered chairs.

"I'll tell her," said the woman, and went away shutting the door after having given Lucy a look of profound disfavour.

After a few minutes the door opened again. From the

first moment Lucy decided that she liked Emma Crackenthorpe.

She was a middle-aged woman with no very outstanding characteristics, neither good-looking nor plain,
sensibly dressed in tweeds and pullover, with dark hair
swept back from her forehead, steady hazel eyes and a
very pleasant voice.

She said: "Miss Eyelesbarrow?" and held out her
hand.

Then she looked doubtful.

"I wonder," she said, "if this post is really what you're
looking for? I don't want a housekeeper, you know, to
supervise things. I want someone to do the work."

Lucy said that that was what most people needed.

Emma Crackenthorpe said apologetically:

"So many people, you know, seem to think that just a
little light dusting will answer the case—but I can do all
the light dusting myself."

"I quite understand," said Lucy. "You want cooking
and washing up, and housework and stoking the boiler.
That's all right. That's what I do. I'm not at all afraid
of work."

"It's a big house, I'm afraid, and inconvenient. Of
course we only live in a portion of it—my father and
myself, that is. He is rather an invalid. We live quite
quietly, and there is an Aga stove. I have several brothers,
but they are not here very often. Two women come in,
a Mrs. Kidder in the morning, and Mrs. Hart three days
a week to do brasses and things like that. You have your
own car?"

"Yes. It can stand out in the open if there's nowhere
to put it. It's used to it."

"Oh, there are any amount of old stables. There's no
trouble about that." She frowned a moment, then said,

"Eyelesbarrow—rather an unusual name. Some friends of mine were telling me about a Lucy Eyelesbarrow—the Kennedys?"

"Yes. I was with them in North Devon when Mrs. Kennedy was having a baby."

Emma Crackenthorpe smiled.

"I know they said they'd never had such a wonderful time as when you were there seeing to everything. But I had the idea that you were terribly expensive. The sum I mentioned——"

"That's quite all right," said Lucy. "I want particularly, you see, to be near Brackhampton. I have an elderly aunt in a critical state of health and I want to be within easy distance of her. That's why the salary is a secondary consideration. I can't afford to do nothing. If I could be sure of having some time off most days?"

"Oh, of course. Every afternoon, till six, if you like?"

"That seems perfect."

Miss Crackenthorpe hesitated a moment before saying: "My father is elderly and a little—difficult sometimes. He is very keen on economy, and he says things sometimes that upset people. I wouldn't like——"

Lucy broke in quickly:

"I'm quite used to elderly people, of all kinds," she said. "I always manage to get on well with them."

Emma Crackenthorpe looked relieved.

"Trouble with father!" diagnosed Lucy. "I bet he's an old tartar."

She was apportioned a large gloomy bedroom which a small electric heater did its inadequate best to warm, and was shown round the house, a vast uncomfortable mansion. As they passed a door in the hall a voice roared out:

"That you, Emma? Got the new girl there? Bring her in. I want to look at her."

Emma flushed, glanced at Lucy apologetically.

The two women entered the room. It was richly upholstered in dark velvet, the narrow windows let in very little light, and it was full of heavy mahogany Victorian furniture.

Old Mr. Crackenthorpe was stretched out in an invalid chair, a silver-headed stick by his side.

He was a big gaunt man, his flesh hanging in loose folds. He had a face rather like a bulldog, with a pugnacious chin. He had thick dark hair flecked with grey, and small suspicious eyes.

"Let's have a look at you, young lady."

Lucy advanced, composed and smiling.

"There's just one thing you'd better understand straight away. Just because we live in a big house doesn't mean we're rich. We're *not* rich. We live simply—do you hear?—*simply!* No good coming here with a lot of high-falutin ideas. Cod's as good a fish as turbot any day, and don't you forget it. I don't stand for waste. I live here because my father built the house and I like it. After I'm dead they can sell it up if they want to—and I expect they will want to. No sense of family. This house is well built—it's solid, and we've got our own land round us. Keeps us private. It would bring in a lot if sold for building land but not while *I'm* alive. You won't get me out of here until you take me out feet first."

He glared at Lucy.

"Your house is your castle," said Lucy.

"Laughing at me?"

"Of course not. I think it's very exciting to have a real country place all surrounded by town."

"Quite so. Can't see another house from here, can you?

42

Fields with cows in them—right in the middle of Brackhampton. You hear the traffic a bit when the wind's that way—but otherwise it's still country."

He added, without pause or change of tone, to his daughter:

"Ring up that damn' fool of a doctor. Tell him that last medicine's no good at all."

Lucy and Emma retired. He shouted after them:

"And don't let that damned woman who sniffs dust in here. She's disarranged all my books."

Lucy asked:

"Has Mr. Crackenthorpe been an invalid long?"

Emma said, rather evasively:

"Oh, for years now. . . . This is the kitchen."

The kitchen was enormous. A vast kitchen range stood cold and neglected. An Aga stood demurely beside it.

Lucy asked times of meals and inspected the larder. Then she said cheerfully to Emma Crackenthorpe:

"I know everything now. Don't bother. Leave it all to me."

Emma Crackenthorpe heaved a sigh of relief as she went up to bed that night.

"The Kennedys were quite right," she said. "She's wonderful."

Lucy rose at six the next morning. She did the house, prepared vegetables, assembled, cooked and served breakfast. With Mrs. Kidder she made the beds and at eleven o'clock they sat down to strong tea and biscuits in the kitchen. Mollified by the fact that Lucy "had no airs about her" and also by the strength and sweetness of the tea, Mrs. Kidder relaxed into gossip. She was a small spare woman with a sharp eye and tight lips.

"Regular old skinflint *he* is. What she has to put up

43

with! All the same, she's not what I call down-trodden.
Can hold her own all right when she has to. When the
gentlemen come down she sees to it there's something
decent to eat."

"The gentlemen?"

"Yes. Big family it was. The eldest, Mr. Edmund, he
was killed in the war. Then there's Mr. Cedric, he lives
abroad somewhere. He's not married. Paints pictures in
foreign parts. Mr. Harold's in the City, lives in London
—married an earl's daughter. Then there's Mr. Alfred,
he's got a nice way with him, but he's a bit of a black
sheep, been in trouble once or twice—and there's Miss
Edith's husband, Mr. Bryan, ever so nice, he is—she died
some years ago, but he's always stayed one of the family,
and there's Master Alexander, Miss Edith's little boy.
He's at school, comes here for part of the holidays always;
Miss Emma's terribly set on him."

Lucy digested all this information, continuing to press
tea on her informant. Finally, reluctantly, Mrs. Kidder
rose to her feet.

"Seem to have got along a treat, we do, this morning,"
she said wonderingly. "Want me to give you a hand with
the potatoes, dear?"

"They're all done ready."

"Well, you are a one for getting on with things! I
might as well be getting along myself as there doesn't
seem anything else to do."

Mrs. Kidder departed and Lucy, with time on her
hands, scrubbed the kitchen table which she had been
longing to do, but which she had put off so as not to
offend Mrs. Kidder whose job it properly was. Then she
cleaned the silver till it shone radiantly. She cooked
lunch, cleared it away, washed it up, and at two-thirty
was ready to start exploration. She had set out the tea

things ready on a tray, with sandwiches and bread and butter covered with a damp napkin to keep them moist.

She strolled first round the gardens which would be the normal thing to do. The kitchen garden was sketchily cultivated with a few vegetables. The hot-houses were in ruins. The paths everywhere were overgrown with weeds. A herbaceous border near the house was the only thing that showed free of weeds and in good condition and Lucy suspected that that had been Emma's hand. The gardener was a very old man, somewhat deaf, who was only making a show of working. Lucy spoke to him pleasantly. He lived in a cottage adjacent to the big stableyard.

Leading out of the stableyard a back drive led through the park which was fenced on either side of it, and under a railway arch into a small back lane.

Every few minutes a train thundered along the main line over the railway arch. Lucy watched the trains as they slackened speed going round the sharp curve that encircled the Crackenthorpe property. She passed under the railway arch and out into the lane. It seemed a little-used track. On the one side was the railway embankment, on the other was a high wall which enclosed some tall factory buildings. Lucy followed the lane until it came out into a street of small houses. She could hear a short distance away the busy hum of main road traffic. She glanced at her watch. A woman came out of a house nearby and Lucy stopped her.

" Excuse me, can you tell me if there is a public telephone near here ? "

"Post office just at the corner of the road."

Lucy thanked her and walked along until she came to the post office which was a combination shop and post office. There was a telephone box at one side. Lucy went

45

into it and made a call. She asked to speak to Miss Marple.
A woman's voice spoke in a sharp bark.

"She's resting. And I'm not going to disturb her!
She needs her rest—she's an old lady. Who shall I say
called?"

"Miss Eyelesbarrow. There's no need to disturb her.
Just tell her that I've arrived and everything is going on
well and that I'll let her know when I've any news."

She replaced the receiver and made her way back to
Rutherford Hall.

CHAPTER V

"I suppose it will be all right if I just practise a few iron
shots in the park?" asked Lucy.

"Oh, yes, certainly. Are you fond of golf?"

"I'm not much good, but I like to keep in practice.
It's a more agreeable form of exercise than just going for
a walk."

"Nowhere to walk outside this place," growled Mr.
Crackenthorpe. "Nothing but pavements and miserable
little band boxes of houses. Like to get hold of my land
and build more of them. But they won't until I'm dead.
And I'm not going to die to oblige anybody. I can tell
you that! Not to oblige *anybody*!"

Emma Crackenthorpe said mildly:

"Now, Father."

"*I* know what they think—and what they're waiting
for. All of 'em. Cedric, and that sly fox Harold with his
smug face. As for Alfred, I wonder he hasn't had a shot
at bumping me off himself. Not sure he didn't, at

Christmas-time. That was a very odd turn I had. Puzzled old Quimper. He asked me a lot of discreet questions."

"Everyone gets these digestive upsets now and again, Father."

"All right, all right, say straight out that I ate too much! That's what you mean. And *why* did I eat too much? Because there was too much food on the table, far too much. Wasteful and extravagant. And that reminds me—you, young woman. Five potatoes you sent in for lunch—good-sized ones too. Two potatoes are enough for anybody. So don't send in more than four in future. The extra one was wasted to-day."

"It wasn't wasted, Mr. Crackenthorpe. I've planned to use it in a Spanish omelet to-night."

"Urgh!" As Lucy went out of the room carrying the coffee tray she heard him say, "Slick young woman, that, always got all the answers. Cooks well, though—and she's a handsome kind of girl."

Lucy Eyelesbarrow took a light iron out of the set of golf clubs she had had the forethought to bring with her, and strolled out into the park, climbing over the fencing.

She began playing a series of shots. After five minutes or so, a ball, apparently sliced, pitched on the side of the railway embankment. Lucy went up and began to hunt about for it. She looked back towards the house. It was a long way away and nobody was in the least interested in what she was doing. She continued to hunt for the ball. Now and then she played shots from the embankment down into the grass. During the afternoon she searched about a third of the embankment. Nothing. She played her ball back towards the house.

Then, on the next day, she came upon something. A thorn bush growing about half-way up the bank had been snapped off. Bits of it lay scattered about. Lucy examined

47

the tree itself. Impaled on one of the thorns was a torn scrap of fur. It was almost the same colour as the wood, a pale brownish colour. Lucy looked at it from a moment, then she took a pair of scissors out of her pocket and snipped it carefully in half. The half she had snipped off she put in an envelope which she had in her pocket. She came down the steep slope searching about for anything else. She looked carefully at the rough grass of the field. She thought she could distinguish a kind of track which someone had made walking through the long grass. But it was very faint—not nearly so clear as her own tracks were. It must have been made some time ago and it was too sketchy for her to be sure that it was not merely imagination on her part.

She began to hunt carefully down in the grass at the foot of the embankment just below the broken thorn bush. Presently her search was rewarded. She found a powder compact, a small cheap enamelled affair. She wrapped it in her handkerchief and put it in her pocket. She searched on but did not find anything more.

On the following afternoon, she got into her car and went to see her invalid aunt. Emma Crackenthorpe said kindly, "Don't hurry back. We shan't want you until dinner-time."

"Thank you, but I shall be back by six at the latest."

No. 4 Madison Road was a small drab house in a small drab street. It had very clean Nottingham lace curtains, a shining white doorstep and a well-polished brass door handle. The door was opened by a tall, grim-looking woman, dressed in black with a large knob of iron-grey hair.

She eyed Lucy in suspicious appraisal as she showed her in to Miss Marple.

Miss Marple was occupying the back sitting-room

which looked out on to a small tidy square of garden. It was aggressively clean with a lot of mats and doilies, a great many china ornaments, a rather big Jacobean suite and two ferns in pots. Miss Marple was sitting in a big chair by the fire busily engaged in crocheting.

Lucy came in and shut the door. She sat down in the chair facing Miss Marple.

"Well!" she said. "It looks as though you were right."

She produced her finds and gave the details of their finding.

A faint flush of achievement came into Miss Marple's cheeks.

"Perhaps one ought not to feel so," she said, "but it *is* rather gratifying to form a theory and get proof that it is correct!"

She fingered the small tuft of fur. "Elspeth said the woman was wearing a light-coloured fur coat. I suppose the compact was in the pocket of the coat and fell out as the body rolled down the slope. It doesn't seem distinctive in any way, but it may help. You didn't take all the fur?"

"No, I left half of it on the thorn bush."

Miss Marple nodded approval.

"Quite right. You are very intelligent, my dear. The police will want to check exactly."

"You are going to the police—with these things?"

"Well—not quite yet. . . ." Miss Marple considered: "It would be better, I think, to find the body first. Don't you?"

"Yes, but isn't that rather a tall order? I mean, granting that your estimate is correct. The murderer pushed the body out of the train, then presumably got out himself at Brackhampton and at some time—probably that same night—came along and removed the body. But what happened after that? He may have taken it *anywhere*."

49

"Not *anywhere*," said Miss Marple. "I don't think you've followed the thing to its logical conclusion, my dear Miss Eyelesbarrow."

"Do call me Lucy. Why not anywhere?"

"Because, if so, he might much more easily have killed the girl in some lonely spot and driven the body away from there. You haven't appreciated——"

Lucy interrupted.

"Are you saying—do you mean—that this was a pre-meditated crime?"

"I didn't think so at first," said Miss Marple. "One wouldn't—naturally. It seemed like a quarrel and a man losing control and strangling the girl and then being faced with the problem of disposing of his victim—a problem which he had to solve within a very few minutes. But it really is too much of a coincidence that he should kill the girl in a fit of passion, and then look out of the window and find the train was going round a curve exactly at a spot where he could tip the body out, *and* where he could be sure of finding his way later and removing it! If he'd just thrown her out there by chance, he'd have done no more about it, and the body would, long before now, have been found."

She paused. Lucy stared at her.

"You know," said Miss Marple thoughtfully, "it's really quite a clever way to have planned a crime—and I think it was very carefully planned. There's something so anonymous about a train. If he'd killed her in the place where she lived, or was staying, somebody might have noticed him come or go. Or if he'd driven her out in the country somewhere, someone might have noticed the car and its number and make. But a train is full of strangers coming and going. In a non-corridor carriage, alone with her, it was quite easy—especially if you realise that

he knew exactly what he was going to do next. He knew
—he *must* have known—all about Rutherford Hall—its
geographical position, I mean, its queer isolation—an
island bounded by railway lines."

"It is exactly like that," said Lucy. "It's an anachronism
out of the past. Bustling urban life goes on all around it,
but doesn't touch it. The tradespeople deliver in the
mornings and that's all."

"So we assume, as you said, that the murderer comes
to Rutherford Hall that night. It is already dark when the
body falls and no one is likely to discover it before the
next day."

"No, indeed."

"The murderer would come—how? In a car? Which
way?"

Lucy considered.

"There's a rough lane, alongside a factory wall. He'd
probably come that way, turn in under the railway arch
and along the back drive. Then he could climb the fence,
go along at the foot of the embankment, find the body,
and carry it back to the car."

"And then," continued Miss Marple. "He took it to
some place he had already chosen beforehand. This was
all thought out, you know. And I don't think, as I say,
that he would take it away from Rutherford Hall, or if
so, not very far. The obvious thing, I suppose, would be
to bury it somewhere?" She looked inquiringly at Lucy.

"I suppose so," said Lucy considering. "But it wouldn't
be quite as easy as it sounds."

Miss Marple agreed.

"He couldn't bury it in the park. Too hard work and
very noticeable. Somewhere where the earth was turned
already?"

"The kitchen garden, perhaps, but that's very close to

the gardener's cottage. He's old and deaf—but still it might be risky."

"Is there a dog?"

"No."

"Then in a shed, perhaps, or an outhouse?"

"That would be simpler and quicker. . . . There are a lot of unused old buildings; broken down pig sties, harness rooms, workshops that nobody ever goes near. Or he might perhaps thrust it into a clump of rhododendrons or shrubs somewhere."

Miss Marple nodded.

"Yes, I think that's *much* more probable."

There was a knock on the door and the grim Florence came in with a tray.

"Nice for you to have a visitor," she said to Miss Marple, "I've made you my special scones you used to like."

"Florence always made the most delicious tea cakes," said Miss Marple.

Florence, gratified, creased her features into a totally unexpected smile and left the room.

"I think, my dear," said Miss Marple, "we won't talk any more about murder during tea. Such an *unpleasant* subject!"

II

After tea, Lucy rose.

"I'll be getting back," she said. "As I've already told you, there's no one actually living at Rutherford Hall who could be the man we're looking for. There's only an old man and a middle-aged woman, and an old deaf gardener."

"I didn't say he was actually *living* there," said Miss Marple. "All I mean is, that he's someone who knows Rutherford Hall very well. But we can go into that after you've found the body."

"You seem to assume quite confidently that I *shall* find it," said Lucy. "I don't feel nearly so optimistic."

"I'm sure you will succeed, my dear Lucy. You are such an efficient person."

"In some ways, but I haven't had any experience in looking for bodies."

"I'm sure all it needs is a little common sense," said Miss Marple encouragingly.

Lucy looked at her, then laughed. Miss Marple smiled back at her.

Lucy set to work systematically the next afternoon.

She poked round outhouses, prodded the briars which wreathed the old pigsties, and was peering into the boiler room under the greenhouse when she heard a dry cough and turned to find old Hillman, the gardener, looking at her disapprovingly.

"You be careful you don't get a nasty fall, miss," he warned her. "Them steps isn't safe, and you was up in the loft just now and the floor there ain't safe neither."

Lucy was careful to display no embarrassment.

"I expect you think I'm very nosy," she said cheerfully. "I was just wondering if something couldn't be made out of this place—growing mushrooms for the market, that sort of thing. Everything seems to have been let go terribly."

"That's the master, that is. Won't spend a penny. Ought to have two men and a boy here, I ought, to keep the place proper, but won't hear of it, he won't. Had all I could do to make him get a motor mower. Wanted me to mow all that front grass by hand, he did."

"But if the place could be made to pay—with some repairs?"

"Won't get a place like this to pay—too far gone. And he wouldn't care about that, anyway. Only cares about saving. Knows well enough what'll happen after he's gone—the young gentlemen'll sell up as fast as they can. Only waiting for him to pop off, they are. Going to come into a tidy lot of money when he dies, so I've heard."

"I suppose he's a very rich man?" said Lucy.

"Crackenthorpe's Fancies, that's what they are. The old gentleman started it, Mr. Crackenthorpe's father. A sharp one he was, by all accounts. Made his fortune, and built this place. Hard as nails, they say, and never forgot an injury. But with all that, *he* was open-handed. Nothing of the miser about him. Disappointed in both his sons, so the story goes. Give 'em an education and brought 'em up to be gentlemen—Oxford and all. But they were too much of gentlemen to want to go into the business. The younger one married an actress and then smashed himself up in a car accident when he'd been drinking. The elder one, our one here, his father never fancied so much. Abroad a lot, he was, bought a lot of heathen statues and had them sent home. Wasn't so close with his money when he was young—come on him more in middle age, it did. No, they never did hit it off, him and his father, so I've heard."

Lucy digested this information with an air of polite interest. The old man leant against the wall and prepared to go on with his saga. He much preferred talking to doing any work.

"Died afore the war, the old gentleman did. Terrible temper he had. Didn't do to give him any sauce, he wouldn't stand for it."

"And after he died, this Mr. Crackenthorpe came and lived here?"

"Him and his family, yes. Nigh to grown up they was by then."

"But surely . . . Oh, I see, you mean the 1914 war."

"No, I don't. Died in 1928, that's what I mean."

Lucy supposed that 1928 qualified as "before the war" though it was not the way she would have described it herself.

She said: "Well, I expect you'll be wanting to go on with your work. You mustn't let me keep you."

"Ar," said old Hillman without enthusiasm, "not much you can do this time of day. Light's too bad."

Lucy went back to the house, pausing to investigate a likely-looking copse of birch and azalea on her way.

She found Emma Crackenthorpe standing in the hall reading a letter. The afternoon post had just been delivered.

"My nephew will be here to-morrow—with a schoolfriend. Alexander's room is the one over the porch. The one next to it will do for James Stoddart-West. They'll use the bathroom just opposite."

"Yes, Miss Crackenthorpe. I'll see the rooms are prepared."

"They'll arrive in the morning before lunch." She hesitated. "I expect they'll be hungry."

"I bet they will," said Lucy. "Roast beef, do you think? And perhaps treacle tart?"

"Alexander's very fond of treacle tart."

The two boys arrived on the following morning. They both had well-brushed hair, suspiciously angelic faces, and perfect manners. Alexander Eastley had fair hair and blue eyes, Stoddart-West was dark and spectacled.

They discoursed gravely during lunch on events in the

sporting world, with occasional references to the latest space fiction. Their manner was that of elderly professors discussing palæolithic implements. In comparison with them, Lucy felt quite young.

The sirloin of beef vanished in no time and every crumb of the treacle tart was consumed.

Mr. Crackenthorpe grumbled: "You two will eat me out of house and home."

Alexander gave him a blue-eyed reproving glance.

"We'll have bread and cheese if you can't afford meat, Grandfather."

"Afford it? I can *afford* it. I don't like waste."

"We haven't wasted any, sir," said Stoddart-West, looking down at his place which bore clear testimony of that fact.

"You boys both eat twice as much as I do."

"We're at the body-building stage," Alexander explained. "We need a big intake of proteins."

The old man grunted.

As the two boys left the table, Lucy heard Alexander say apologetically to his friend:

"You mustn't pay any attention to my grandfather. He's on a diet or something and that makes him rather peculiar. He's terribly mean, too. I think it must be a complex of some kind."

Stoddart-West said comprehendingly:

"I had an aunt who kept thinking she was going bankrupt. Really, she had oodles of money. Pathological, the doctor said. Have you got that football, Alex?"

After she had cleared away and washed up lunch, Lucy went out. She could hear the boys calling out in the distance on the lawn. She herself went in the opposite direction, down the front drive and from there she struck across to some clumped masses of rhododendron bushes.

She began to hunt carefully, holding back the leaves and peering inside. She moved from clump to clump systematically, and was raking inside with a golf club when the polite voice of Alexander Eastley made her start.

"Are you looking for something, Miss Eyelesbarrow?"

"A golf ball," said Lucy promptly. "Several golf balls in fact. I've been practising golf shots most afternoons and I've lost quite a lot of balls. I thought that to-day I really must find some of them."

"We'll help you," said Alexander obligingly.

"That's very kind of you. I thought you were playing football."

"One can't go *on* playing footer," explained Stoddart-West. "One gets too hot. Do you play a lot of golf?"

"I'm quite fond of it. I don't get much opportunity."

"I suppose you don't. You do the cooking here, don't you?"

"Yes."

"Did you cook the lunch to-day?"

"Yes. Was it all right?"

"Simply wizard," said Alexander. "We get awful meat at school, all dried up. I love beef that's pink and juicy inside. That treacle tart was pretty smashing, too."

"You must tell me what things you like best."

"Could we have apple meringue one day? It's my favourite thing."

"Of course."

Alexander sighed happily.

"There a clock golf set under the stairs," he said. "We could fix it up on the lawn and do some putting. What about it, Stodders?"

"Good-oh!" said Stoddart-West.

"He isn't really Australian," explained Alexander

57

courteously. "But he's practising talking that way in case his people take him out to see the Test Match next year."

Encouraged by Lucy, they went off to get the clock golf set. Later, as she returned to the house, she found them setting it out on the lawn and arguing about the position of the numbers.

"We don't want it like a clock," said Stoddart-West. "That's kid stuff. We want to make a course of it. Long holes and short ones. It's a pity the numbers are so rusty. You can hardly see them."

"They need a lick of white paint," said Lucy. "You might get some to-morrow and paint them."

"Good idea." Alexander's face lit up. "I say, I believe there are some old pots of paint in the Long Barn—left there by the painters last hols. Shall we see?"

"What's the Long Barn?" asked Lucy.

Alexander pointed to a long stone building a little way from the house near the back drive.

"It's quite old," he said. "Grandfather calls it a Leak Barn and says it's Elizabethan, but that's just swank. It belonged to the farm that was here originally. My great-grandfather pulled it down and built this awful house instead."

He added: "A lot of grandfather's collection is in the barn. Things he had sent home from abroad when he was a young man. Most of them are pretty frightful, too. The Long Barn is used sometimes for whist drives and things like that. Women's Institute stuff. And Conservative Sales of Work. Come and see it."

Lucy accompanied them willingly.

There was a big nail-studded oak door to the barn.

Alexander raised his hand and detached a key on a nail just under some ivy to the right hand of the top of the door. He turned it in the lock, pushed the door open and they went in.

At a first glance Lucy felt that she was in a singularly bad museum. The heads of two Roman emperors in marble glared at her out of bulging eyeballs, there was a huge sarcophagus of a decadent Greco-Roman period, a simpering Venus stood on a pedestal clutching her falling draperies. Besides these works of art, there were a couple of trestle tables, some stacked-up chairs, and sundry oddments such as a rusted hand-mower, two buckets, a couple of moth-eaten car seats, and a green-painted iron garden seat that had lost a leg.

"I think I saw the paint over here," said Alexander vaguely. He went to a corner and pulled aside a tattered curtain that shut it off.

They found a couple of paint pots and brushes, the latter dry and stiff.

"You really need some turps," said Lucy.

They could not, however, find any turpentine. The boys suggested bicycling off to get some, and Lucy urged them to do so. Painting the clock golf numbers would keep them amused for some time, she thought.

The boys went off, leaving her in the barn.

"This really could do with a clear up," she had murmured.

"I shouldn't bother," Alexander advised her. "It gets cleaned up if it's going to be used for anything, but it's practically never used this time of year."

"Do I hang the key up outside the door again? Is that where it's kept?"

"Yes. There's nothing to pinch here, you see. Nobody would want those awful marble things and, anyway, they weigh a ton."

Lucy agreed with him. She could hardly admire old

Mr. Crackenthorpe's taste in art. He seemed to have an unerring instinct for selecting the worst specimen of any period.

She stood looking round her after the boys had gone. Her eyes came to rest on the sarcophagus and stayed there.

That sarcophagus . . .

The air in the barn was faintly musty as though un-aired for a long time. She went over to the sarcophagus. It had a heavy close-fitting lid. Lucy looked at it speculatively.

Then she left the barn, went to the kitchen, found a heavy crowbar, and returned.

It was not an easy task, but Lucy toiled doggedly.

Slowly the lid began to rise, prised up by the crowbar.

It rose sufficiently for Lucy to see what was inside. . . .

CHAPTER VI

A few minutes later Lucy, rather pale, left the barn, locked the door and put the key back on the nail.

She went rapidly to the stables, got out her car and drove down the back drive. She stopped at the post office at the end of the road. She went into the telephone box, put in the money and dialled.

"I want to speak to Miss Marple."

"She's resting, miss. It's Miss Eyelesbarrow, isn't it?"

"Yes."

"I'm not going to disturb her and that's flat, miss. She's an old lady and she needs her rest."

"You must disturb her. It's urgent."

"I'm not——"

"Please do what I say at once."

When she chose, Lucy's voice could be as incisive as steel. Florence knew authority when she heard it.

Presently Miss Marple's voice spoke.

"Yes, Lucy?"

Lucy drew a deep breath.

"You were quite right," she said. "I've found it."

"A woman's body?"

"Yes. A woman in a fur coat. It's in a stone sarcophagus in a kind of barn-cum-museum near the house. What do you want me to do? I ought to inform the police, I think."

"Yes. You must inform the police. At once."

"But what about the rest of it? About you? The first thing they'll want to know is *why* I was prying up a lid that weighs tons for apparently no reason. Do you want me to invent a reason? I can."

"No. I think, you know," said Miss Marple in her gentle serious voice, "that the only thing to do is to tell the exact truth."

"About you?"

"About everything."

A sudden grin split the whiteness of Lucy's face.

"That will be quite simple for me," she said. "But I imagine they'll find it quite hard to believe!"

She rang off, waited a moment, and then rang and got the police station.

"I have just discovered a dead body in a sarcophagus in the Long Barn at Rutherford Hall."

"What's that?"

Lucy repeated her statement and anticipating the next question gave her name.

She drove back, put the car away and entered the house. She paused in the hall for a moment, thinking.

Then she gave a brief sharp nod of the head and went to the library where Miss Crackenthorpe was sitting helping her father to do *The Times* crossword.

"Can I speak to you a moment, Miss Crackenthorpe?"

Emma looked up, a shade of apprehension on her face. The apprehension was, Lucy thought, purely domestic. In such words do useful household staff announce their imminent departure.

"Well, speak up, girl, speak up," said old Mr. Crackenthorpe irritably.

Lucy said to Emma:

"I'd like to speak to you alone, please."

"Nonsense," said Mr. Crackenthorpe. "You say straight out here what you've got to say."

"Just a moment, Father." Emma rose and went towards the door.

"All nonsense. It can wait," said the old man angrily.

"I'm afraid it can't wait," said Lucy.

Mr. Crackenthorpe said, "What impertinence!"

Emma came out into the hall, Lucy followed her and shut the door behind them.

"Yes?" said Emma. "What is it? If you think there's too much to do with the boys here, I can help you and——"

"It's not that at all," said Lucy. "I didn't want to speak before your father because I understand he is an invalid and it might give him a shock. You see, I've just discovered the body of a murdered woman in that big sarcophagus in the Long Barn."

Emma Crackenthorpe stared at her.

"In the sarcophagus? A murdered woman? It's impossible!"

"I'm afraid it's quite true. I've rung up the police. They will be here at any minute."

A slight flush came into Emma's cheek.

"You should have told me first—before notifying the police."

"I'm sorry," said Lucy.

"I didn't hear you ring up——" Emma's glance went to the telephone on the hall table.

"I rang up from the post office just down the road."

"But how extraordinary. Why not from here?"

Lucy thought quickly.

"I was afraid the boys might be about—might hear—if I rang up from the hall here."

"I see. . . . Yes. . . . I see. . . . They are coming—the police, I mean?"

"They're here now," said Lucy, as with a squeal of brakes a car drew up at the front door and the front-door bell pealed through the house.

II

"I'm sorry, very sorry—to have asked this of you," said Inspector Bacon.

His hand under her arm, he led Emma Crackenthorpe out of the barn. Emma's face was very pale, she looked sick, but she walked firmly erect.

"I'm quite sure that I've never seen the woman before in my life."

"We're very grateful to you, Miss Crackenthorpe. That's all I wanted to know. Perhaps you'd like to lie down?"

"I must go to my father. I telephoned to Dr. Quimper as soon as I heard about this and the doctor is with him now."

Dr. Quimper came out of the library as they crossed the hall. He was a tall genial man, with a casual off-hand, cynical manner that his patients found very stimulating.

He and the inspector nodded to each other.

"Miss Crackenthorpe has performed an unpleasant task very bravely," said Bacon.

"Well done, Emma," said the doctor, patting her on the shoulder. "You can take things. I've always known that. Your father's all right. Just go in and have a word with him, and then go into the dining-room and get yourself a glass of brandy. That's a prescription."

Emma smiled at him gratefully and went into the library.

"That woman's the salt of the earth," said the doctor, looking after her. "A thousand pities she's never married. The penalty of being the only female in a family of men. The other sister got clear, married at seventeen, I believe. This one's quite a handsome woman really. She'd have been a success as a wife and mother."

"Too devoted to her father, I suppose," said Inspector Bacon.

"She's not really as devoted as all that—but she's got the instinct some women have to make their menfolk happy. She sees that her father likes being an invalid, so she lets him be an invalid. She's the same with her brothers. Cedric feels he's a good painter, whatshisname—Harold—knows how much she relies on his sound judgment—she lets Alfred shock her with his stories of his clever deals. Oh, yes, she's a clever woman—no fool. Well, do you want me for anything? Want me to have a look at your corpse now Johnstone has done with it" (Johnstone was the police surgeon) "and see if it happens to be one of my medical mistakes?"

"I'd like you to have a look, yes, Doctor. We want to

get her identified. I suppose it's impossible for old Mr. Crackenthorpe? Too much of a strain?"

"Strain? Fiddlesticks. He'd never forgive you or me if you didn't let him have a peep. He's all agog. Most exciting thing that's happened to him for fifteen years or so—*and* it won't cost him anything!"

"There's nothing really much wrong with him then?"

"He's seventy-two," said the doctor. "That's all, really, that's the matter with him. He has odd rheumatic twinges—who doesn't? So he calls it arthritis. He has palpitations after meals—as well he may—he puts them down to 'heart.' But he can always do anything he wants to do! I've plenty of patients like that. The ones who are really ill usually insist desperately that they're perfectly well. Come on, let's go and see this body of yours. Unpleasant, I suppose?"

"Johnstone estimates she's been dead between a fortnight and three weeks."

"Quite unpleasant, then."

The doctor stood by the sarcophagus and looked down with frank curiosity, professionally unmoved by what he had named the "unpleasantness."

"Never seen her before. No patient of mine. I don't remember ever seeing her about in Brackhampton. She must have been quite good-looking once—hm—*somebody* had it in for her all right."

They went out again into the air. Doctor Quimper glanced up at the building.

"Found in the—what do they call it?—the Long Barn —in a sarcophagus! Fantastic! Who found her?"

"Miss Lucy Eyelesbarrow."

"Oh, the latest lady help? What was *she* doing, poking about in sarcophagi?"

"That," said Inspector Bacon grimly, "is just what I am

65   c

going to ask her. Now, about Mr. Crackenthorpe. Will you——?"

"I'll bring him along."

Mr. Crackenthorpe, muffled in scarves, came walking at a brisk pace, the doctor beside him.

"Disgraceful," he said. "Absolutely disgraceful! I brought back that sarcophagus from Florence in—let me see—it must have been in 1908—or was it 1909?"

"Steady now," the doctor warned him. "This isn't going to be nice, you know."

"No matter how ill I am, I've got to do my duty, haven't I?"

A very brief visit inside the Long Barn was, however, quite long enough. Mr. Crackenthorpe shuffled out into the air again with remarkable speed.

"Never saw her before in my life!" he said. "What's it mean? Absolutely disgraceful. It wasn't Florence—I remember now—it was Naples. A very fine specimen. And some fool of a woman has to come and get herself killed in it!"

He clutched at the folds of his overcoat on the left side.

"Too much for me. . . . My heart. . . . Where's Emma? Doctor . . ."

Doctor Quimper took his arm.

"You'll be all right," he said. "I prescribe a little stimulant. Brandy."

They went back together towards the house.

"Sir. Please, sir."

Inspector Bacon turned. Two boys had arrived, breathless, on bicycles. Their faces were full of eager pleading.

"Please, sir, can we see the body?"

"No, you can't," said Inspector Bacon.

"Oh, sir, *please*, sir. You never know. We might know

who she was. Oh, please, sir, do be a sport. It's not fair. Here's a murder, right in our own barn. It's the sort of chance that might never happen again. Do be a sport, sir."

"Who are you two?"

"I'm Alexander Eastley, and this is my friend James Stoddart-West."

"Have you ever seen a blonde woman wearing a light-coloured dyed squirrel coat anywhere about the place?"

"Well, I can't remember exactly," said Alexander astutely. "If I were to have a look——"

"Take 'em in, Sanders," said Inspector Bacon to the constable who was standing by the barn door. "One's only young once!"

"Oh, sir, thank you, sir." Both boys were vociferous. "It's *very* kind of you, sir."

Bacon turned away towards the house.

"And now," he said to himself grimly, "for Miss Lucy Eyelesbarrow!"

III

After leading the police to the Long Barn, and giving a brief account of her actions, Lucy had retired into the background, but she was under no illusion that the police had finished with her.

She had just finished preparing potatoes for chips that evening when word was brought to her that Inspector Bacon required her presence. Putting aside the large bowl of cold water and salt in which the chips were reposing, Lucy followed the policeman to where the Inspector awaited her. She sat down and awaited his questions composedly.

She gave her name—and her address in London, and added of her own accord:

"I will give you some names and addresses of references if you want to know all about me."

The names were very good ones. An Admiral of the Fleet, the Provost of an Oxford College, and a Dame of the British Empire. In spite of himself Inspector Bacon was impressed.

"Now, Miss Eyelesbarrow, you went into the Long Barn to find some paint. Is that right? And after having found the paint you got a crowbar, forced up the lid of this sarcophagus and found the body. What were you looking for in the sarcophagus?"

"I was looking for a body," said Lucy.

"You were looking for a body—and you found one! Doesn't that seem to you a very extraordinary story?"

"Oh, yes, it is an extraordinary story. Perhaps you will let me explain it to you."

"I certainly think you had better do so."

Lucy gave him a precise recital of the events which had led up to her sensational discovery.

The inspector summed it up in an outraged voice.

"You were engaged by an elderly lady to obtain a post here and to search the house and grounds for *a dead body*? Is that right?"

"Yes."

"Who is this elderly lady?"

"Miss Jane Marple. She is at present living at 4 Madison Road."

The Inspector wrote it down.

"You expect me to believe this story?"

Lucy said gently:

"Not, perhaps, until after you have interviewed Miss Marple and got her confirmation of it."

"I shall interview her all right. She must be cracked."

Lucy forbore to point out that to be proved right is not really a proof of mental incapacity. Instead she said:

"What are you proposing to tell Miss Crackenthorpe? About *me*, I mean?"

"Why do you ask?"

"Well, as far as Miss Marple is concerned I've *done* my job, I've found the body she wanted found. But I'm still engaged by Miss Crackenthorpe, and there are two hungry boys in the house and probably some more of the family will soon be coming down after all this upset. She needs domestic help. If you go and tell her that I only took this post in order to hunt for dead bodies she'll probably throw me out. Otherwise I can get on with my job and be useful."

The Inspector looked hard at her.

"I'm not saying anything to *anyone* at present," he said. "I haven't verified your statement yet. For all I know you may be making the whole thing up."

Lucy rose.

"Thank you. Then I'll go back to the kitchen and get on with things."

CHAPTER VII

"WE'D BETTER have the Yard in on it, is that what you think, Bacon?"

The Chief Constable looked inquiringly at Inspector Bacon. The inspector was a big solid man—his expression was that of one utterly disgusted with humanity.

"The woman wasn't a local, sir," he said. "There's some reason to believe—from her underclothing—that she might have been a foreigner. Of course," added Inspector Bacon hastily, "I'm not letting on about that yet awhile. We're keeping it up our sleeves until after the inquest."

The Chief Constable nodded.

"The inquest will be purely formal, I suppose?"

"Yes, sir. I've seen the Coroner."

"And it's fixed for—when?"

"To-morrow. I understand the other members of the Crackenthorpe family will be here for it. There's just a chance *one* of them might be able to identify her. They'll all be here."

He consulted a list he held in his hand.

"Harold Crackenthorpe, he's something in the City— quite an important figure, I understand. Alfred—don't quite know what he does. Cedric—that's the one who lives abroad. Paints!" The inspector invested the word with its full quota of sinister significance. The Chief Constable smiled into his moustache.

"No reason, is there, to believe the Crackenthorpe family are connected with the crime in any way?" he asked.

"Not apart from the fact that the body was found on the premises," said Inspector Bacon. "And of course it's just possible that this artist member of the family might be able to identify her. What beats me is this extraordinary rigmarole about the train."

"Ah, yes. You've been to see this old lady, this—er—" (he glanced at the memorandum lying on his desk) "Miss Marple?"

"Yes, sir. And she's quite set and definite about the whole thing. Whether she's barmy or not, I don't know, but she sticks to her story—about what her friend saw and all the rest of it. As far as all that goes, I dare say it's just make-believe—sort of thing old ladies do make up, like seeing flying saucers at the bottom of the garden, and Russian agents in the lending library. But it seems quite clear that she *did* engage this young woman, the lady help, and told her to look for a body—which the girl did."

"*And* found one," observed the Chief Constable. "Well, it's all a very remarkable story. Marple, Miss Jane Marple —the name seems familiar somehow. . . . Anyway, I'll get on to the Yard. I think you're right about its not being a local case—though we won't advertise the fact just yet. For the moment we'll tell the Press as little as possible."

II

The inquest was a purely formal affair. No one came forward to identify the dead woman. Lucy was called to give evidence of finding the body and medical evidence was given as to the cause of death—strangulation. The proceedings were then adjourned.

It was a cold blustery day when the Crackenthorpe family came out of the hall where the inquest had been held. There were five of them all told, Emma, Cedric, Harold, Alfred, and Bryan Eastley, the husband of the dead daughter Edith. There was also Mr. Wimborne, the senior partner of the firm of solicitors who dealt with the Crackenthorpes' legal affairs. He had come down specially from London at great inconvenience to attend the inquest. They all stood for a moment on the pavement, shivering. Quite a crowd had assembled; the piquant details of the "Body in the Sarcophagus" had been fully reported in both the London and the local Press.

A murmur went round: "That's them. . . ."

Emma said sharply: "Let's get away."

The big hired Daimler drew up to the kerb. Emma got in and motioned to Lucy. Mr. Wimborne, Cedric and Harold followed. Bryan Eastley said: "I'll take Alfred with me in my little bus." The chauffeur shut the door and the Daimler prepared to roll away.

"Oh, stop!" cried Emma. "There are the boys!"

The boys, in spite of aggrieved protests, had been left behind at Rutherford Hall, but they now appeared grinning from ear to ear.

"We came on our bicycles," said Stoddart-West. "The policeman was very kind and let us in at the back of the hall. I hope you don't mind, Miss Crackenthorpe," he added politely.

"She doesn't mind," said Cedric, answering for his sister. "You're only young once. Your first inquest, I expect?"

"It was rather disappointing," said Alexander. "All over so soon."

"We can't stay here talking," said Harold irritably. "There's quite a crowd. And all those men with cameras."

At a sign from him, the chauffeur pulled away from the kerb. The boys waved cheerfully.

"All over so soon!" said Cedric. "That's what *they* think, the young innocents! It's just beginning."

"It's all very unfortunate. *Most* unfortunate," said Harold. "I suppose——"

He looked at Mr. Wimborne who compressed his thin lips and shook his head with distaste.

"I hope," he said sententiously, "that the whole matter will soon be cleared up satisfactorily. The police are very efficient. However, the whole thing, as Harold says, has been most unfortunate."

He looked, as he spoke, at Lucy, and there was distinct disapproval in his glance. "If it had not been for this young woman," his eyes seemed to say, "poking about where she had no business to be—none of this would have happened."

This sentiment, or one closely resembling it, was voiced by Harold Crackenthorpe.

"By the way—er—Miss—er—er—Eyelesbarrow, just what *made* you go looking in that sarcophagus?"

Lucy had already wondered just when this thought would occur to one of the family. She had known that the police would ask it first thing: what surprised her was that it seemed to have occurred to no one else until this moment.

Cedric, Emma, Harold and Mr. Wimborne all looked at her.

Her reply, for what it was worth, had naturally been prepared for some time.

"Really," she said in a hesitating voice, "I hardly

know . . . I *did* feel that the whole place needed a thorough clearing out and cleaning. And there was "—she hesitated —"a very peculiar and disagreeable smell. . . ."

She had counted accurately on the immediate shrinking of everyone from the unpleasantness of this idea. . . .

Mr. Wimborne murmured: "Yes, yes, of course . . . about three weeks the police surgeon said . . . I think, you know, we must all try and not let our minds *dwell* on this thing." He smiled encouragingly at Emma who had turned very pale. "Remember," he said, "this wretched young woman was nothing to do with any of *us*."

"Ah, but you can't be so sure of that, can you?" said Cedric.

Lucy Eyelesbarrow looked at him with some interest. She had already been intrigued by the rather startling differences between the three brothers. Cedric was a big man with a weather-beaten rugged face, unkempt dark hair, and a jocund manner. He had arrived from the airport unshaven, and though he had shaved in preparation for the inquest, he was still wearing the clothes in which he had arrived and which seemed to be the only ones he had; old grey flannel trousers, and a patched and rather threadbare baggy jacket. He looked the stage Bohemian to the life and proud of it.

His brother Harold, on the contrary, was the perfect picture of a City gentleman and a director of important companies. He was tall with a neat erect carriage, had dark hair going slightly bald on the temples, a small black moustache, and was impeccably dressed in a dark well-cut suit and a pearl-grey tie. He looked what he was, a shrewd and successful business man.

He now said stiffly:

"Really, Cedric, that seems a *most* uncalled for remark."

"Don't see why? She was in our barn after all. What did she come there for?"

Mr. Wimborne coughed, and said:

"Possibly some—er—assignation. I understand that it was a matter of local knowledge that the key was kept outside on a nail."

His tone indicated outrage at the carelessness of such procedure. So clearly marked was this that Emma spoke apologetically.

"It started during the war. For the A.R.P. wardens. There was a little spirit stove and they made themselves hot cocoa. And afterwards, since there was really nothing there anybody could have wanted to take, we went on leaving the key hanging up. It was convenient for the Women's Institute people. If we'd kept it in the house it might have been awkward—when there was no one at home to give it them when they wanted it to get the place ready. With only daily women and no resident servants. . . ."

Her voice tailed away. She had spoken mechanically, giving a wordy explanation without interest, as though her mind was elsewhere.

Cedric gave her a quick puzzled glance.

"You're worried, sis. What's up?"

Harold spoke with exasperation:

"Really, Cedric, can you ask?"

"Yes, I do ask. Granted a strange young woman has got herself killed in the barn at Rutherford Hall (sounds like a Victorian melodrama) and granted it gave Emma a shock at the time—but Emma's always been a sensible girl—I don't see why she goes on being worried *now*. Dash it, one gets used to everything."

"Murder takes a little more getting used to by some people than it may in your case," said Harold acidly. "I

75

dare say murders are two a penny in Majorca and——"

"Iviza, not Majorca."

"It's the same thing."

"Not at all—it's quite a different island."

Harold went on talking:

"My point is that though murder may be an everyday commonplace to *you*, living amongst hot-blooded Latin people, nevertheless in England we take such things seriously." He added with increasing irritation, "And really, Cedric, to appear at a public inquest in those clothes——"

"What's wrong with my clothes? They're comfortable."

"They're unsuitable."

"Well, anyway, they're the only clothes I've got with me. I didn't pack my wardrobe trunk when I came rushing home to stand in with the family over this business. I'm a painter and painters like to be comfortable in their clothes."

"So you're still trying to paint?"

"Look here, Harold, when you say trying to paint——"

Mr. Wimborne cleared his throat in an authoritative manner.

"This discussion is unprofitable," he said reprovingly. "I hope, my dear Emma, that you will tell me if there is any further way in which I can be of service to you before I return to town?"

The reproof had its effect. Emma Crackenthorpe said quickly:

"It was most kind of you to come down."

"Not at all. It was advisable that someone should be at the inquest to watch the proceedings on behalf of the family. I have arranged for an interview with the inspector at the house. I have no doubt that, distressing as all this has been, the situation will soon be clarified.

In my own mind, there seems little doubt as to what occurred. As Emma has told us, the key of the Long Barn was known locally to hang outside the door. It seems highly probable that the place was used in the winter months as a place of assignation by local couples. No doubt there was a quarrel and some young man lost control of himself. Horrified at what he had done, his eye lit on the sarcophagus and he realised that it would make an excellent place of concealment."

Lucy thought to herself, " Yes, it sounds most plausible. That's just what one might think."

Cedric said, " You say a local couple—but nobody's been able to identify the girl locally."

" It's early days yet. No doubt we shall get an identification before long. And it is possible, of course, that the *man* in question was a local resident, but that the girl came from elsewhere, perhaps from some other part of Brackhampton. Brackhampton's a big place—it's grown enormously in the last twenty years."

" If I were a girl coming to meet my young man, I'd not stand for being taken to a freezing cold barn miles from anywhere," Cedric objected. " I'd stand out for a nice bit of cuddle in the cinema, wouldn't you, Miss Eyelesbarrow ? "

" Do we need to go into all this ? " Harold demanded plaintively.

And with the voicing of the question the car drew up before the front door of Rutherford Hall and they all got out.

CHAPTER VIII

ON ENTERING the library Mr. Wimborne blinked a little as his shrewd old eyes went past Inspector Bacon whom he had already met, to the fair-haired, good-looking man beyond him.

Inspector Bacon performed introductions.

"This is Detective-Inspector Craddock of New Scotland Yard," he said.

"New Scotland Yard—hm." Mr. Wimborne's eyebrows rose.

Dermot Craddock, who had a pleasant manner, went easily into speech.

"We have been called in on the case, Mr. Wimborne," he said. "As you are representing the Crackenthorpe family, I feel it is only fair that we should give you a little confidential information."

Nobody could make a better show of presenting a very small portion of the truth and implying that it was the whole truth than Inspector Craddock.

"Inspector Bacon will agree, I am sure," he added, glancing at his colleague.

Inspector Bacon agreed with all due solemnity and not at all as though the whole matter were prearranged.

"It's like this," said Craddock. "We have reason to believe, from information that has come into our possession, that the dead woman is not a native of these parts, that she travelled down here from London and that she had recently come from abroad. Probably (though we are not sure of that) from France."

Mr. Wimborne again raised his eyebrows.

"Indeed," he said. "Indeed?"

"That being the case," explained Inspector Bacon, "the Chief Constable felt that the Yard were better fitted to investigate the matter."

"I can only hope," said Mr. Wimborne, "that the case will be solved quickly. As you can no doubt appreciate, the whole business has been a source of much distress to the family. Although not *personally* concerned in any way, they are——"

He paused for a bare second, but Inspector Craddock filled the gap quickly.

"It's not a pleasant thing to find a murdered woman on your property? I couldn't agree with you more. Now I should like to have a brief interview with the various members of the family——"

"I really cannot see——"

"What they can tell me? Probably nothing of interest —but one never knows. I dare say I can get most of the information I want from you, sir. Information about this house and the family."

"And what can that possibly have to do with an unknown young woman coming from abroad and getting herself killed here."

"Well, that's rather the point," said Craddock. "*Why* did she come here? Had she once had some connection with this house? Had she been, for instance, a servant here at one time? A lady's maid, perhaps. Or did she come here to meet a former occupant of Rutherford Hall?"

Mr. Wimborne said coldly that Rutherford Hall had

been occupied by the Crackenthorpes ever since Josiah Crackenthorpe built it in 1884.

"That's interesting in itself," said Craddock. "If you'd just give me a brief outline of the family history——"

Mr. Wimborne shrugged his shoulders.

"There is very little to tell. Josiah Crackenthorpe was a manufacturer of sweet and savoury biscuits, relishes, pickles, etc. He accumulated a vast fortune. He built this house. Luther Crackenthorpe, his eldest son, lives here now."

"Any other sons?"

"One other son, Henry, who was killed in a motor accident in 1911."

"And the present Mr. Crackenthorpe has never thought of selling the house?"

"He is unable to do so," said the lawyer dryly. "By the terms of his father's will."

"Perhaps you'll tell me about the will?"

"Why should I?"

Inspector Craddock smiled.

"Because I can look it up myself if I want to, at Somerset House."

Against his will, Mr. Wimborne gave a crabbed little smile.

"Quite right, Inspector. I was merely protesting that the information you ask for is quite irrelevant. As to Josiah Crackenthorpe's will, there is no mystery about it. He left his very considerable fortune in trust, the income from it to be paid to his son Luther for life, and after Luther's death the capital to be divided equally between Luther's children, Edmund, Cedric, Harold, Alfred, Emma and Edith. Edmund was killed in the war, and Edith died four years ago, so that on Luther Cracken-thorpe's decease the money will be divided between

Cedric, Harold, Alfred, Emma and Edith's son Alexander Eastley."

"And the house?"

"That will go to Luther Crackenthorpe's eldest surviving son or his issue."

"Was Edmund Crackenthorpe married?"

"No."

"So the property will actually go——?"

"To the next son—Cedric."

"Mr. Luther Crackenthorpe himself cannot dispose of it?"

"No."

"And he has no control of the capital."

"No."

"Isn't that rather unusual? I suppose," said Inspector Craddock shrewdly, "that his father didn't like him."

"You suppose correctly," said Mr. Wimborne. "Old Josiah was disappointed that his eldest son showed no interest in the family business—or indeed in business of any kind. Luther spent his time travelling abroad and collecting *objets d'art*. Old Josiah was very unsympathetic to that kind of thing. So he left his money in trust for the next generation."

"But in the meantime the next generation have no income except what they make or what their father allows them, and their father has a considerable income but no power of disposal of the capital."

"Exactly. And what all this has to do with the murder of an unknown young woman of foreign origin I cannot imagine!"

"It doesn't seem to have anything to do with it," Inspector Craddock agreed promptly, "I just wanted to ascertain all the facts."

Mr. Wimborne looked at him sharply, then, seemingly

satisfied with the result of his scrutiny, rose to his feet.

"I am proposing now to return to London," he said. "Unless there is anything further you wish to know?"

He looked from one man to the other.

"No, thank you, sir."

The sound of the gong rose fortissimo from the hall outside.

"Dear me," said Mr. Wimborne. "One of the boys, I think, must be performing."

Inspector Craddock raised his voice, to be heard above the clamour, as he said:

"We'll leave the family to have lunch in peace, but Inspector Bacon and I would like to return after it—say at two-fifteen—and have a short interview with every member of the family."

"You think that is necessary?"

"Well . . ." Craddock shrugged his shoulders. "It's just an off chance. *Somebody* might remember something that would give us a clue to the woman's identity."

"I doubt it, Inspector. I doubt it very much. But I wish you good luck. As I said just now, the sooner this distasteful business is cleared up, the better for everybody."

Shaking his head, he went slowly out of the room.

II

Lucy had gone straight to the kitchen on getting back from the inquest, and was busy with preparations for lunch when Bryan Eastley put his head in.

"Can I give you a hand in any way?" he asked. "I'm handy about the house."

Lucy gave him a quick, slightly preoccupied glance. Bryan had arrived at the inquest direct in his small M.G. car, and she had not as yet had much time to size him up.

What she saw was likeable enough. Eastley was an amiable-looking young man of thirty-odd with brown hair, rather plaintive blue eyes and an enormous fair moustache.

"The boys aren't back yet," he said, coming in and sitting on the end of the kitchen table. "It will take 'em another twenty minutes on their bikes."

Lucy smiled.

"They were certainly determined not to miss anything."

"Can't blame them. I mean to say—first inquest in their young lives and right in the family so to speak."

"Do you mind getting off the table, Mr. Eastley? I want to put the baking dish down there."

Bryan obeyed.

"I say, that fat's corking hot. What are you going to put in it?"

"Yorkshire pudding."

"Good old Yorkshire. Roast beef of old England, is that the menu for to-day?"

"Yes."

"The funeral baked meats, in fact. Smells good." He sniffed appreciatively. "Do you mind my gassing away?"

"If you came in to help I'd rather you helped." She drew another pan from the oven. "Here—turn all these potatoes over so that they brown on the other side. . . ."

Bryan obeyed with alacrity.

"Have all these things been fizzling away in here while we've been at the inquest? Supposing they'd been all burnt up."

"Most improbable. There's a regulating number on the oven."

"Kind of electric brain, eh, what? Is that right?"

Lucy threw a swift look in his direction.

"Quite right. Now put the pan in the oven. Here, take the cloth. On the second shelf—I want the top one for the Yorkshire pudding."

Bryan obeyed, but not without uttering a shrill yelp.

"Burn yourself?"

"Just a bit. It doesn't matter. What a dangerous game cooking is!"

"I suppose you never do your own cooking?"

"As a matter of fact I do—quite often. But not this sort of thing. I can boil an egg—if I don't forget to look at the clock. And I can do eggs and bacon. And I can put a steak under the grill or open a tin of soup. I've got one of those little electric whatnots in my flat."

"You live in London?"

"If you call it living—yes."

His tone was despondent. He watched Lucy shoot in the dish with the Yorkshire pudding mixture.

"This is awfully jolly," he said and sighed.

Her immediate preoccupations over, Lucy looked at him with more attention.

"What is—this kitchen?"

"Yes. Reminds me of our kitchen at home—when I was a boy."

It struck Lucy that there was something strangely forlorn about Bryan Eastley. Looking closely at him, she realised that he was older than she had at first thought. He must be close on forty. It seemed difficult to think of him as Alexander's father. He reminded her of innumerable young pilots she had known during the war when she had been at the impressionable age of fourteen.

She had gone on and grown up into a post-war world—but she felt as though Bryan had not gone on, but had been passed by in the passage of years. His next words confirmed this. He had subsided on to the kitchen table again.

"It's a difficult sort of world," he said, "isn't it? To get your bearings in, I mean. You see, one hasn't been trained for it."

Lucy recalled what she had heard from Emma.

"You were a fighter pilot, weren't you?" she said. "You've got a D.F.C."

"That's the sort of thing that puts you wrong. You've got a gong and so people try to make it easy for you. Give you a job and all that. Very decent of them. But they're all admin. jobs, and one simply isn't any good at that sort of thing. Sitting at a desk getting tangled up in figures. I've had ideas of my own, you know, tried out a wheeze or two. But you can't get the backing. Can't get the chaps to come in and put down the money. If I had a bit of capital——"

He brooded.

"You didn't know Edie, did you? My wife. No, of course you didn't. She was quite different from all this lot. Younger, for one thing. She was in the W.A.A.F. She always said her old man was crackers. He is, you know. Mean as hell over money. And it's not as though he could take it with him. It's got to be divided up when he dies. Edie's share will go to Alexander, of course. He won't be able to touch the capital until he's twenty-one, though."

"I'm sorry, but will you get off the table again? I want to dish up and make gravy."

At that moment Alexander and Stoddart-West arrived with rosy faces and very much out of breath.

"Hallo, Bryan," said Alexander kindly to his father. "So this is where you've got to. I say, what a smashing piece of beef. Is there Yorkshire pudding?"

"Yes, there is."

"We have awful Yorkshire pudding at school—all damp and limp."

"Get out of my way," said Lucy. "I want to make the gravy."

"Make lots of gravy. Can we have two sauce-boats full?"

"Yes."

"Good-oh!" said Stoddart-West, pronouncing the word carefully.

"I don't like it pale," said Alexander anxiously.

"It won't be pale."

"She's a smashing cook," said Alexander to his father.

Lucy had a momentary impression that their rôles were reversed. Alexander spoke like a kindly father to his son.

"Can we help you, Miss Eyelesbarrow?" asked Stoddart-West politely.

"Yes, you can. Alexander, go and sound the gong. James, will you carry this tray into the dining-room? And will you take the joint in, Mr. Eastley? I'll bring the potatoes and the Yorkshire pudding."

"There's a Scotland Yard man here," said Alexander. "Do you think he will have lunch with us?"

"That depends on what your aunt arranges."

"I don't suppose Aunt Emma would mind. . . . She's very hospitable. But I suppose Uncle Harold wouldn't like it. He's being very sticky over this murder." Alexander went out through the door with the tray adding a little additional information over his shoulder. "Mr. Wimborne's in the library with the Scotland Yard man now. But he isn't staying to lunch. He said he had to get back to London. Come on, Stodders. Oh, he's gone to do the gong."

At that moment the gong took charge. Stoddart-West was an artist. He gave it everything he had, and all further conversation was inhibited.

Bryan carried in the joint, Lucy followed with the vegetables—returned to the kitchen to get the two brimming sauce-boats of gravy.

Mr. Wimborne was standing in the hall putting on his gloves—as Emma came quickly down the stairs.

"Are you really sure you won't stop for lunch, Mr. Wimborne? It's all ready."

"No. I've an important appointment in London. There is a restaurant car on the train."

"It was very good of you to come down," said Emma gratefully.

The two police officers emerged from the library.

Mr. Wimborne took Emma's hand in his.

"There's nothing to worry about, my dear," he said. "This is Detective-Inspector Craddock from New Scotland Yard who has come down to take charge of the case. He is coming back at two-fifteen to ask you for any facts that may assist him in his inquiry. But, as I say, you have nothing to worry about." He looked towards Craddock. "I may repeat to Miss Crackenthorpe what you have told me?"

"Certainly, sir."

"Inspector Craddock has just told me that this almost certainly was not a local crime. The murdered woman is thought to have come from London and was probably a foreigner."

Emma Crackenthorpe said sharply:

"A foreigner. Was she French?"

Mr. Wimborne had clearly meant his statement to be consoling. He looked slightly taken aback. Dermot Craddock's glance went quickly from him to Emma's face.

He wondered why she had leaped to the conclusion that the murdered woman was French, and why that thought disturbed her so much?

CHAPTER IX

THE ONLY people who really did justice to Lucy's excellent lunch were the two boys and Cedric Crackenthorpe who appeared completely unaffected by the circumstances which had caused him to return to England. He seemed, indeed, to regard the whole thing as a rather good joke of a macabre nature.

This attitude, Lucy noted, was most unpalatable to his brother Harold. Harold seemed to take the murder as a kind of personal insult to the Crackenthorpe family and so great was his sense of outrage that he ate hardly any lunch. Emma looked worried and unhappy and also ate very little. Alfred seemed lost in a train of thought of his own and spoke very little. He was quite a good-looking man with a thin dark face and eyes set rather too close together.

After lunch the police officers returned and politely asked if they could have a few words with Mr. Cedric Crackenthorpe.

Inspector Craddock was very pleasant and friendly.

"Sit down, Mr. Crackenthorpe. I understand you have just come back from the Balearics? You live out there?"

"Have done for the last six years. In Iviza. Suits me better than this dreary country."

"You get a good deal more sunshine than we do, I expect," said Inspector Craddock agreeably. "You were home not so very long ago, I understand—for Christmas, to be exact. What made it necessary for you to come back again so soon?"

Cedric grinned.

"Got a wire from Emma—my sister. We've never had a murder on the premises before. Didn't want to miss anything—so along I came."

"You are interested in criminology?"

"Oh, we needn't put it in such highbrow terms! I just like murders—Whodunnits, and all that! With a Whodunnit parked right on the family doorstep, it seemed the chance of a lifetime. Besides, I thought poor old Em might need a spot of help—managing the old man and the police and all the rest of it."

"I see. It appealed to your sporting instincts and also to your family feelings. I've no doubt your sister will be very grateful to you—although her two other brothers have also come to be with her."

"But not to cheer and comfort," Cedric told him. "Harold is terrifically put out. It's not at all the thing for a City magnate to be mixed up with the murder of a questionable female."

Craddock's eyebrows rose gently.

"Was she—a questionable female?"

"Well, you're the authority on that point. Going by the facts, it seemed to me likely."

"I thought perhaps you might have been able to make a guess at who she was?"

"Come now, Inspector, you already know—or your

89

colleagues will tell you, that I haven't been able to identify her."

"I said a guess, Mr. Crackenthorpe. You might never have *seen* the woman before—but you might have been able to make a guess at who she was—or who she might have been?"

Cedric shook his head.

"You're barking up the wrong tree. I've absolutely no idea. You're suggesting, I suppose, that she may have come to the Long Barn to keep an assignation with one of us? But we none of us live here. The only people in the house were a woman and an old man. You don't seriously believe that she came here to keep a date with my revered Pop?"

"Our point is—Inspector Bacon agrees with me—that the woman may once have had some association with this house. It may have been a considerable number of years ago. Cast your mind back, Mr. Crackenthorpe."

Cedric thought a moment or two, then shook his head.

"We've had foreign help from time to time, like most people, but I can't think of any likely possibility. Better ask the others—they'd know more than I would."

"We shall do that, of course."

Craddock leaned back in his chair and went on:

"As you have heard at the inquest, the medical evidence cannot fix the time of death very accurately. Longer than two weeks, less than four—which brings it somewhere around Christmas-time. You have told me you came home for Christmas. When did you arrive in England and when did you leave?"

Cedric reflected.

"Let me see. . . . I flew. Got here on the Saturday before Christmas—that would be the 21st."

"You flew straight from Majorca?"

"Yes. Left at five in the morning and got here midday."

"And you left?"

"I flew back on the following Friday, the 27th."

"Thank you."

Cedric grinned.

"Leaves me well within the limit, unfortunately. But really, Inspector, strangling young women is *not* my favourite form of Christmas fun."

"I hope not, Mr. Crackenthorpe."

Inspector Bacon merely looked disapproving.

"There would be a remarkable absence of peace and good will about such an action, don't you agree?"

Cedric addressed this question to Inspector Bacon who merely grunted. Inspector Craddock said politely:

"Well, thank you, Mr. Crackenthorpe. That will be all."

"And what do you think of him?" Craddock asked as Cedric shut the door behind him.

Bacon grunted again.

"Cocky enough for anything," he said. "I don't care for the type, myself. A loose-living lot, these artists, and very likely to be mixed up with a disreputable class of woman."

Craddock smiled.

"I don't like the way he dresses, either," went on Bacon. "No respect—going to an inquest like that. Dirtiest pair of trousers I've seen in a long while. And did you see his tie? Looked as though it was made of coloured string. If you ask me, he's the kind that would easily strangle a woman and make no bones about it."

"Well, he didn't strangle this one—if he didn't leave Majorca until the 21st. And that's a thing we can verify easily enough."

Bacon threw him a sharp glance.

"I notice that you're not tipping your hand yet about the actual date of the crime."

"No, we'll keep that dark for the present. I always like to have something up my sleeve in the early stages."

Bacon nodded in full agreement.

"Spring it on 'em when the time comes," he said. "That's the best plan."

"And now," said Craddock, "we'll see what our correct City gentleman has to say about it all."

Harold Crackenthorpe, thin-lipped, had very little to say about it. It was most distasteful—a very unfortunate incident. The newspapers, he was afraid . . . Reporters, he understood, had already been asking for interviews. . . . All that sort of thing. . . . Most regrettable. . . .

Harold's staccato unfinished sentences ended. He leaned back in his chair with the expression of a man confronted with a very bad smell.

The inspector's probing produced no result. No, he had no idea who the woman was or could be. Yes, he had been at Rutherford Hall for Christmas. He had been unable to come down until Christmas Eve—but had stayed on over the following week-end.

"That's that, then," said Inspector Craddock, without pressing his questions further. He had already made up his mind that Harold Crackenthorpe was not going to be helpful.

He passed on to Alfred, who came into the room with a nonchalance that seemed just a trifle overdone.

Craddock looked at Alfred Crackenthorpe with a faint feeling of recognition. Surely he had seen this particular member of the family somewhere before? Or had it been his picture in the paper? There was something discreditable attached to the memory. He asked Alfred his occupation and Alfred's answer was vague.

"I'm in insurance at the moment. Until recently I've been interested in putting a new type of talking machine on the market. Quite revolutionary. I did very well out of that as a matter of fact."

Inspector Craddock looked appreciative—and no one could have had the least idea that he was noticing the superficially smart appearance of Alfred's suit and gauging correctly the low price it had cost. Cedric's clothes had been disreputable, almost threadbare, but they had been originally of good cut and excellent material. Here there was a cheap smartness that told its own tale. Craddock passed pleasantly on to his routine questions. Alfred seemed interested—even slightly amused.

"It's quite an idea, that the woman might once have had a job here. Not as a lady's maid; I doubt if my sister has ever had such a thing. I don't think anyone has nowadays. But, of course, there is a good deal of foreign domestic labour floating about. We've had Poles—and a temperamental German or two. As Emma definitely didn't recognise the woman, I think that washes your idea out, Inspector, Emma's got a very good memory for a face. No, if the woman came from London . . . What gives you the idea she came from London, by the way?"

He slipped the question in quite casually, but his eyes were sharp and interested.

Inspector Craddock smiled and shook his head.

Alfred looked at him keenly.

"Not telling, eh? Return ticket in her coat pocket, perhaps, is that it?"

"It could be, Mr. Crackenthorpe."

"Well, granting she came from London, perhaps the chap she came to meet had the idea that the Long Barn would be a nice place to do a quiet murder. He knows

93

the set up here, evidently. I should go looking for *him* if I were you, Inspector."

"We are," said Inspector Craddock, and made the two little words sound quiet and confident.

He thanked Alfred and dismissed him.

"You know," he said to Bacon, "I've seen that chap somewhere before. . . ."

Inspector Bacon gave his verdict.

"Sharp customer," he said. "So sharp that he cuts himself sometimes."

II

"I don't suppose you want to see me," said Bryan Eastley apologetically, coming into the room and hesitating by the door. "I don't exactly belong to the family——"

"Let me see, you are Mr. Bryan Eastley, the husband of Miss Edith Crackenthorpe, who died five years ago?"

"That's right."

"Well, it's very kind of you, Mr. Eastley, especially if you know something that you think could assist us in some way?"

"But I don't. Wish I did. Whole thing seems so ruddy peculiar, doesn't it? Coming along and meeting some fellow in that draughty old barn in the middle of winter. Wouldn't be my cup of tea!"

"It is certainly very perplexing," Inspector Craddock agreed.

"Is it true that she was a foreigner? Word seems to have got round to that effect."

"Does that fact suggest anything to you?" The

inspector looked at him sharply, but Bryan seemed amiably vacuous.

"No, it doesn't, as a matter of fact."

"Maybe she was French," said Inspector Bacon, with dark suspicion.

Bryan was roused to slight animation. A look of interest came into his blue eyes, and he tugged at his big fair moustache.

"Really? Gay Paree?" He shook his head. "On the whole it seems to make it even more unlikely, doesn't it? Messing about in the barn, I mean. You haven't had any other sarcophagus murders, have you? One of these fellows with an urge—or a complex? Thinks he's Caligula or someone like that?"

Inspector Craddock did not even trouble to reject this speculation. Instead he asked in a casual manner:

"Nobody in the family got any French connections, or —or—relationships that you know of?"

Bryan said that the Crackenthorpes weren't a very gay lot.

"Harold's respectably married," he said. "Fish-faced woman, some impoverished peer's daughter. Don't think Alfred cares about women much—spends his life going in for shady deals which usually go wrong in the end. I dare say Cedric's got a few Spanish señoritas jumping through hoops for him in Iviza. Women rather fall for Cedric. Doesn't always shave and looks as though he never washes. Don't see why that should be attractive to women, but apparently it is—I say, I'm not being very helpful, am I?"

He grinned at them.

"Better get young Alexander on the job. He and James Stoddart-West are out hunting for clues in a big way. Bet you they turn up something."

Inspector Craddock said he hoped they would. Then he thanked Bryan Eastley and said he would like to speak to Miss Emma Crackenthorpe.

III

Inspector Craddock looked with more attention at Emma Crackenthorpe than he had done previously. He was still wondering about the expression that he had surprised on her face before lunch.

A quiet woman. Not stupid. Not brilliant either. One of those comfortable pleasant women whom men were inclined to take for granted, and who had the art of making a house into a home, giving it an atmosphere of restfulness and quiet harmony. Such, he thought, was Emma Crackenthorpe.

Women such as this were often underrated. Behind their quiet exterior they had force of character, they were to be reckoned with. Perhaps, Craddock thought, the clue to the mystery of the dead woman in the sarcophagus was hidden away in the recesses of Emma's mind.

Whilst these thoughts were passing through his head, Craddock was asking various unimportant questions.

"I don't suppose there is much that you haven't already told Inspector Bacon," he said. "So I needn't worry you with many questions."

"Please ask me anything you like."

"As Mr. Wimborne told you, we have reached the conclusion that the dead women was not a native of these parts. That may be a relief to you—Mr. Wimborne seemed to think it would be—but it makes it really more difficult for us. She's less easily identified."

"But didn't she have anything—a handbag? Papers?"

Craddock shook his head.

"No handbag, nothing in her pockets."

"You've no idea of her name—of where she came from
—anything at all?"

Craddock thought to himself: She wants to know—
she's very anxious to know—who the woman is. Has she
felt like that all along, I wonder? Bacon didn't give me
that impression—and he's a shrewd man. . . .

"We know nothing about her," he said. "That's why
we hoped one of you could help us. Are you sure you
can't? Even if you didn't recognise her—can you think
of anyone she might be?"

He thought, but perhaps he imagined it, that there was
a very slight pause before she answered.

"I've absolutely no idea," she said.

Imperceptibly, Inspector Craddock's manner changed.
It was hardly noticeable except as a slight hardness in his
voice.

"When Mr. Wimborne told you that the woman
was a foreigner, why did you assume that she was
French?"

Emma was not disconcerted. Her eyebrows rose
slightly.

"Did I? Yes, I believe I did. I don't really know why—
except that one always tends to think foreigners *are* French
until one finds out what nationality they really are. Most
foreigners in this country are French, aren't they?"

"Oh, I really wouldn't say that was so, Miss Crackenthorpe. Not nowadays. We have so many nationalities
over here, Italians, Germans, Austrians, all the Scandi-
navian countries——"

"Yes, I suppose you're right."

"You didn't have some special reason for thinking that
this woman was likely to be French."

She didn't hurry to deny it. She just thought a moment and then shook her head almost regretfully.

"No," she said. "I really don't think so."

Her glance met his placidly, without flinching. Craddock looked towards Inspector Bacon. The latter leaned forward and presented a small enamel powder compact.

"Do you recognise this, Miss Crackenthorpe?"

She took it and examined it.

"No. It's certainly not mine."

"You've no idea to whom it belonged?"

"No."

"Then I don't think we need worry you any more—for the present."

"Thank you."

She smiled briefly at them, got up, and left the room. Again he may have imagined it, but Craddock thought she moved rather quickly, as though a certain relief hurried her.

"Think she knows anything?" asked Bacon.

Inspector Craddock said ruefully:

"At a certain stage one is inclined to think everyone knows a little more than they are willing to tell you."

"They usually do, too," said Bacon out of the depth of his experience. "Only," he added, "it quite often isn't anything to do with the business in hand. It's some family peccadillo or some silly scrape that people are afraid is going to be dragged into the open."

"Yes, I know. Well, at least——"

But whatever Inspector Craddock had been about to say never got said, for the door was flung open and old Mr. Crackenthorpe shuffled in in a high state of indignation.

"A pretty pass," he said. "Things have come to a pretty pass, when Scotland Yard comes down and doesn't have the courtesy to talk to the head of the family first! Who's the master of this house, I'd like to know? Answer me that? Who's master here?"

"You are, of course, Mr. Crackenthorpe," said Craddock soothingly and rising as he spoke. "But we understood that you had already told Inspector Bacon all you knew, and that, your health not being good, we must not make too many demands upon it. Dr. Quimper said——"

"I dare say—I dare say. I'm not a strong man. . . . As for Dr. Quimper, he's a regular old woman—perfectly good doctor, understands my case—but inclined to wrap me up in cotton-wool. Got a bee in his bonnet about food. Went on at me Christmas-time when I had a bit of a turn —what did I eat? When? Who cooked it? Who served it? Fuss, fuss, fuss! But though I may have indifferent health, I'm well enough to give you all the help that's in my power. Murder in my own house—or at any rate in my own barn! Interesting building, that. Elizabethan. Local architect says not—but fellow doesn't know what he's talking about. Not a day later than 1580—but that's not what we're talking about. What do you want to know? What's your present theory?"

"It's a little too early for theories, Mr. Crackenthorpe. We are still trying to find out who the woman was?"

"Foreigner, you say?"

"We think so."

"Enemy agent?"

"Unlikely, I should say."

"You'd say—you'd say! They're everywhere, these people. Infiltrating! Why the Home Office lets them in beats me. Spying on industrial secrets, I'd bet. That's what she was doing."

"In Brackhampton?"

"Factories everywhere. One outside my own back gate."

Craddock shot an inquiring glance at Bacon who responded.

"Metal Boxes."

"How do you know that's what they're really making? Can't swallow all these fellows tell you. All right, if she wasn't a spy, who do you think she was? Think she was mixed up with one of my precious sons? It would be Alfred, if so. Not Harold, he's too careful. And Cedric doesn't condescend to live in this country. All right, then, she was Alfred's bit of skirt. And some violent fellow followed her down here, thinking she was coming to meet him and did her in. How's that?"

Inspector Craddock said diplomatically that it was certainly a theory. But Mr. Alfred Crackenthorpe, he said, had not recognised her.

"Pah! Afraid, that's all! Alfred always was a coward. But he's a liar, remember, always was! Lie himself black in the face. None of my sons are any good. Crowd of vultures, waiting for me to die, that's their real occupation in life." He chuckled. "*And* they can wait. I won't die to oblige *them*! Well, if that's all I can do for you ... I'm tired. Got to rest."

He shuffled out again.

"Alfred's bit of skirt?" said Bacon questioningly. "In my opinion the old man just made that up." He paused, hesitated. "I think, personally, Alfred's quite all right—perhaps a shifty customer in some ways—but not our present cup of tea. Mind you—I did just wonder about that Air Force chap."

"Bryan Eastley?"

"Yes. I've run into one or two of his type. They're what you might call adrift in the world—had danger and death and excitement too early in life. Now they find life tame. Tame and unsatisfactory. In a way, we've given them a raw deal. Though I don't really know what we could do about it. But there they are, all past and no future, so to speak. And they're the kind that don't mind taking chances—the ordinary fellow plays safe by instinct, it's not so much morality as prudence. But these fellows aren't afraid—playing safe isn't really in their vocabulary. If Eastley were mixed up with a woman and wanted to kill her . . ." He stopped, threw out a hand hopelessly. "But why should he want to kill her? And if you do kill a woman, why plant her in your father-in-law's sarcophagus? No, if you ask me, none of this lot had anything to do with the murder. If they had, they wouldn't have gone to all the trouble of planting the body on their own back door step, so to speak."

Craddock agreed that that hardly made sense.

"Anything more you want to do here?"

Craddock said there wasn't.

Bacon suggested coming back to Brackhampton and having a cup of tea—but Inspector Craddock said that he was going to call on an old acquaintance.

CHAPTER X

MISS MARPLE, sitting erect against a background of china dogs and presents from Margate, smiled approvingly at Inspector Dermot Craddock.

"I'm so glad," she said, "that you have been assigned to the case. I hoped you would be."

"When I got your letter," said Craddock, "I took it straight to the A.C. As it happened he had just heard from the Brackhampton people calling us in. They seemed to think it wasn't a local crime. The A.C. was very interested in what I had to tell him about you. He'd heard about you, I gather, from my godfather."

"Dear Sir Henry," murmured Miss Marple affectionately.

"He got me to tell him all about the Little Paddocks business. Do you want to hear what he said next?"

"Please tell me if it is not a breach of confidence."

"He said, ' Well, as this seems a completely cockeyed business, all thought up by a couple of old ladies who've turned out, against all probability, to be right, and since you already know one of these old ladies, I'm sending you down on the case.' So here I am! And now, my dear Miss Marple, where do we go from here? This is not, as you probably appreciate, an official visit. I haven't got my henchmen with me. I thought you and I might take down our back hair together first."

Miss Marple smiled at him.

"I'm sure," she said, "that no one who only knows you officially would ever guess that you could be so human, and better-looking than ever—don't blush. . . . Now, what, exactly, have you been told so far?"

"I've got everything, I think. Your friend, Mrs. Mc-Gillicuddy's original statement to the police at St. Mary Mead, confirmation of her statement by the ticket collector, and also the note to the station master at Brackhampton. I may say that all the proper inquiries were made by the people concerned—the railway people and the police. But there's no doubt that you outsmarted them all by a most fantastic process of guesswork."

"*Not* guesswork," said Miss Marple. "And I had a great advantage. I *knew* Elspeth McGillicuddy. Nobody else did. There was no obvious confirmation of her story, and if there was no question of any woman being reported missing, then quite naturally they would think it was just an elderly lady imagining things—as elderly ladies often do—but not Elspeth McGillicuddy."

"Not Elspeth McGillicuddy," agreed the Inspector. "I'm looking forward to meeting her, you know. I wish she hadn't gone to Ceylon. We're arranging for her to be interviewed there, by the way."

"My own process of reasoning was not really original," said Miss Marple. "It's all in Mark Twain. The boy who found the horse. He just imagined where he would go if he were a horse and he went there and there was the horse."

"You imagined what you'd do if you were a cruel and cold-blooded murderer?" said Craddock looking thoughtfully at Miss Marple's pink and white elderly fragility. "Really, your mind——"

"Like a sink, my nephew Raymond used to say," Miss

Marple agreed, nodding her head briskly. "But as I always told him, sinks are necessary domestic equipment and actually very hygienic."

"Can you go a little further still, put yourself in the murderer's place, and tell me just where he is now?"

Miss Marple sighed.

"I wish I could. I've no idea—no idea at all. But he must be someone who has lived in, or knows all about, Rutherford Hall."

"I agree. But that opens up a very wide field. Quite a succession of daily women have worked there. There's the Women's Institute—and the A.R.P. Wardens before them. They all know the Long Barn and the sarcophagus and where the key was kept. The whole set up there is widely known locally. *Anybody* living round about might hit on it as a good spot for his purpose."

"Yes, indeed. I *quite* understand your difficulties."

Craddock said: "We'll never get anywhere until we identify the body."

"And that, too, may be difficult?"

"Oh, we'll get there—in the end. We're checking up on all the reported disappearances of a woman of that age and appearance. There's no one outstanding who fits the bill. The M.O. puts her down as about thirty-five, healthy, probably a married woman, has had at least one child. Her fur coat is a cheap one purchased at a London store. Hundreds of such coats were sold in the last three months, about sixty per cent of them to blonde women. No sales girl can recognise the photograph of the dead woman, or is likely to if the purchase were made just before Christmas. Her other clothes seem mainly of foreign manufacture, mostly purchased in Paris. There are no English laundry marks. We've communicated with Paris and they are checking up there for us. Sooner or later, of course, someone will come forward with a missing relative or lodger. It's just a matter of time."

"The compact wasn't any help?"

"Unfortunately, no. It's a type sold by the hundred in the Rue de Rivoli, quite cheap. By the way, you ought to have turned that over to the police at once, you know—or rather Miss Eyelesbarrow should have done so."

Miss Marple shook her head.

"But at that moment there wasn't any question of a crime having been committed," she pointed out. "If a young lady, practising golf shots, picks up an old compact of no particular value in the long grass, surely she doesn't rush straight off to the police with it?" Miss Marple paused, and then added firmly: "I thought it *much* wiser to find the body first."

Inspector Craddock was tickled.

"You don't seem ever to have had any doubts but that it would be found?"

"I was sure it would. Lucy Eyelesbarrow is a most efficient and intelligent person."

"I'll say she is! She scares the life out of me, she's so devastatingly efficient. No man will ever dare marry that girl."

"Now you know, I wouldn't say *that*. . . . It would have to be a special type of man, of course." Miss Marple brooded on this thought a moment. "How is she getting on at Rutherford Hall?"

"They're completely dependent upon her as far as I can see. Eating out of her hand—literally as you might say. By the way, they know nothing about her connection with you. We've kept that dark."

"She has no connection *now* with me. She has done what I asked her to do."

"So she could hand in her notice and go if she wanted to?"

"Yes."

"But she stops on. Why?"

"She has not mentioned her reasons to me. She is a very intelligent girl. I suspect that she has become interested."

"In the problem? Or in the family?"

"It may be," said Miss Marple, "that it is rather difficult to separate the two."

Craddock looked hard at her.

"Have you got anything particular in mind?"

"Oh, no—oh, dear me, no."

"I think you have."

Miss Marple shook her head.

Dermot Craddock sighed. "So all I can do is to ' prosecute my inquiries '—to put it in jargon. A policeman's life is a dull one!"

"You'll get results, I'm sure."

"Any ideas for me? More inspired guesswork?"

"I was thinking of things like theatrical companies," said Miss Marple rather vaguely. "Touring from place to place and perhaps not many home ties. One of those young women would be much less likely to be missed."

"Yes. Perhaps you've got something there. We'll pay special attention to that angle." He added, "What are you smiling about?"

"I was just thinking," said Miss Marple, "of Elspeth McGillicuddy's face when she hears we've found the body!"

II

"Well!" said Mrs. McGillicuddy. "*Well!*"

Words failed her. She looked across at the nicely spoken pleasant young man who had called upon her with official credentials and then down at the photographs that he had handed her.

"That's her all right," she said. "Yes, that's her. Poor soul. Well, I must say I'm glad you've found her body. Nobody believed a word I said! The police, or the railway people or anyone else. It's very galling not to be believed. At any rate, nobody could say I didn't do all I possibly could."

The nice young man made sympathetic and appreciative noises.

"Where did you say the body was found?"

"In a barn at a house called Rutherford Hall, just outside Brackhampton."

"Never heard of it. How did it get there, I wonder?"

The young man did not reply.

"Jane Marple found it, I suppose. Trust Jane."

"The body," said the young man, referring to some notes, "was found by a Miss Lucy Eyelesbarrow."

"Never heard of her either," said Mrs. McGillicuddy. "I still think Jane Marple had something to do with it."

"Anyway, Mrs. McGillicuddy, you definitely identify this picture as that of the woman whom you saw in a train?"

"Being strangled by a man. Yes, I do."

"Now, can you describe this man?"

"He was a tall man," said Mrs. McGillicuddy.

"Yes?"

" And dark."

" Yes? "

" That's all I can tell you," said Mrs. McGillicuddy.
" He had his back to me. I didn't see his face."

" Would you be able to recognise him if you saw him? "

" Of course I shouldn't! He had his back to me. I never
saw his face."

" You've no idea at all as to his age? "

Mrs. McGillicuddy considered.

" No—not really. I mean, I don't *know*. . . . He wasn't,
I'm almost sure—very young. His shoulders looked—well,
set, if you know what I mean." The young man nodded.
" Thirty and upward, I can't get closer than that. I wasn't
really looking at him, you see. It was *her*—with those
hands round her throat and her face—all blue. . . . You
know, sometimes I dream of it even now. . . ."

" It must have been a distressing experience," said the
young man sympathetically.

He closed his notebook and said:

" When are you returning to England? "

" Not for another three weeks. It isn't necessary, is it,
for me? "

He quickly reassured her.

" Oh, no. There's nothing you could do at present. Of
course, if we make an arrest——"

It was left like that.

The mail brought a letter from Miss Marple to her
friend. The writing was spiky and spidery and heavily
underlined. Long practice made it easy for Mrs. Mc-
Gillicuddy to decipher. Miss Marple wrote a very full
account to her friend who devoured every word with
great satisfaction.

She and Jane had shown them all right!

CHAPTER VI

"I SIMPLY can't make you out," said Cedric Crackenthorpe.

He eased himself down on the decaying wall of a long derelict pigsty and stared at Lucy Eyelesbarrow.

"What can't you make out?"

"What you're doing here."

"I'm earning my living."

"As a skivvy?" He spoke disparagingly.

"You're out of date," said Lucy. "Skivvy, indeed! I'm a Household Help, a Professional Domestician, or an Answer to Prayer, mainly the latter."

"You can't like all the things you have to do—cooking and making beds and whirring about with a hoopla or whatever you call it, and sinking your arms up to the elbows in greasy water."

Lucy laughed.

"Not the details, perhaps, but cooking satisfies my creative instincts, and there's something in me that really revels in clearing up mess."

"I live in a permanent mess," said Cedric. "I like it," he added defiantly.

"You look as though you did."

"My cottage in Iviza is run on simple straightforward lines. Three plates, two cups and saucers, a bed, a table and a couple of chairs. There's dust everywhere and smears of paint and chips of stone—I sculpt as well as paint—and nobody's allowed to touch a thing. I won't have a woman near the place."

"Not in any capacity?"

"Just what do you mean by that?"

"I was assuming that a man of such artistic tastes presumably had some kind of love life."

"My love life, as you call it, is my own business," said Cedric with dignity. "What I won't have is woman in her tidying-up interfering *bossing* capacity!"

"How I'd love to have a go at your cottage," said Lucy. "It would be a challenge!"

"You won't get the opportunity."

"I suppose not."

Some bricks fell out of the pigsty. Cedric turned his head and looked into its nettle-ridden depths.

"Dear old Madge," he said. "I remember her well. A sow of most endearing disposition and a prolific mother. Seventeen in the last litter, I remember. We used to come here on fine afternoons and scratch Madge's back with a stick. She loved it."

"Why has this whole place been allowed to get into the state it's in? It can't only be the war?"

"You'd like to tidy this up, too, I suppose? What an interfering female you are. I quite see now why you *would* be the person to discover a body! You couldn't even leave a Greco-Roman sarcophagus alone." He paused and then went on. "No, it's not only the war. It's my father. What do you think of him, by the way?"

"I haven't had much time for thinking."

"Don't evade the issue. He's as mean as hell, and in my opinion a bit crazy as well. Of course he hates all of us—except perhaps Emma. That's because of my grandfather's will."

Lucy looked inquiring.

"My grandfather was the man who mada-da-monitch. With the Crunchies and the Cracker Jacks and the Cosy Crisps. All the afternoon tea delicacies, and then, being far sighted, he switched on very early to Cheesies and Canapés so that now we cash in on cocktail parties in a big way. Well, the time came when father intimated that he had a soul above Crunchies. He travelled in Italy and the Balkans and Greece and dabbled in art. My grandfather was peeved. He decided my father was no man of business and a rather poor judge of art (quite right in both cases), so left all his money in trust for his grandchildren. Father had the income for life, but he couldn't touch the capital. Do you know what he did? He stopped spending money. He came here and began to save. I'd say that by now he's accumulated nearly as big a fortune as my grandfather left. And in the meantime all of us, Harold, myself, Alfred and Emma haven't got a penny of grandfather's money. I'm a stony-broke painter. Harold went into business and is now a prominent man in the City—he's the one with the money-making touch, though I've heard rumours that he's in Queer Street lately. Alfred—well, Alfred is usually known in the privacy of the family as Flash Alf——"

"Why?"

"What a lot of things you want to know! The answer is that Alf is the black sheep of the family. He's not actually been to prison yet, but he's been very near it. He was in the Ministry of Supply during the war, but left it rather abruptly under questionable circumstances. And after that there were some dubious deals in tinned fruits—and trouble over eggs. Nothing in a big way— just a few doubtful deals on the side."

"Isn't it rather unwise to tell strangers all these things?"

"Why? Are you a police spy?"

"I might be."

"I don't think so. You were here slaving away before the police began to take an interest in us. I should say——"

He broke off as his sister Emma came through the door of the kitchen garden.

"Hallo, Em? You're looking very perturbed about something."

"I am. I want to talk to you, Cedric."

"I must get back to the house," said Lucy, tactfully.

"Don't go," said Cedric. "Murder has made you practically one of the family."

"I've got a lot to do," said Lucy. "I only came out to get some parsley."

She beat a rapid retreat to the kitchen garden. Cedric's eyes followed her.

"Good-looking girl," he said. "Who is she really?"

"Oh, she's quite well known," said Emma. "She's made a speciality of this kind of thing. But never mind Lucy Eyelesbarrow, Cedric, I'm terribly worried. Apparently the police think that the dead woman was a foreigner, perhaps French. Cedric, you don't think that she could possibly be—*Martine*?"

II

For a moment or two Cedric stared at her as though uncomprehending.

"Martine? But who on earth—oh, you mean *Martine*?"

"Yes. Do you think——"

"Why on earth should it be *Martine*?"

"Well, her sending that telegram was odd when you come to think of it. It must have been roughly about the same time. . . . Do you think that she may, after all, have come down here and——"

"Nonsense. Why should Martine come down here and find her way into the Long Barn? What for? It seems wildly unlikely to me."

"You don't think, perhaps, that I ought to tell Inspector Bacon—or the other one?"

"Tell him what?"

"Well—about Martine. About her letter."

"Now don't you go complicating things, sis, by bringing up a lot of irrelevant stuff that has nothing to do with all this. I was never very convinced about that letter from Martine, anyway."

"I was."

"You've always been good at believing impossible things before breakfast, old girl. My advice to you is, sit tight, and keep your mouth shut. It's up to the police to identify their precious corpse. And I bet Harold would say the same."

"Oh, I know Harold would. And Alfred, also. But I'm worried, Cedric, I really *am* worried. I don't know what I ought to do."

"Nothing," said Cedric promptly. "You keep your mouth shut, Emma. Never go half-way to meet trouble, that's my motto."

Emma Crackenthorpe sighed. She went slowly back to the house uneasy in her mind.

As she came into the drive, Doctor Quimper emerged from the house and opened the door of his battered Austin car. He paused when he saw her, then leaving the car, he came towards her.

"Well, Emma," he said. "Your father's in splendid shape. Murder suits him. It's given him an interest in life. I must recommend it for more of my patients."

Emma smiled mechanically. Dr. Quimper was always quick to notice reactions.

"Anything particular the matter?" he asked.

Emma looked up at him. She had come to rely a lot on the kindliness and sympathy of the doctor. He had become a friend on whom to lean, not only a medical attendant. His calculated brusqueness did not deceive her —she knew the kindness that lay behind it.

"I am worried, yes," she admitted.

"Care to tell me? Don't if you don't want to."

"I'd like to tell you. Some of it you know already. The point is I don't know what to do."

"I should say your judgment was usually most reliable. What's the trouble?"

"You remember—or perhaps you don't—what I once told you about my brother—the one who was killed in the war?"

"You mean about his having married—or wanting to marry—a French girl? Something of that kind?"

"Yes. Almost immediately after I got that letter, he was killed. We never heard anything of or about the girl. All we knew, actually, was her Christian name. We always expected her to write or to turn up, but she didn't. We never heard *anything*—until about a month ago, just before Christmas."

"I remember. You got a letter, didn't you?"

"Yes. Saying she was in England and would like to come and see us. It was all arranged and then, at the last minute, she sent a wire that she had to return unexpectedly to France."

"Well?"

"The police think that this woman who was killed—was French."

"They do, do they? She looked more of an English type

114

to me, but one can't really judge. What's worrying you then, is that just possibly the dead woman might be your brother's girl?"

"Yes."

"I think it's most unlikely," said Dr. Quimper, adding: "But all the same, I understand what you feel."

"I'm wondering if I ought not to tell the police about —about it all. Cedric and the others say it's quite unnecessary. What do you think?"

"Hm." Dr. Quimper pursed up his lips. He was silent for a moment or two, deep in thought. Then he said, almost unwillingly, "It's much *simpler*, of course, if you say nothing. I can understand what your brothers feel about it. All the same——"

"Yes?"

Quimper looked at her. His eyes had an affectionate twinkle in them.

"I'd go ahead and tell 'em," he said. "You'll go on worrying if you don't. I know you."

Emma flushed a little.

"Perhaps I'm foolish."

"You do what you want to do, my dear—and let the rest of the family go hang! I'd back your judgment against the lot of them any day."

CHAPTER XII

"GIRL! You, girl! Come in here."

Lucy turned her head, surprised. Old Mr. Crackenthorpe was beckoning to her fiercely from just inside a door.

"You want me, Mr. Crackenthorpe?"

"Don't talk so much. Come in here."

Lucy obeyed the imperative finger. Old Mr. Crackenthorpe took hold of her arm and pulled her inside the door and shut it.

"Want to show you something," he said.

Lucy looked round her. They were in a small room evidently designed to be used as a study, but equally evidently not used as such for a very long time. There were piles of dusty papers on the desk and cobwebs festooned from the corners of the ceiling. The air smelt damp and musty.

"Do you want me to clean this room?" she asked.

Old Mr. Crackenthorpe shook his head fiercely.

"No, you don't! I keep this room locked up. Emma would like to fiddle about in here, but I don't let her. It's *my* room. See these stones? They're geological specimens."

Lucy looked at a collection of twelve or fourteen lumps of rock, some polished and some rough.

"Lovely," she said kindly. "Most interesting."

"You're quite right. They are interesting. You're an intelligent girl. I don't show them to everybody. I'll show you some more things."

"It's very kind of you, but I ought really to get on with what I was doing. With six people in the house——"

"Eating me out of house and home. . . . That's all they do when they come down here! *Eat*. They don't offer to pay for what they eat, either. Leeches! All waiting for me to die. Well, I'm not going to die just yet—I'm not going to die to please *them*. I'm a lot stronger than even Emma knows."

"I'm sure you are."

"I'm not so old, either. She makes out I'm an old man, treats me as an old man. You don't think I'm old, do you?"

"Of course not," said Lucy.

"Sensible girl. Take a look at this."

He indicated a large faded chart which hung on the wall. It was, Lucy saw, a genealogical tree; some of it done so finely that one would have had to have a magnifying glass to read the names. The remote forebears, however, were written in large proud capitals with crowns over the names.

"Descended from Kings," said Mr. Crackenthorpe. "My mother's family tree, that is—not my father's. He was a vulgarian! Common old man! Didn't like me. I was a cut above him always. Took after my mother's side. Had a natural feeling for art and classical sculpture —*he* couldn't see anything in it—silly old fool. Don't remember my mother—died when I was two. Last of her family. They were sold up and she married my father. But you look there—Edward the Confessor—Ethelred the Unready—whole lot of them. And that was before the Normans came. *Before the Normans*—that's something, isn't it?"

"It is indeed."

"Now I'll show you something else." He guided her

across the room to an enormous piece of dark oak furniture. Lucy was rather uneasily conscious of the strength of the fingers clutching her arm. There certainly seemed nothing feeble about old Mr. Crackenthorpe to-day. "See this? Came out of Lushington—that was my mother's people's place. Elizabethan, this is. Takes four men to move it. You don't know what I keep inside it, do you? Like me to show you?"

"Do show me," said Lucy politely.

"Curious, aren't you? All women are curious." He took a key from his pocket and unlocked the door of the lower cupboard. From this he took out a surprisingly new-looking cash box. This, again, he unlocked.

"Take a look here, my dear. Know what these are?"

He lifted out a small paper-wrapped cylinder and pulled away the paper from one end. Gold coins trickled out into his palm.

"Look at these, young lady. Look at 'em, hold 'em, touch 'em. Know what they are? Bet you don't! You're too young. Sovereigns—that's what they are. Good golden sovereigns. What we used before all these dirty bits of paper came into fashion. Worth a lot more than silly pieces of paper. Collected them a long time back. I've got other things in this box, too. Lots of things put away in here. All ready for the future. Emma doesn't know—nobody knows. It's our secret, see, girl? D'you know why I'm telling you and showing you?"

"Why?"

"Because I don't want you to think I'm a played-out sick old man. Lots of life in the old dog yet. My wife's been dead a long time. Always objecting to everything, she was. Didn't like the names I gave the children—good Saxon names—no interest in that family tree. I never paid any attention to what she said, though—and she was a poor-spirited creature—always gave in. Now you're a spirited filly—a very nice filly indeed. I'll give you some advice. Don't throw yourself away on a young man. Young men are fools! You want to take care of your future. You *wait. . . .*" His fingers pressed into Lucy's arm. He leaned to her ear. "I don't say more than that. *Wait.* Those silly fools think I'm going to die soon. I'm not. Shouldn't be surprised if I outlived the lot of them. And then we'll see! Oh, yes, then we'll see. Harold's got no children. Cedric and Alfred aren't married. Emma— Emma will never marry now. She's a bit sweet on Quimper—but Quimper will never think of marrying Emma. There's Alexander, of course. Yes, there's Alexander. . . . But, you know, I'm fond of Alexander. . . . Yes, that's awkward. I'm fond of Alexander."

He paused for a moment, frowning, then said:

"Well, girl, what about it? What about it, eh?"

"Miss Eyelesbarrow. . . ."

Emma's voice came faintly through the closed study door. Lucy seized gratefully at the opportunity.

"Miss Crackenthorpe's calling me. I must go. Thank you so much for all you have shown me. . . ."

"Don't forget . . . our secret . . ."

"I won't forget," said Lucy, and hurried out into the hall not quite certain as to whether she had or had not just received a conditional proposal of marriage.

II

Dermot Craddock sat at his desk in his room at New Scotland Yard. He was slumped sideways in an easy attitude, and was talking into the telephone receiver which he held with one elbow propped up on the table. He was speaking in French, a language in which he was tolerably proficient.

"It was only an idea, you understand," he said.

"But decidedly it is an idea," said the voice at the other end, from the Prefecture in Paris. "Already I have set inquiries in motion in those circles. My agent reports that he has two or three promising lines of inquiry. Unless there is some family life—or a lover, these women drop out of circulation very easily and no one troubles about them. They have gone on tour, or there is some new man—it is no one's business to ask. It is a pity that the photograph you sent me is so difficult for anyone to recognise. Strangulation, it does not improve the appearance. Still, that cannot be helped. I go now to study the latest reports of my agents on this matter. There will be, perhaps, something. *Au revoir, mon cher.*"

As Craddock reiterated the farewell politely, a slip of paper was placed before him on the desk. It read:

Miss Emma Crackenthorpe.
To see Detective-Inspector Craddock.
Rutherford Hall case.

He replaced the receiver and said to the police constable: "Bring Miss Crackenthorpe up."

As he waited, he leaned back in his chair, thinking.

So he had not been mistaken—there was something that Emma Crackenthorpe knew—not much, perhaps, but something. And she had decided to tell him.

He rose to his feet as she was shown in, shook hands, settled her in a chair and offered her a cigarette which she refused. Then there was a momentary pause. She was trying, he decided, to find just the words she wanted. He leaned forward.

"You have come to tell me something, Miss Cracken-thorpe? Can I help you? You've been worried about something, haven't you? Some little thing, perhaps, that you feel probably has nothing to do with the case, but on the other hand, just might be related to it. You've come here to tell me about it, haven't you? It's to do, perhaps, with the identity of the dead woman. You think you know who she was?"

"No, no, not quite that. I think really it's most un-likely. But——"

"But there is some possibility that worries you. You'd better tell me about it—because we may be able to set your mind at rest."

Emma took a moment of two before speaking. Then she said:

"You have seen three of my brothers. I had another brother, Edmund, who was killed in the war. Shortly before he was killed, he wrote to me from France."

She opened her handbag and took out a worn and faded letter. She read from it:

"I hope this won't be a shock to you, Emmie, but I'm getting married—to a French girl. It's all been very sudden—but I know you'll be fond of Martine—and look after her if anything happens to me. Will write you all the details in my next—by which time I shall be a married man. Break it gently to the old man, won't you? He'll probably go up in smoke."

Inspector Craddock held out a hand. Emma hesi-tated, then put the letter into it. She went on, speaking rapidly.

"Two days after receiving this letter, we had a telegram saying Edmund was *Missing, believed killed*. Later he was definitely reported killed. It was just before Dunkirk—and a time of great confusion. There was no Army record, as far as I could find out, of his having been married—but as I say, it was a confused time. I never heard anything from the girl. I tried, after the war, to make some inquiries, but I only knew her Christian name and that part of France had been occupied by the Germans and it was difficult to find out anything, without knowing the girl's surname and more about her. In the end I assumed that the marriage had never taken place and that the girl had probably married someone else before the end of the war, or might possibly herself have been killed."

Inspector Craddock nodded. Emma went on.

"Imagine my surprise to receive a letter just about a month ago, signed *Martine Crackenthorpe*."

"You have it?"

Emma took it from her bag and handed it to him. Craddock read it with interest. It was written in a slanting French hand—an educated hand.

DEAR MADEMOISELLE,

I hope it will not be a shock to you to get this letter. I do not even know if your brother Edmund told you that we were married. He said he was going to do so. He was killed only a few days after our marriage and at the same time the Germans occupied our village. After the war ended, I decided that I would not write to you or approach you, though Edmund had told me to do so. But by then I had made a new life for myself, and it was not necessary. But now things have changed. For my son's sake I write this letter. He is your brother's son, you see, and I—I can no longer give him the advantages he ought to have. I am coming to England early next week. Will you let me know if I can come and see you? My address for letters is 126 Elvers

Crescent, N.10. I hope again this will not be the great shock to you.

I remain with assurance of my excellent sentiments,
MARTINE CRACKENTHORPE

Craddock was silent for a moment or two. He reread the letter carefully before handing it back.

"What did you do on receipt of this letter, Miss Crackenthorpe?"

"My brother-in-law, Bryan Eastley, happened to be staying with me at the time and I talked to him about it. Then I rang up my brother Harold in London and consulted him about it. Harold was rather sceptical about the whole thing and advised extreme caution. We must, he said, go carefully into this woman's credentials."

Emma paused and then went on:

"That, of course, was only common sense and I quite agreed. But if this girl—woman—was really the Martine about whom Edmund had written to me, I felt that we must make her welcome. I wrote to the address she gave in her letters, inviting her to come down to Rutherford Hall and meet us. A few days later I received a telegram from London: *Very sorry forced to return to France unexpectedly. Martine.* There was no further letter or news of any kind."

"All this took place—when?"

Emma frowned.

"It was shortly before Christmas. I know, because I wanted to suggest her spending Christmas with us—but my father would not hear of it—so I suggested she should come down the week-end after Christmas while the family would still be there. I think the wire saying she was returning to France came actually a few days before Christmas."

"And you believe that this woman whose body was found in the sarcophagus might be this Martine?"

"No, of course I don't. But when you said she was probably a foreigner—well, I couldn't help wondering . . . if perhaps . . ."

Her voice died away.

Craddock spoke quickly and reassuringly.

"You did quite right to tell me about this. We'll look into it. I should say there is probably little doubt that the woman who wrote to you actually *did* go back to France and is there now alive and well. On the other hand, there *is* a certain coincidence of dates, as you yourself have been clever enough to realise. As you heard at the inquest, the woman's death according to the police surgeon's evidence must have occurred about three to four weeks ago. Now don't worry, Miss Crackenthorpe, just leave it to us." He added casually, "You consulted Mr. Harold Crackenthorpe. What about your father and your other brothers?"

"I had to tell my father, of course. He got very worked up," she smiled faintly. "He was convinced it was a put-up thing to get money out of us. My father gets very excited about money. He believes, or pretends to believe, that he is a very poor man, and that he must save every penny he can. I believe elderly people do get obsessions of that kind sometimes. It's not true, of course, he has a very large income and doesn't actually spend a quarter of it—or used not to until these days of high income tax. Certainly he has a large amount of savings put by." She paused and then went on. "I told my other two brothers also. Alfred seemed to consider it rather a joke, though he, too, thought it was almost certainly an imposture. Cedric just wasn't interested—he's inclined to be self-centred. Our idea was that the family would receive

Martine, and that our lawyer, Mr. Wimborne, should also be asked to be present."

"What did Mr. Wimborne think about the matter?"

"We hadn't got as far as discussing the matter with him. We were on the point of doing so when Martine's telegram arrived."

"You have taken no further steps?"

"Yes. I wrote to the address in London with *Please forward* on the envelope, but I have had no reply of any kind."

"Rather a curious business. . . . Hm . . ."

He looked at her sharply.

"What do you yourself think about it?"

"I don't know what to think."

"What were your reactions at the time? Did you think the letter was genuine—or did you agree with your father and brothers? What about your brother-in-law, by the way, what did he think?"

"Oh, Bryan thought that the letter was genuine."

"And you?"

"I—wasn't sure."

"And what were your feelings about it—supposing that this girl really *was* your brother Edmund's widow?"

Emma's face softened.

"I was very fond of Edmund. He was my favourite brother. The letter seemed to me exactly the sort of letter that a girl like Martine would write under the circumstances. The course of events she described was entirely natural. I assumed that by the time the war ended she had either married again or was with some man who was protecting her and the child. Then perhaps, this man had died, or left her, and it then seemed right to her to apply to Edmund's family—as he himself had wanted her to do. The letter seemed genuine and natural to me—but, of course, Harold pointed out that if it was written by an impostor, it would be written by some woman who had known Martine and who was in possession of all the facts, and so could write a thoroughly plausible letter. I had to admit the justice of that—but all the same . . ."

She stopped.

"You wanted it to be true?" said Craddock gently.

She looked at him gratefully.

"Yes, I wanted it to be true. I would be so glad if Edmund had left a son."

Craddock nodded.

"As you say, the letter, on the face of it, sounds genuine enough. What *is* surprising is the sequel; Martine Crackenthorpe's abrupt departure for Paris and the fact that you have never heard from her since. You had replied kindly to her, were prepared to welcome her. Why, even if she had to return to France, did she not write again? That is, presuming her to be the genuine article. If she were an impostor, of course, it's easier to explain. I thought perhaps that you might have consulted Mr. Wimborne, and that he might have instituted inquiries which alarmed the woman. That, you tell me, is not so. But it's still possible that one or other of your brothers may have done something of the kind. It's possible that this Martine may have had a background that would not stand investigation. She may have assumed that she would be dealing only with Edmund's affectionate sister, not with hard-headed suspicious business men. She may have hoped to get sums of money out of you for the child (hardly a child now—a boy presumably of fifteen or sixteen) without many questions being asked. But instead she found she was going to run up against something quite different. After all, I should imagine that serious legal aspects would arise. If Edmund Crackenthorpe left a son, born in wedlock, he would be one of the heirs to your grandfather's estate? "

Emma nodded.

"Moreover, from what I have been told, he would in due course inherit Rutherford Hall and the land round it —very valuable building land, probably, by now."

Emma looked slightly startled.

"Yes, I hadn't thought of that."

"Well, I shouldn't worry," said Inspector Craddock. "You did quite right to come and tell me. I shall make inquiries, but it seems to me highly probable that there is no connection between the woman who wrote the letter (and who was probably trying to cash in on a swindle) and the woman whose body was found in the sarcophagus."

Emma rose with a sigh of relief.

"I'm so glad I've told you. You've been very kind."

Craddock accompanied her to the door.

Then he rang for Detective-Sergeant Wetherall.

"Bob, I've got a job for you. Go to 126 Elvers Crescent, N.10. Take photographs of the Rutherford Hall woman with you. See what you can find out about a woman calling herself Mrs. Crackenthorpe—Mrs. Martine Crackenthorpe, who was either living there, or calling for letters there, between the dates of, say, 15th to the end of December."

"Right, sir."

Craddock busied himself with various other matters that were waiting attention on his desk. In the afternoon he went to see a theatrical agent who was a friend of his. His inquiries were not fruitful.

Later in the day when he returned to his office he found a wire from Paris on his desk.

Particulars given by you might apply to Anna Stravinska of Ballet Maritski. Suggest you come over. Dessin, Prefecture.

Craddock heaved a big sigh of relief, and his brow cleared.

At last! So much, he thought, for the Martine Crackenthorpe hare. . . . He decided to take the night ferry to Paris.

CHAPTER XIII

"IT's so very kind of you to have asked me to take tea with you," said Miss Marple to Emma Crackenthorpe.

Miss Marple was looking particularly woolly and fluffy —a picture of a sweet old lady. She beamed as she looked round her—at Harold Crackenthorpe in his well-cut dark suit, at Alfred handing her sandwiches with a charming smile, at Cedric standing by the mantelpiece in a ragged tweed jacket scowling at the rest of his family.

"We are very pleased that you could come," said Emma politely.

There was no hint of the scene which had taken place after lunch that day when Emma had exclaimed: "Dear me, I quite forgot. I told Miss Eyelesbarrow that she could bring her old aunt to tea to-day."

"Put her off," said Harold brusquely. "We've still got a lot to talk about. We don't want strangers here."

"Let her have tea in the kitchen or somewhere with the girl," said Alfred.

"Oh, no, I couldn't do that," said Emma firmly. "That would be very rude."

"Oh, let her come," said Cedric. "We can draw her out a little about the wonderful Lucy. I should like to know more about that girl, I must say. I'm not sure that I trust her. Too smart by half."

"She's very well connected and quite genuine," said Harold. "I've made it my business to find out. One wanted to be sure. Poking about and finding the body the way she did."

"If we only knew who this damned woman was," said Alfred.

Harold added angrily:

"I must say, Emma, that I think you were out of your senses, going and suggesting to the police that the dead woman might be Edmund's French girl friend. It will make them convinced that she came here, and that probably one or other of *us* killed her."

"Oh, no, Harold. Don't exaggerate."

"Harold's quite right," said Alfred. "Whatever possessed you, I don't know. I've a feeling I'm being followed everywhere I go by plain-clothes men."

"I told her not to do it," said Cedric. "Then Quimper backed her up."

"It's no business of his," said Harold angrily. "Let him stick to pills and powders and National Health."

"Oh, do stop quarrelling," said Emma wearily. "I'm really glad this old Miss Whatshername is coming to tea. It will do us all good to have a stranger here and be prevented from going over and over the same things again and again. I must go and tidy myself up a little."

She left the room.

"This Lucy Eyelesbarrow," said Harold, and stopped. "As Cedric says, it *is* odd that she should nose about in the barn and go opening up a sarcophagus—really a Herculean task. Perhaps we ought to take steps. Her attitude, I thought, was rather antagonistic at lunch——"

"Leave her to me," said Alfred. "I'll soon find out if she's up to anything."

"I mean, *why* open up that sarcophagus?"

"Perhaps she isn't really Lucy Eyelesbarrow at all," suggested Cedric.

"But what would be the point——?" Harold looked thoroughly upset. "Oh, damn!"

They looked at each other with worried faces.

"And here's this pestilential old woman coming to tea. Just when we want to *think*."

"We'll talk things over this evening," said Alfred. "In the meantime, we'll pump the old aunt about Lucy."

So Miss Marple had duly been fetched by Lucy and installed by the fire and she was now smiling up at Alfred as he handed her sandwiches with the approval she always showed towards a good-looking man.

"Thank you so much. . . . May I ask . . .? Oh, egg and sardine, yes, that will be very nice. I'm afraid I'm always rather greedy over my tea. As one gets on, you know . . . And, of course, at night only a very light meal. . . . I have to be careful." She turned to her hostess once more. "What a beautiful house you have. And so many beautiful things in it. Those bronzes, now, they remind me of some my father bought—at the Paris Exhibition. Really, your grandfather did? In the classical style, aren't they? Very handsome. How delightful for you having your brothers with you? So often families are scattered— India, though I suppose that is all done with now—and Africa—the west coast, such a bad climate."

"Two of my brothers live in London."

"That is very nice for you."

"But my brother Cedric is a painter and lives in Iviza, one of the Balearic Islands."

"Painters are so fond of islands, are they not?" said Miss Marple. "Chopin—that was Majorca, was it not? But he was a musician. It is Gauguin I am thinking of. A sad life—misspent, one feels. I myself never really care for paintings of native women—and although I know he is very much admired—I have never cared for that lurid mustard colour. One really feels quite bilious looking at his pictures."

She eyed Cedric with a slightly disapproving air.

"Tell us about Lucy as a child, Miss Marple," said Cedric.

She smiled up at him delightedly.

"Lucy was always so clever," she said. "Yes, you were, dear—now don't interrupt. Quite remarkable at arithmetic. Why, I remember when the butcher overcharged me for topside of beef . . ."

Miss Marple launched full steam ahead into reminiscences of Lucy's childhood and from there to experiences of her own in village life.

The stream of reminiscence was interrupted by the entry of Bryan and the boys rather wet and dirty as a result of an enthusiastic search for clues. Tea was brought in and with it came Dr. Quimper who raised his eyebrows slightly as he looked round after acknowledging his introduction to the old lady.

"Hope your father's not under the weather, Emma?"

"Oh, no—that is, he was just a little tired this afternoon——"

"Avoiding visitors, I expect," said Miss Marple with a roguish smile. "How well I remember my own dear father. ' Got a lot of old pussies coming? ' he would say to my mother. ' Send my tea into the study.' Very naughty about it, he was."

"Please don't think——" began Emma, but Cedric cut in.

"It's always tea in the study when his dear sons come down. Psychologically to be expected, eh, Doctor?"

Dr. Quimper, who was devouring sandwiches and coffee

cake with the frank appreciation of a man who has usually too little time to spend on his meals, said:

"Psychology's all right if it's left to the psychologists. Trouble is, everyone is an amateur psychologist nowadays. My patients tell *me* exactly what complexes and neuroses they're suffering from, without giving me a chance to tell them. Thanks, Emma, I will have another cup. No time for lunch to-day."

"A doctor's life, I always think, is so noble and self-sacrificing," said Miss Marple.

"You can't know many doctors," said Dr. Quimper. "Leeches they used to be called, and leeches they often are! At any rate, we do get paid nowadays, the State sees to that. No sending in of bills that you know won't ever be met. Trouble is that all one's patients are determined to get everything they can 'out of the Government,' and as a result, if little Jenny coughs twice in the night, or little Tommy eats a couple of green apples, out the poor doctor has to come in the middle of the night. Oh, well! Glorious cake, Emma. What a cook you are!"

"Not mine. Miss Eyelesbarrow's."

"You make 'em just as good," said Quimper loyally.

"Will you come and see Father?"

She rose and the doctor followed her. Miss Marple watched them leave the room.

"Miss Crackenthorpe is a very devoted daughter, I see," she said.

"Can't imagine how she sticks the old man, myself," said the outspoken Cedric.

"She has a very comfortable home here, and father is very much attached to her," said Harold quickly.

"Em's all right," said Cedric. "Born to be an old maid."

There was a faint twinkle in Miss Marple's eye as she said:

"Oh, do you think so?"

Harold said quickly:

"My brother didn't use the term old maid in any derogatory sense, Miss Marple."

"Oh, I wasn't offended," said Miss Marple. "I just wondered if he was right. I shouldn't say myself that Miss Crackenthorpe would be an old maid. She's the type, I think, that's quite likely to marry late in life—and make a success of it."

"Not very likely living here," said Cedric. "Never sees anybody she could marry."

Miss Marple's twinkle became more pronounced than ever.

"There are always clergymen—and doctors."

Her eyes, gentle and mischievous, went from one to another.

It was clear that she had suggested to them something that they had never thought of and which they did not find overpleasing.

Miss Marple rose to her feet, dropping as she did so, several little woolly scarves and her bag.

The three brothers were most attentive picking things up.

"So kind of you," fluted Miss Marple. "Oh, yes, and my little blue muffler. Yes—as I say—so kind to ask me here. I've been picturing, you know, just what your home was like—so that I can visualise dear Lucy working here."

"Perfect home conditions—with murder thrown in," said Cedric.

"Cedric!" Harold's voice was angry.

Miss Marple smiled up at Cedric.

"Do you know who you remind me of? Young Thomas Eade, our bank manager's son. Always out to shock people. It didn't do in banking circles, of course, so he went to the West Indies. . . . He came home when his father died and inherited quite a lot of money. So nice for him. He was always better at spending money than making it."

II

Lucy took Miss Marple home. On her way back a figure stepped out of the darkness and stood in the glare of the headlights just as she was about to turn into the back lane. He held up his hand and Lucy recognised Alfred Crackenthorpe.

"That's better," he observed, as he got in. "Brrr, it's cold! I fancied I'd like a nice bracing walk. I didn't. Taken the old lady home all right?"

"Yes. She enjoyed herself very much."

"One could see that. Funny what a taste old ladies have for any kind of society, however dull. And, really, nothing could be duller than Rutherford Hall. Two days here is about as much as I can stand. How do you manage to stick it out, Lucy? Don't mind if I call you Lucy, do you?"

"Not at all. I don't find it dull. Of course with me it's not a permanency."

"I've been watching you—you're a smart girl, Lucy. Too smart to waste yourself cooking and cleaning."

"Thank you, but I prefer cooking and cleaning to the office desk."

"So would I. But there are other ways of living. You could be a freelance."

"I am."

"Not this way. I mean, working for yourself, pitting your wits against——"

"Against what?"

"The powers that be! All the silly pettifogging rules and regulations that hamper us all nowadays. The interesting thing is there's always a way round them if you're smart enough to find it. And you're smart. Come now, does the idea appeal to you?"

"Possibly."

Lucy manœuvred the car into the stableyard.

"Not going to commit yourself?"

"I'd have to hear more."

"Frankly, my dear girl, I could use you. You've got the sort of manner that's invaluable—creates confidence."

"Do you want me to help you sell gold bricks?"

"Nothing so risky. Just a little by-passing of the law —no more." His hand slipped up her arm. "You're a damned attractive girl, Lucy. I'd like you as a partner."

"I'm flattered."

"Meaning nothing doing? Think about it. Think of the fun, the pleasure you'd get out of outwitting all the sobersides. The trouble is, one needs capital."

"I'm afraid I haven't got any."

"Oh, it wasn't a touch! I'll be laying my hands on some before long. My revered Papa can't live for ever, mean old brute. When he pops off, I lay my hands on some real money. What about it, Lucy?"

"What are the terms?"

"Marriage if you fancy it. Women seem to, no matter how advanced and self-supporting they are. Besides, married women can't be made to give evidence against their husbands."

"Not so flattering!"

"Come off it, Lucy. Don't you realise I've fallen for you?"

Rather to her surprise Lucy was aware of a queer

fascination. There was a quality of charm about Alfred, perhaps due to sheer animal magnetism. She laughed and slipped from his encircling arm.

"This is no time for dalliance. There's dinner to think about."

"So there is, Lucy, and you're a lovely cook. What's for dinner?"

"Wait and see! You're as bad as the boys!"

They entered the house and Lucy hurried to the kitchen. She was rather surprised to be interrupted in her preparations by Harold Crackenthorpe.

"Miss Eyelesbarrow, can I speak to you about something?"

"Would later do, Mr. Crackenthorpe? I'm rather behind hand."

"Certainly. Certainly. After dinner?"

"Yes, that will do."

Dinner was duly served and appreciated. Lucy finished washing up and came out into the hall to find Harold Crackenthorpe waiting for her.

"Yes, Mr. Crackenthorpe?"

"Shall we come in here?" He opened the door of the drawing-room and led the way. He shut the door behind her.

"I shall be leaving early in the morning," he explained, "but I want to tell you how struck I have been by your ability."

"Thank you," said Lucy, feeling a little surprised.

"I feel that your talents are wasted here—definitely wasted."

"Do you? I don't."

At any rate, *he* can't ask me to marry him, thought Lucy. He's got a wife already.

"I suggest that having very kindly seen us through this

lamentable crisis, you call upon me in London. If you will ring up and make an appointment, I will leave instructions with my secretary. The truth is that we could use someone of your outstanding ability in the firm. We could discuss fully in what field your talents would be most ably employed. I can offer you, Miss Eyelesbarrow, a very good salary indeed with brilliant prospects. I think you will be agreeably surprised."

His smile was magnanimous.

Lucy said demurely:

"Thank you, Mr. Crackenthorpe, I'll think about it."

"Don't wait too long. These opportunities should not be missed by a young woman anxious to make her way in the world."

Again his teeth flashed.

"Good night, Miss Eyelesbarrow, sleep well."

"Well," said Lucy to herself, "well . . . this is all very interesting. . . ."

On her way up to bed, Lucy encountered Cedric on the stairs.

"Look here, Lucy, there's something I want to say to you."

"Do you want me to marry you and come to Iviza and look after you?"

Cedric looked very much taken aback, and slightly alarmed.

"I never thought of such a thing."

"Sorry. My mistake."

"I just wanted to know if you've a timetable in the house?"

"Is that all? There's one on the hall table."

"You know," said Cedric, reprovingly, "you shouldn't go about thinking everyone wants to marry you. You're quite a good-looking girl but not as good-looking as all that. There's a name for that sort of thing—it grows on you and you get worse. Actually, you're the last girl in the world I should care to marry. The last girl."

"Indeed?" said Lucy. "You needn't rub it in. Perhaps you'd prefer me as a stepmother?"

"What's that?" Cedric stared at her stupefied.

"You heard me," said Lucy, and went into her room and shut the door.

CHAPTER VIX

DERMOT CRADDOCK was fraternising with Armand Dessin of the Paris Prefecture. The two men had met on one or two occasions and got on well together. Since Craddock spoke French fluently, most of their conversation was conducted in that language.

"It is an idea only," Dessin warned him, "I have a picture here of the corps de ballet—that is she, the fourth from the left—it says anything to you, yes?"

Inspector Craddock said that actually it didn't. A strangled young woman is not easy to recognise, and in this picture all the young women concerned were heavily made up and were wearing extravagant bird headdresses.

"It could be," he said. "I can't go further than that. Who was she? What do you know about her?"

"Almost less than nothing," said the other cheerfully. "She was not important, you see. And the Ballet Maritski —it is not important, either. It plays in suburban theatres and goes on tour—it has no real names, no stars, no famous ballerinas. But I will take you to see Madame Joliet who runs it."

Madame Joliet was a brisk business-like Frenchwoman with a shrewd eye, a small moustache, and a good deal of adipose tissue.

"Me, I do not like the police!" She scowled at them, without camouflaging her dislike of the visit. "Always, if they can, they make me embarrassments."

"No, no, Madame, you must not say that," said Dessin, who was a tall thin melancholy-looking man. "When have I ever caused you embarrassments?"

"Over that little fool who drank the carbolic acid," said Madame Joliet promptly. "And all because she has fallen in love with the chef d'orchestre—who does not care for women and has other tastes. Over that you made the big brouhaha! Which is not good for my beautiful Ballet."

"On the contrary, big box-office business," said Dessin, "And that was three years ago. You should not bear malice. Now about this girl, Anna Stravinska."

"Well, what about her?" said Madame cautiously.

"Is she Russian?" asked Inspector Craddock.

"No, indeed. You mean, because of her name? But they all call themselves names like that, these girls. She was not important, she did not dance well, she was not particularly good-looking. *Elle était assez bien, c'est tout.* She danced well enough for the corps de ballet—but no solos."

"Was she French?"

"Perhaps. She had a French passport. But she told me once that she had an English husband."

"She told you that she had an English husband? Alive —or dead?"

Madame Joliet shrugged her shoulders.

"Dead, or he had left her. How should I know which?

These girls—there is always some trouble with men——"

"When did you last see her?"

"I take my company to London for six weeks. We play at Torquay, at Bournemouth, at Eastbourne, at somewhere else I forget and at Hammersmith. Then we come back to France, but Anna—she does not come. She sends a message only that she leaves the company, that she goes to live with her husband's family—some nonsense of that kind. I did not think it is true, myself. I think it more likely that she has met a man, you understand."

Inspector Craddock nodded. He perceived that that was what Madame Joliet would invariably think.

"And it is no loss to me. I do not care. I can get girls just as good and better to come and dance, so I shrug the shoulders and do not think of it any more. Why should I? They are all the same, these girls, mad about men."

"What date was this?"

"When we return to France? It was—yes—the Sunday before Christmas. And Anna she leaves two—or is it three—days before that? I cannot remember exactly. . . . But the end of the week at Hammersmith we have to dance without her—and it means rearranging things. . . . It was very naughty of her—but these girls—the moment they meet a man they are all the same. Only I say to everybody, ' Zut, I do not take her back, that one!' "

"Very annoying for you."

"Ah! Me—I do not care. No doubt she passes the Christmas holiday with some man she has picked up. It is not my affair. I can find other girls—girls who will leap at the chance of dancing in the Ballet Maritski and who can dance as well—or better than Anna."

Madame Joliet paused and then asked with a sudden gleam of interest:

"Why do you want to find her? Has she come into money?"

"On the contrary," said Inspector Craddock politely. "We think she may have been murdered."

Madame Joliet relapsed into indifference.

"*Ça se peut!* It happens. Ah, well! She was a good Catholic. She went to Mass on Sundays, and no doubt to confession."

"Did she ever speak to you, Madame, of a son?"

"A son? Do you mean she had a child? That, now, I should consider most unlikely. These girls, all—*all* of them know a useful address to which to go. M. Dessin knows that as well as I do."

"She may have had a child before she adopted a stage life," said Craddock. "During the war, for instance."

"*Ah! dans la guerre.* That is always possible. But if so, I know nothing about it."

"Who amongst the other girls were her closest friends?"

"I can give you two or three names—but she was not very intimate with anyone."

They could get nothing else useful from Madame Joliet.

Shown the compact, she said Anna had one of that kind, but so had most of the other girls. Anna had perhaps bought a fur coat in London—she did not know. "Me, I occupy myself with the rehearsals, with the stage lighting, with all the difficulties of my business. I have not time to notice what my artists wear."

After Madame Joliet, they interviewed the girls whose names she had given them. One or two of them had known Anna fairly well, but they all said that she had not been one to talk much about herself, and that when she did, it was, so one girl said, mostly lies.

"She liked to pretend things—stories about having

been the mistress of a Grand Duke—or of a great English financier—or how she worked for the Resistance in the war. Even a story about being a film star in Hollywood."

Another girl said:

"I think that really she had had a very tame bourgeois existence. She liked to be in ballet because she thought it was romantic, but she was not a good dancer. You understand that if she were to say, ' My father was a draper in Amiens,' that would not be romantic! So instead she made up things."

"Even in London," said the first girl, "she threw out hints about a very rich man who was going to take her on a cruise round the world, because she reminded him of his dead daughter who had died in a car accident. *Quelle blague!* "

"She told *me* she was going to stay with a rich lord in Scotland," said the second girl. "She said she would shoot the deer there."

None of this was helpful. All that seemed to emerge from it was that Anna Stravinska was a proficient liar. She was certainly not shooting deer with a peer in Scotland, and it seemed equally unlikely that she was on the sun deck of a liner cruising round the world. But neither was there any real reason to believe that her body had been found in a sarcophagus at Rutherford Hall. The identification by the girls and Madame Joliet was very uncertain and hesitating. It looked something like Anna, they all agreed. But really! All swollen up—it might be anybody!

The only fact that was established was that on the 19th of December Anna Stravinska had decided not to return to France, and that on the 20th December a woman resembling her in appearance had travelled to Brackhampton by the 4.33 train and had been strangled.

If the woman in the sarcophagus was *not* Anna Stravinska, where was Anna now?

To that, Madame Joliet's answer was simple and inevitable.

"With a man!"

And it was probably the correct answer, Craddock reflected ruefully.

One other possibility had to be considered—raised by the casual remark that Anna had once referred to having an English husband.

Had that husband been Edmund Crackenthorpe?

It seemed unlikely, considering the word picture of Anna that had been given him by those who knew her. What was much more probable was that Anna had at one time known the girl Martine sufficiently intimately to be acquainted with the necessary details. It *might* have been Anna who wrote that letter to Emma Crackenthorpe and, if so, Anna would have been quite likely to have taken fright at any question of an investigation. Perhaps she had even thought it prudent to sever her connection with the Ballet Maritski. Again, where was she now?

And again, inevitably, Madame Joliet's answer seemed the most likely.

With a man. . . .

II

Before leaving Paris, Craddock discussed with Dessin the question of the woman named Martine. Dessin was inclined to agree with his English colleague that the matter had probably no connection with the woman found in the sarcophagus. All the same, he agreed, the matter ought to be investigated.

He assured Craddock that the Sûreté would do their best to discover if there actually was any record of a marriage between Lieutenant Edmund Crackenthorpe of the 4th Southshire Regiment and a French girl whose Christian name was Martine. Time—just prior to the fall of Dunkirk.

He warned Craddock, however, that a definite answer was doubtful. The area in question had not only been occupied by the Germans at almost exactly that time, but subsequently that part of France had suffered severe war damage at the time of the invasion. Many buildings and records had been destroyed.

"But rest assured, my dear colleague, we shall do our best."

With this, he and Craddock took leave of each other.

III

On Craddock's return Sergeant Wetherall was waiting to report with gloomy relish:

"Accommodation address, sir—that's what 126 Elvers Crescent is. Quite respectable and all that."

"Any identifications?"

"No, nobody could recognise the photograph as that of a woman who had called for letters, but I don't think they would anyway—it's a month ago, very near, and a good many people use the place. It's actually a boarding-house for students."

"She might have stayed there under another name."

"If so, they didn't recognise her as the original of the photograph."

He added:

"We circularised the hotels—nobody registering as

Martine Crackenthorpe anywhere. On receipt of your call from Paris, we checked up on Anna Stravinska. She was registered with other members of the company in a cheap hotel off Brook Green. Mostly theatricals there. She cleared out on the night of Thursday 19th after the show. No further record."

Craddock nodded. He suggested a line of further inquiries—though he had little hope of success from them.

After some thought, he rang up Wimborne, Henderson and Carstairs and asked for an appointment with Mr Wimborne.

In due course, he was ushered into a particularly airless room where Mr. Wimborne was sitting behind a large old-fashioned desk covered with bundles of dusty-looking papers. Various deed boxes labelled *Sir John ffouldes, dec. Lady Derrin, George Rowbotham, Esq.*, ornamented the walls; whether as relics of a bygone era or as part of present-day legal affairs, the inspector did not know.

Mr. Wimborne eyed his visitor with the polite wariness characteristic of a family lawyer towards the police.

"What can I do for you, Inspector?"

"This letter . . ." Craddock pushed Martine's letter across the table. Mr. Wimborne touched it with a distasteful finger but did not pick it up. His colour rose very slightly and his lips tightened.

"Quite so," he said; "*quite* so! I received a letter from Miss Emma Crackenthorpe yesterday morning, informing me of her visit to Scotland Yard and of—ah—all the circumstances. I may say that I am at a loss to understand —quite at a loss—why I was not consulted about this letter at the time of its arrival! *Most* extraordinary! I should have been informed immediately. . . ."

Inspector Craddock repeated soothingly such platitudes

as seemed best calculated to reduce Mr. Wimborne to an amenable frame of mind.

"I'd no idea that there was ever any question of Edmund's having married," said Mr. Wimborne in an injured voice.

Inspector Craddock said that he supposed—in war time —and left it to trail away vaguely.

"War time!" snapped Mr. Wimborne with waspish acerbity. "Yes, indeed, we were in Lincoln's Inn Fields at the outbreak of war and there was a direct hit on the house next door, and a great number of our records were destroyed. Not the really important documents, of course; they had been removed to the country for safety. But it caused a great deal of confusion. Of course, the Crackenthorpe business was in my father's hands at that time. He died six years ago. I dare say *he* may have been told about this so-called marriage of Edmund's—but on the face of it, it looks as though that marriage, even if contemplated, never took place, and so, no doubt, my father did not consider the story of any importance. I must say, all this sounds very fishy to me. This coming forward, after all these years, and claiming a marriage and a legitimate son. Very fishy indeed. What proofs had she got, I'd like to know?"

"Just so," said Craddock. "What would her position, or her son's position be?"

"The idea was, I suppose, that she would get the Crackenthorpes to provide for her and for the boy."

"Yes, but I meant, what would she and the son be entitled to, legally speaking—if she could prove her claim?"

"Oh, I see." Mr. Wimborne picked up his spectacles which he had laid aside in his irritation, and put them on, staring through them at Inspector Craddock with shrewd attention. "Well, at the moment, nothing. But if she could prove that the boy was the son of Edmund Crackenthorpe, born in lawful wedlock, then the boy would be entitled to his share of Josiah Crackenthorpe's trust on the death of Luther Crackenthorpe. More than that, he'd inherit Rutherford Hall, since he's the son of the eldest son."

"Would anyone want to inherit the house?"

"To live in? I should say, certainly not. But that estate, my dear Inspector, is worth a considerable amount of money. Very considerable. Land for industrial and building purposes. Land which is now in the heart of Brackhampton. Oh, yes, a very considerable inheritance."

"If Luther Crackenthorpe dies, I believe you told me that Cedric gets it?"

"He inherits the real estate—yes, as the eldest surviving son."

"Cedric Crackenthorpe, I have been given to understand, is not interested in money?"

Mr. Wimborne gave Craddock a cold stare.

"Indeed? I am inclined, myself, to take statements of such a nature with what I might term a grain of salt. There are doubtless certain unworldly people who are indifferent to money. I myself have never met one."

Mr. Wimborne obviously derived a certain satisfaction from this remark.

Inspector Craddock hastened to take advantage of this ray of sunshine.

"Harold and Alfred Crackenthorpe," he ventured, "seem to have been a good deal upset by the arrival of this letter?"

"Well they might be," said Mr. Wimborne. "Well they might be."

"It would reduce their eventual inheritance?"

"Certainly. Edmund Crackenthorpe's son—always presuming there is a son—would be entitled to a fifth share of the trust money."

"That doesn't really seem a very serious loss?"

Mr. Wimborne gave him a shrewd glance.

"It is a totally inadequate motive for murder, if that is what you mean."

"But I suppose they're both pretty hard up," Craddock murmured.

He sustained Mr. Wimborne's sharp glance with perfect impassivity.

"Oh! So the police have been making inquiries? Yes, Alfred is almost incessantly in low water. Occasionally he is very flush of money for a short time—but it soon goes. Harold, as you seem to have discovered, is at present somewhat precariously situated."

"In spite of his appearance of financial prosperity?"

"Façade. All façade! Half these city concerns don't even know if they're solvent or not. Balance sheets can be made to look all right to the inexpert eye. But when the assets that are listed aren't really assets—when those assets are trembling on the brink of a crash—where are you?"

"Where, presumably, Harold Crackenthorpe is, in bad need of money."

"Well, he wouldn't have got it by strangling his late brother's widow," said Mr. Wimborne. "And nobody's murdered Luther Crackenthorpe which is the only murder that would do the family any good. So, really, Inspector, I don't quite see where your ideas are leading you?"

The worst of it was, Inspector Craddock thought, that he wasn't very sure himself.

CHAPTER XV

INSPECTOR CRADDOCK had made an appointment with Harold Crackenthorpe at his office, and he and Sergeant Wetherall arrived there punctually. The office was on the fourth floor of a big block of City offices. Inside everything showed prosperity and the acme of modern business taste.

A neat young woman took his name, spoke in a discreet murmur through a telephone, and then, rising, showed them into Harold Crackenthorpe's own private office.

Harold was sitting behind a large leather-topped desk and was looking as impeccable and self-confident as ever. If, as the inspector's private knowledge led him to surmise, he was close upon Queer Street, no trace of it showed.

He looked up with a frank welcoming interest.

"Good morning, Inspector Craddock. I hope this means that you have some definite news for us at last?"

"Hardly that, I am afraid, Mr. Crackenthorpe. It's just a few more questions I'd like to ask."

"More questions? Surely by now we have answered everything imaginable."

"I dare say it feels like that to you, Mr. Crackenthorpe, but it's just a question of our regular routine."

"Well, what is it this time?" He spoke impatiently.

"I should be glad if you could tell me exactly what you were doing on the afternoon and evening of 20th

December last—say between the hours of 3 p.m. and midnight."

Harold Crackenthorpe went an angry shade of plum-red.

"That seems to be a most extraordinary question to ask me. What does it mean, I should like to know?"

Craddock smiled gently.

"It just means that I should like to know where you were between the hours of 3 p.m. and midnight on Friday, 20th December."

"Why?"

"It would help to narrow things down."

"Narrow them down? You have extra information, then?"

"We hope that we're getting a little closer, sir."

"I'm not at all sure that I ought to answer your question. Not, that is, without having my solicitor present."

"That, of course, is entirely up to you," said Craddock. "You are not bound to answer any questions, and you have a perfect right to have a solicitor present before you do so."

"You are not—let me be quite clear—er—warning me in any way?"

"Oh, no, sir." Inspector Craddock looked properly shocked. "Nothing of that kind. The questions I am asking you, I am asking of several other people as well. There's nothing directly personal about this. It's just a matter of necessary eliminations."

"Well, of course—I'm anxious to assist in any way I can. Let me see now. Such a thing isn't easy to answer offhand, but we're very systematic here. Miss Ellis, I expect, can help."

He spoke briefly into one of the telephones on his desk

and almost immediately a streamlined young woman in a well-cut black suit entered with a notebook.

"My secretary, Miss Ellis, Inspector Craddock. Now, Miss Ellis, the inspector would like to know what I was doing on the afternoon and evening of—what was the date?"

"Friday, 20th December."

"Friday, 20th December. I expect you will have some record."

"Oh, yes." Miss Ellis left the room, returned with an office memorandum calendar and turned the pages.

"You were in the office in the morning of 20th December. You had a conference with Mr. Goldie about the Cromartie merger, you lunched with Lord Forthville at the Berkeley——"

"Ah, it was that day, yes."

"You returned to the office at about 3 o'clock and dictated half a dozen letters. You then left to attend Sotheby's sale rooms where you were interested in some rare manuscripts which were coming up for sale that day. You did not return to the office again, but I have a note to remind you that you were attending the Catering Club dinner that evening." She looked up interrogatively.

"Thank you, Miss Ellis."

Miss Ellis glided from the room.

"That is all quite clear in my mind," said Harold. "I went to Sotheby's that afternoon but the items I wanted there went for far too high a price. I had tea in a small place in Jermyn Street—Russells, I think, it is called. I dropped into a News Theatre for about half an hour or so, then went home—I live at 43 Cardigan Gardens. The Catering Club dinner took place at seven-thirty at Caterers' Hall, and after it I returned home to bed. I think that should answer your questions."

"That's all very clear, Mr. Crackenthorpe. What time was it when you returned home to dress?"

"I don't think I can remember exactly. Soon after six, I should think."

"And after the dinner?"

"It was, I think, half-past eleven when I got home."

"Did your manservant let you in? Or perhaps Lady Alice Crackenthorpe——"

"My wife, Lady Alice, is abroad in the South of France and has been since early in December. I let myself in with my latch key."

"So there is no one who can vouch for your returning home when you say you did?"

Harold gave him a cold stare.

"I dare say the servants heard me come in. I have a man and wife. But, really, Inspector——"

"Please, Mr. Crackenthorpe, I know these kind of questions are annoying, but I have nearly finished. Do you own a car?"

"Yes, a Humber Hawk."

"You drive it yourself?"

"Yes. I don't use it much except at week-ends. Driving in London is quite impossible nowadays."

"I presume you use it when you go down to see your father and sister at Brackhampton?"

"Not unless I am going to stay there for some length of time. If I just go down for the night—as, for instance, to the inquest the other day—I always go by train. There is an excellent train service and it is far quicker than going by car. The car my sister hires meets me at the station."

"Where do you keep your car?"

"I rent a garage in the Mews behind Cardigan Gardens. Any more questions?"

"I think that's all for now," said Inspector Craddock, smiling and rising. "I'm very sorry for having to bother you."

When they were outside, Sergeant Wetherall, a man who lived in a state of dark suspicion of all and sundry, remarked meaningly:

"He didn't *like* those questions—didn't like them at all. Put out, he was."

"If you have not committed a murder, it naturally annoys you if it seems someone thinks that you have," said Inspector Craddock mildly. "It would particularly annoy an ultra respectable man like Harold Crackenthorpe. There's nothing in that. What we've got to find out now is if anyone actually saw Harold Crackenthorpe at the sale that afternoon, and the same applies to the tea-shop place. He could easily have travelled by the 4.33, pushed the woman out of the train and caught a train back to London in time to appear at the dinner. In the same way he could have driven his car down that night, moved the body to the sarcophagus and driven back again. Make inquiries in the Mews."

"Yes, sir. Do you think that's what he did do?"

"How do I know?" asked Inspector Craddock. "He's a tall dark man. He *could* have been on that train and he's got a connection with Rutherford Hall. He's a possible suspect in this case. Now for Brother Alfred."

II

Alfred Crackenthorpe had a flat in West Hampstead, in a big modern building of slightly jerry-built type with a large courtyard in which the owners of flats parked their cars with a certain lack of consideration for others.

The flat was of the modern built-in type, evidently rented furnished. It had a long plywood table that let down from the wall, a divan bed, and various chairs of improbable proportions.

Alfred Crackenthorpe met them with engaging friendliness but was, the inspector thought, nervous.

"I'm intrigued," he said. "Can I offer you a drink, Inspector Craddock?" He held up various bottles invitingly.

"No, thank you, Mr. Crackenthorpe."

"As bad as that?" He laughed at his own little joke, then asked what it was all about.

Inspector Craddock said his little piece.

"What was I doing on the afternoon and evening of 20th December. How should I know? Why, that's—what —over three weeks ago."

"Your brother Harold has been able to tell us very exactly."

"Brother Harold, perhaps. Not Brother Alfred." He added with a touch of something—envious malice possibly: "Harold is the successful member of the family —busy, useful, fully employed—a time for everything, and everything at that time. Even if he were to commit a—murder, shall we say?—it would be carefully timed and exact."

"Any particular reason for using that example?"

"Oh, no. It just came into my mind—as a supreme absurdity."

"Now about yourself."

Alfred spread out his hands.

"It's as I tell you—I've no memory for times or places. If you were to say Christmas Day now—then I *should* be able to answer you—there's a peg to hang it on. I know where I was Christmas Day. We spend that with my father at Brackhampton. I really don't know why. He grumbles at the expense of having us—and would grumble that we never came near him if we didn't come. We really do it to please my sister."

"And you did it this year?"

"Yes."

"But unfortunately your father was taken ill, was he not?"

Craddock was pursuing a sideline deliberately, led by the kind of instinct that often came to him in his profession.

"He was taken ill. Living like a sparrow in the glorious cause of economy, sudden full eating and drinking had its effect."

"That was all it was, was it?"

"Of course. What else?"

"I gathered that his doctor was—worried."

"Oh, that old fool Quimper," Alfred spoke quickly and scornfully. "It's no use listening to *him*, Inspector. He's an alarmist of the worst kind."

"Indeed? He seemed a rather sensible kind of man to me."

"He's a complete fool. Father's not really an invalid, there's nothing wrong with his heart, but he takes in Quimper completely. Naturally, when father really felt ill, he made a terrific fuss, and had Quimper going and coming, asking questions, going into everything he'd eaten and drunk. The whole thing was ridiculous!" Alfred spoke with unusual heat.

Craddock was silent for a moment or two, rather effectively. Alfred fidgeted, shot him a quick glance, and then said petulantly:

"Well, what *is* all this? Why do you want to know

where I was on a particular Friday, three or four weeks ago?"

"So you do remember that it was a Friday?"

"I thought you said so."

"Perhaps I did," said Inspector Craddock. "At any rate, Friday 20th is the day I am asking about."

"Why?"

"A routine inquiry."

"That's nonsense. Have you found out something more about this woman? About where she came from?"

"Our information is not yet complete."

Alfred gave him a sharp glance.

"I hope you're not being led aside by this wild theory of Emma's that she might have been my brother Edmund's widow. That's complete nonsense."

"This—Martine, did not at any time apply to you?"

"To me? Good lord, no! That would have been a laugh."

"She would be more likely, you think, to go to your brother Harold?"

"Much more likely. His name's frequently in the papers. He's well off. Trying a touch there wouldn't surprise me. Not that she'd have got anything. Harold's as tight-fisted as the old man himself. Emma, of course, is the soft-hearted one of the family, and she was Edmund's favourite sister. All the same, Emma isn't credulous. She was quite alive to the possibility of this woman being phoney. She had it all laid on for the entire family to be there—and a hard-headed solicitor as well."

"Very wise," said Craddock. "Was there a definite date fixed for this meeting?"

"It was to be soon after Christmas—the week-end of the 27th . . ." He stopped.

"Ah," said Craddock pleasantly. "So I see some dates have a meaning to you."

"I've told you—no definite date was fixed."

"But you talked about it—when?"

"I really can't remember."

"And you can't tell me what you yourself were doing on Friday, 20th December?"

"Sorry—my mind's an absolute blank."

"You don't keep an engagement book?"

"Can't stand the things."

"The Friday before Christmas—it shouldn't be too difficult."

"I played golf one day with a likely prospect." Alfred shook his head. "No, that was the week before. I probably just mooched around. I spend a lot of my time doing that. I find one's business gets done in bars more than anywhere else."

"Perhaps the people here, or some of your friends, may be able to help?"

"Maybe. I'll ask them. Do what I can."

Alfred seemed more sure of himself now.

"I can't tell you what I was doing that day," he said; "but I can tell you what I *wasn't* doing. I wasn't murdering anyone in the Long Barn."

"Why should you say that, Mr. Crackenthorpe?"

"Come now, my dear Inspector. You're investigating this murder, aren't you? And when you begin to ask ' Where were you on such and such a day at such and such a time?' you're narrowing down things. I'd very much like to know why you've hit on Friday the 20th between —what? Lunch-time and midnight? It couldn't be medical evidence, not after all this time. Did somebody see the deceased sneaking into the barn that afternoon? She went in and she never came out, etc.? Is that it?"

The sharp black eyes were watching him narrowly, but Inspector Craddock was far too old a hand to react to that sort of thing.

"I'm afraid we'll have to let you guess about that," he said pleasantly.

"The police are so secretive."

"Not only the police. I think, Mr. Crackenthorpe, you *could* remember what you were doing on that Friday if you tried. Of course you may have reasons for not wishing to remember——"

"You won't catch me that way, Inspector. It's very suspicious, of course, very suspicious, indeed, that I can't remember—but there it is! Wait a minute now—I went to Leeds that week—stayed at a hotel close to the Town Hall—can't remember its name—but you'd find it easily enough. That *might* have been on the Friday."

"We'll check up," said the inspector unemotionally.

He rose. "I'm sorry you couldn't have been more co-operative, Mr. Crackenthorpe."

"Most unfortunate for *me*! There's Cedric with a safe alibi in Iviza, and Harold, no doubt, checked with business appointments and public dinners every hour—and here am I with no alibi at all. Very sad. And all so silly. I've already told you I don't murder people. And why should I murder an unknown woman, anyway? What for? Even if the corpse *is* the corpse of Edmund's widow, why should any of us wish to do away with her? Now if she'd been married to *Harold* in the war, and had suddenly reappeared—then it might have been awkward for the respectable Harold—bigamy and all that. But Edmund! Why, we'd all have *enjoyed* making Father stump up a bit to give her an allowance and send the boy to a decent school. Father would have been wild, but he couldn't in decency refuse to do something. Won't you have a drink before you go, Inspector? Sure? Too bad I haven't been able to help you."

III

"Sir, listen, do you know what?"

Inspector Craddock looked at his excited sergeant.

"Yes, Wetherall, what is it?"

"I've placed him, sir. That chap. All the time I was trying to fix it and suddenly it came. He was mixed up in that tinned food business with Dicky Rogers. Never got anything on him—too cagey for that. And he's been in with one or more of the Soho lot. Watches and that Italian sovereign business."

Of course! Craddock realised now why Alfred's face had seemed vaguely familiar from the first. It had all been small-time stuff—never anything that could be proved. Alfred had always been on the outskirts of the racket with a plausible innocent reason for having been mixed up in it at all. But the police had been quite sure that a small steady profit came his way.

"That throws rather a light on things," Craddock said.

"Think he did it?"

"I shouldn't have said he was the type to do murder. But it explains other things—the reason why he couldn't come up with an alibi."

"Yes, that looks bad for him."

"Not really," said Craddock. "It's quite a clever line— just to say firmly you can't remember. Lots of people can't remember what they did and where they were even a week ago. It's especially useful if you don't particularly want to call attention to the way you spend your time—

interesting rendezvous at lorry pull-ups with the Dicky Rogers crowd, for instance."

"So you think he's all right?"

"I'm not prepared to think anyone's all right just yet," said Inspector Craddock. "You've got to work on it, Wetherall."

Back at his desk, Craddock sat frowning, and making little notes on the pad in front of him.

Murderer (he wrote). . . . A tall dark man!!!

Victim? . . . Could have been Martine, Edmund Crackenthorpe's girl-friend or widow.

Or

Could have been Anna Stravinska. Went out of circulation at appropriate time, right age and appearance, clothing, etc. No connection with Rutherford Hall as far as is known.

Could be Harold's first wife! Bigamy!

„   „   mistress. Blackmail?!

If connection with Alfred, might be blackmail. Had knowledge that could have sent him to gaol?

If Cedric—might have had connection with him abroad—Paris? Balearics?

Or

Victim could be Anna S. posing as Martine

or

Victim is unknown woman killed by unknown murderer!

"And most probably the latter," said Craddock aloud.

He reflected gloomily on the situation. You couldn't get far with a case until you had the motive. All the motives suggested so far seemed either inadequate or far fetched.

Now if only it had been the murder of old Mr. Cracken-thorpe. . . . Plenty of motive there. . . .

Something stirred in his memory. . . .

He made further notes on his pad.

Ask Dr. Q. about Christmas illness.

Cedric—alibi.

Consult Miss M. for latest gossip.

CHAPTER XVI

WHEN CRADDOCK got to 4 Madison Road he found Lucy Eyelesbarrow with Miss Marple.

He hesitated for a moment on his plan of campaign and then decided that Lucy Eyelesbarrow might prove a valuable ally.

After greetings, he solemnly drew out his notecase, extracted three pound notes, added three shillings and pushed them across the table to Miss Marple.

" What's this, Inspector? "

" Consultation fee. You're a consultant—on murder! Pulse, temperature, local reactions, possible deep-seated cause of said murder. I'm just the poor harassed local G.P."

Miss Marple looked at him and twinkled. He grinned at her. Lucy Eyelesbarrow gave a faint gasp and then laughed.

" Why, Inspector Craddock—you're human after all."

" Oh, well, I'm not strictly on duty this afternoon."

" I told you we had met before," said Miss Marple to

Lucy. "Sir Henry Clithering is his godfather—a very old friend of mine."

"Would you like to hear, Miss Eyelesbarrow, what my godfather said about her—the first time we met? He described her as just the finest detective God ever made—natural genius cultivated in a suitable soil. He told me never to despise the "—Dermot Craddock paused for a moment to seek for a synonym for "old pussies "—"—er—elderly ladies. He said they could usually tell you what *might* have happened, what ought to have happened, and even what actually *did* happen! And," he said, "they can tell you *why* it happened," he added, "that this particular —er—elderly lady—was at the top of the class."

"Well!" said Lucy. "That seems to be a testimonial all right."

Miss Marple was pink and confused and looked unusually dithery.

"Dear Sir Henry," she murmured. "Always so kind. Really I'm not at all clever—just, perhaps, a *slight* knowledge of human nature—living, you know, in a *village*——"

She added, with more composure:

"Of course, I am somewhat handicapped, by not actually being on the spot. It is so helpful, I always feel, when people remind you of other people—because types are alike everywhere and that is such a valuable guide."

Lucy looked a little puzzled, but Craddock nodded comprehendingly.

"But you've been to tea there, haven't you?" he said.

"Yes, indeed. Most pleasant. I was a little disappointed that I didn't see old Mr. Crackenthorpe—but one can't have everything."

"Do you feel that if you saw the person who had done the murder, you'd know?" asked Lucy.

"Oh, I wouldn't say *that*, dear. One is always inclined

to guess—and guessing would be very wrong when it is a question of anything as serious as murder. All one can do is to observe the people concerned—or who might have been concerned—and see of whom they remind you."

"Like Cedric and the bank manager?"

Miss Marple corrected her.

"The bank manager's *son*, dear. Mr. Eade himself was far more like Mr. Harold—a very conservative man—but perhaps a little too fond of money—the sort of man, too, who would go a long way to avoid scandal."

Craddock smiled, and said:

"And Alfred?"

"Jenkins at the garage," Miss Marple replied promptly. "He didn't exactly appropriate tools—but he used to exchange a broken or inferior jack for a good one. And I believe he wasn't very honest over batteries—though I don't understand these things very well. I know Raymond left off dealing with him and went to the garage on the Milchester road. As for Emma," continued Miss Marple thoughtfully, "she reminds me very much of Geraldine Webb—always very quiet, almost dowdy—and bullied a good deal by her elderly mother. Quite a surprise to everybody when the mother died unexpectedly and Geraldine came into a nice sum of money and went and had her hair cut and permed, and went off on a cruise, and came back married to a very nice barrister. They had two children."

The parallel was clear enough. Lucy said, rather uneasily: "Do you think you ought to have said what you did about Emma marrying? It seemed to upset the brothers."

Miss Marple nodded.

"Yes," she said. "So like men—quite unable to see

what's going on under their eyes. I don't believe you noticed yourself."

"No," admitted Lucy. "I never thought of anything of that kind. They both seemed to me——"

"So old?" said Miss Marple smiling a little. "But Dr. Quimper isn't much over forty, I should say, though he's going grey on the temples, and it's obvious that he's longing for some kind of home life; and Emma Crackenthorpe is under forty—not too old to marry and have a family. The doctor's wife died quite young having a baby, so I have heard."

"I believe she did. Emma said something about it one day."

"He must be lonely," said Miss Marple. "A busy hardworking doctor needs a wife—someone sympathetic—not too young."

"Listen, darling," said Lucy. "Are we investigating crime, or are we match-making?"

Miss Marple twinkled.

"I'm afraid I *am* rather romantic. Because I am an old maid, perhaps. You know, dear Lucy, that, as far as I am concerned, you have fulfilled your contract. If you really want a holiday abroad before taking up your next engagement, you would have time still for a short trip."

"And leave Rutherford Hall? Never! I'm the complete sleuth by now. Almost as bad as the boys. They spend their entire time looking for clues. They looked all through the dustbins yesterday. Most unsavoury—and they hadn't really the faintest idea what they were looking for. If they come to you in triumph, Inspector Craddock, bearing a torn scrap of paper with *Martine—if you value your life keep away from the Long Barn !* on it, you'll know that I've taken pity on them and concealed it in the pigsty!"

"Why the pigsty, dear?" asked Miss Marple with interest. "Do they keep pigs?"

"Oh, no, not nowadays. It's just—I go there sometimes."

For some reason Lucy blushed. Miss Marple looked at her with increased interest.

"Who's at the house now?" asked Craddock.

"Cedric's there, and Bryan's down for the week-end. Harold and Alfred are coming down to-morrow. They rang up this morning. I somehow got the impression that you had been putting the cat among the pigeons, Inspector Craddock."

Craddock smiled.

"I shook them up a little. Asked them to account for their movements on Friday, 20th December."

"And could they?"

"Harold could. Alfred couldn't—or wouldn't."

"I think alibis must be terribly difficult," said Lucy. "Times and places and dates. They must be hard to check up on, too."

"It takes time and patience—but we manage." He glanced at his watch. "I'll be coming along to Rutherford Hall presently to have a word with Cedric, but I want to get hold of Dr. Quimper first."

"You'll be just about right. He has his surgery at six and he's usually finished about half past. I must get back and deal with dinner."

"I'd like your opinion on one thing, Miss Eyelesbarrow. What's the family view about this Martine business—amongst themselves?"

Lucy replied promptly.

"They're all furious with Emma for going to you about it—and with Dr. Quimper who, it seemed, encouraged her to do so. Harold and Alfred think it was a try on and not genuine. Emma isn't sure. Cedric thinks it was phoney, too, but he doesn't take it as seriously as the other two. Bryan, on the other hand, seems quite sure that it's genuine."

"Why, I wonder?"

"Well, Bryan's rather like that. Just accepts things at their face value. He thinks it was Edmund's wife—or rather widow—and that she had suddenly to go back to France, but that they'll hear from her again sometime. The fact that she hasn't written, or anything, up to now, seems to him to be quite natural because he never writes letters himself. Bryan's rather sweet. Just like a dog that wants to be taken for a walk."

"And do you take him for a walk, dear?" asked Miss Marple. "To the pigsties, perhaps?"

Lucy shot a keen glance at her.

"So many gentlemen in the house, coming and going," mused Miss Marple.

When Miss Marple uttered the word "gentlemen" she always gave it its full Victorian flavour—an echo from an era actually before her own time. You were conscious at once of dashing full-blooded (and probably whiskered) males, sometimes wicked, but always gallant.

"You're such a handsome girl," pursued Miss Marple, appraising Lucy. "I expect they pay you a good deal of attention, don't they?"

Lucy flushed slightly. Scrappy remembrances passed across her mind. Cedric, leaning against the pigsty wall. Bryan sitting disconsolately on the kitchen table. Alfred's fingers touching hers as he helped her collect the coffee cups.

"Gentlemen," said Miss Marple, in the tone of one speaking of some alien and dangerous species, "are all very much alike in some ways—even if they are quite *old. . . .*"

"Darling," cried Lucy. "A hundred years ago you would certainly have been burned as a witch!"

And she told her story of old Mr. Crackenthorpe's conditional proposal of marriage.

"In fact," said Lucy, "they've all made what you might call advances to me in a way. Harold's was very correct —an advantageous financial position in the City. I don't think it's my attractive appearance—they must think I know something."

She laughed.

But Inspector Craddock did not laugh.

"Be careful," he said. "They might murder you instead of making advances to you."

"I suppose it might be simpler," Lucy agreed.

Then she gave a slight shiver.

"One forgets," she said. "The boys have been having such fun that one almost thought of it all as a game. But it's not a game."

"No," said Miss Marple. "Murder isn't a game."

She was silent for a moment or two before she said:

"Don't the boys go back to school soon?"

"Yes, next week. They go to-morrow to James Stoddart-West's home for the last few days of the holidays."

"I'm glad of that," said Miss Marple gravely. "I shouldn't like anything to happen while they're there."

"You mean to old Mr. Crackenthorpe. Do you think *he's* going to be murdered next?"

"Oh, no," said Miss Marple. "*He'll* be all right. I meant to the boys."

"To the boys?"

"Well, to Alexander."

"But surely——"

"Hunting about, you know—looking for clues. Boys love that sort of thing—but it might be very dangerous."

Craddock looked at her thoughtfully.

"You're not prepared to believe, are you, Miss Marple, that it's a case of an unknown woman murdered by an unknown man? You tie it up definitely with Rutherford Hall?"

"I think there's a definite connection, yes."

"All we knew about the murderer is that he's a tall dark man. That's what your friend says and all she can say. There are three tall dark men at Rutherford Hall. On the day of the inquest, you know, I came out to see the three brothers standing waiting on the pavement for the car to draw up. They had their backs to me and it was astonishing how, in their heavy overcoats, they looked all alike. *Three tall dark men.* And yet, actually, they're all three quite different types." He sighed. "It makes it very difficult."

"I wonder," murmured Miss Marple. "I have been wondering—whether it might perhaps be all much *simpler* than we suppose. Murders so often are quite simple—with an obvious rather sordid motive. . . ."

"Do you believe in the mysterious Martine, Miss Marple?"

"I'm quite ready to believe that Edmund Crackenthorpe either married, or meant to marry, a girl called Martine. Emma Crackenthorpe showed you his letter, I understand, and from what I've seen of her and from what Lucy tells me, I should say Emma Crackenthorpe is quite incapable of making up a thing of that kind—indeed, why should she?"

"So granted Martine," said Craddock thoughtfully, "there *is* a motive of a kind. Martine's reappearance with a son would diminish the Crackenthorpe inheritance—

though hardly to a point, one would think, to activate murder. They're all very hard up——"

"Even Harold?" Lucy demanded incredulously.

"Even the prosperous-looking Harold Crackenthorpe is not the sober and conservative financier he appears to be. He's been plunging heavily and mixing himself up in some rather undesirable ventures. A large sum of money, soon, might avoid a crash."

"But if so——" said Lucy, and stopped.

"Yes, Miss Eyelesbarrow——"

"I know, dear," said Miss Marple. "The wrong murder, that's what you mean."

"Yes. Martine's death wouldn't do Harold—or any of the others—any good. Not until——"

"Not until Luther Crackenthorpe died. Exactly. That occurred to me. And Mr. Crackenthorpe, senior, I gather from his doctor, is a much better life than any outsider would imagine."

"He'll last for years," said Lucy. Then she frowned.

"Yes?" Craddock spoke encouragingly.

"He was rather ill at Christmas-time," said Lucy. "He said the doctor made a lot of fuss about it—'Anyone would have thought I'd been poisoned by the fuss he made.' That's what he said."

She looked inquiringly at Craddock.

"Yes," said Craddock. "That's really what I want to ask Dr. Quimper about."

"Well, I must go," said Lucy. "Heavens, it's late."

Miss Marple put down her knitting and picked up *The Times* with a half-done crossword puzzle.

"I wish I had a dictionary here," she murmured. "Tontine and Tokay—I always mix those two words up. One, I believe, is a Hungarian wine."

"That's Tokay," said Lucy, looking back from the door.

"But one's a five-letter word and one's a seven. What's the clue?"

"Oh, it wasn't in the crossword," said Miss Marple vaguely. "It was in my head."

Inspector Craddock looked at her very hard. Then he said good-bye and went.

CHAPTER XVII

CRADDOCK HAD to wait a few minutes whilst Quimper finished his evening surgery, and then the doctor came to him. He looked tired and depressed.

He offered Craddock a drink and when the latter accepted he mixed one for himself as well.

"Poor devils," he said as he sank down in a worn easy-chair. "So scared and so stupid—no sense. Had a painful case this evening. Woman who ought to have come to me a year ago. If she'd come then, she might have been operated on successfully. Now it's too late. Makes me mad. The truth is people are an extraordinary mixture of heroism and cowardice. She's been suffering agony, and borne it without a word, just because she was too scared to come and find out that what she feared might be true. At the other end of the scale are the people who come and waste my time because they've got a dangerous swelling causing them agony on their little finger which they think may be cancer and which turns out to be a common or garden chilblain! Well, don't mind me. I've blown off steam now. What did you want to see me about?"

"First, I've got you to thank, I believe, for advising

Miss Crackenthorpe to come to me with the letter that purported to be from her brother's widow."

"Oh, that? Anything in it? I didn't exactly advise her to come. She wanted to. She was worried. All the dear little brothers were trying to hold her back, of course."

"Why should they?"

The doctor shrugged his shoulders.

"Afraid the lady might be proved genuine, I suppose."

"Do you think the letter was genuine?"

"No idea. Never actually saw it. I should say it was someone who knew the facts, just trying to make a touch. Hoping to work on Emma's feelings. They were dead wrong, there. Emma's no fool. She wouldn't take an unknown sister-in-law to her bosom without asking a few practical questions first."

He added with some curiosity:

"But why ask *my* views? I've got nothing to do with it?"

"I really came to ask you something quite different— but I don't quite know how to put it."

Dr. Quimper looked interested.

"I understand that not long ago—at Christmas-time, I think it was—Mr. Crackenthorpe had rather a bad turn of illness."

He saw a change at once in the doctor's face. It hardened.

"Yes."

"I gather a gastric disturbance of some kind?"

"Yes."

"This is difficult. . . . Mr. Crackenthorpe was boasting of his health, saying he intended to outlive most of his family. He referred to you—you'll excuse me, Doctor..."

"Oh, don't mind me. I'm not sensitive as to what my patients say about me!"

"He spoke of you as an old fuss-pot." Quimper smiled. "He said you had asked him all sorts of questions, not only as to what he had eaten, but as to who prepared it and served it."

The doctor was not smiling now. His face was hard again.

"Go on."

"He used some such phrase as—' Talked as though he believed someone had poisoned me.' "

There was a pause.

"Had you—any suspicion of that kind? "

Quimper did not answer at once. He got up and walked up and down. Finally, he wheeled round on Craddock.

"What the devil do you expect me to say? Do you think a doctor can go about flinging accusations of poisoning here and there without any real evidence? "

"I'd just like to know, off the record, if—that idea—did enter your head? "

Dr. Quimper said evasively:

"Old Crackenthorpe leads a fairly frugal life. When the family comes down, Emma steps up the food. Result—a nasty attack of gastro-enteritis. The symptoms were consistent with that diagnosis."

Craddock persisted.

"I see. You were quite satisfied? You were not at all—shall we say—puzzled? "

"All right. All right. Yes, I was Yours Truly Puzzled! Does that please you? "

"It interests me," said Craddock. "What actually did you suspect—or fear? "

"Gastric cases vary, of course, but there were certain indications that would have been, shall we say, more consistent with arsenical poisoning than with plain gastro enteritis. Mind you, the two things are very much alike. Better men than myself have failed to recognise arsenical poisoning—and have given a certificate in all good faith."

"And what was the result of your inquiries?"

"It seemed that what I suspected could not possibly be true. Mr. Crackenthorpe assured me that he had had similar attacks before I attended him—and from the same cause, he said. They had always taken place when there was too much rich food about."

"Which was when the house was full? With the family? Or guests?"

"Yes. That seemed reasonable enough. But frankly, Craddock, I wasn't happy. I went so far as to write to old Dr. Morris. He was my senior partner and retired soon after I joined him. Crackenthorpe was his patient originally. I asked about these earlier attacks that the old man had had."

"And what response did you get?"

Quimper grinned.

"I got a flea in the ear. I was more or less told not to be a damned fool. Well "—he shrugged his shoulders— "presumably I *was* a damned fool."

"I wonder." Craddock was thoughtful.

Then he decided to speak frankly.

"Throwing discretion aside, Doctor, there are people who stand to benefit pretty considerably from Luther Crackenthorpe's death." The doctor nodded. "He's an old man—and a hale and hearty one. He may live to be ninety odd?"

"Easily. He spends his life taking care of himself, and his constitution is sound."

"And his sons—and daughter—are all getting on, and they are all feeling the pinch?"

"You leave Emma out of it. She's no poisoner. These

attacks only happen when the others are there—not when she and he are alone."

" An elementary precaution—if she's the one," the inspector thought, but was careful not to say aloud.

He paused, choosing his words carefully.

"Surely—I'm ignorant in these matters—but supposing just as a hypothesis that arsenic *was* administered—hasn't Crackenthorpe been very lucky not to succumb?"

"Now there," said the doctor, " you *have* got something odd. It is exactly that fact that leads me to believe that I have been, as old Morris puts it, a damned fool. You see, it's obviously not a case of small doses of arsenic administered regularly—which is what you might call the classic method of arsenic poisoning. Crackenthorpe has never had any chronic gastric trouble. In a way, that's what makes these sudden violent attacks seem unlikely. So, assuming they are not due to natural causes, it looks as though the poisoner is muffing it every time—which hardly makes sense."

" Giving an inadequate dose, you mean?"

"Yes. On the other hand, Crackenthorpe's got a strong constitution and what might do in another man, doesn't do him in. There's always personal idiosyncrasy to be reckoned with. But you'd think that by now the poisoner —unless he's unusually timid—would have stepped up the dose. Why hasn't he?

"That is," he added, " if there *is* a poisoner which there probably isn't! Probably all my ruddy imagination from start to finish."

"It's an odd problem," the inspector agreed. "It doesn't seem to make sense."

II

"Inspector Craddock!"

The eager whisper made the inspector jump.

He had been just on the point of ringing the front-door bell.

Alexander and his friend Stoddart-West emerged cautiously from the shadows.

"We heard your car, and we wanted to get hold of you."

"Well, let's come inside." Craddock's hand went out to the door bell again, but Alexander pulled at his coat with the eagerness of a pawing dog.

"We've found a clue," he breathed.

"Yes, we've found a clue," Stoddart-West echoed.

"Damn that girl," thought Craddock unamiably.

"Splendid," he said in a perfunctory manner. "Let's go inside the house and look at it."

"No." Alexander was insistent. "Someone's sure to interrupt. Come to the harness room. We'll guide you."

Somewhat unwillingly, Craddock allowed himself to be guided round the corner of the house and along to the stable yard. Stoddart-West pushed open a heavy door, stretched up, and turned on a rather feeble electric light. The harness room, once the acme of Victorian spit and polish, was now the sad repository of everything that no one wanted. Broken garden chairs, rusted old garden implements, a vast decrepit mowing-machine, rusted spring mattresses, hammocks, and disintegrated tennis nets.

"We come here a good deal," said Alexander. "One can really be private here."

There were certain tokens of occupancy about. The decayed mattresses had been piled up to make a kind of divan, there was an old rusted table on which reposed a large tin of chocolate biscuits, there was a hoard of apples, a tin of toffee, and a jig-saw puzzle.

"It really *is* a clue, sir," said Stoddart-West eagerly, his eyes gleaming behind his spectacles. "We found it this afternoon."

"We've been hunting for days. In the bushes——"

"And inside hollow trees——"

"And we went all through the ash bins——"

"There were some jolly interesting things there, as a matter of fact——"

"And then we went into the boiler house——"

"Old Hillman keeps a great galvanised tub there full of waste paper——"

"For when the boiler goes out and he wants to start it again——"

"Any odd paper that's blowing about. He picks it up and shoves it in there——"

"And that's where we found it——"

"Found WHAT?" Craddock interrupted the duet.

"*The clue.* Careful, Stodders, get your gloves on."

Importantly, Stoddart-West, in the best detective story tradition, drew on a pair of rather dirty gloves and took from his pocket a Kodak photographic folder. From this he extracted in his gloved fingers with the utmost care a soiled and crumpled envelope which he handed importantly to the inspector.

Both boys held their breath in excitement.

Craddock took it with due solemnity. He liked the boys and he was ready to enter into the spirit of the thing.

The letter had been through the post, there was no enclosure inside, it was just a torn envelope—addressed to

Mrs. Martine Crackenthorpe, 126 Elvers Crescent, N.10.

"You see?" said Alexander breathlessly. "It shows she *was* here—Uncle Edmund's French wife, I mean—the one there's all the fuss about. She must have actually been here and dropped it somewhere. So it looks, doesn't it——"

Stoddart-West broke in:

"It looks as though *she* was the one who got murdered —I mean, don't you think, sir, that it simply *must* have been her in the sarcophagus?"

They waited anxiously.

Craddock played up.

"Possible, very possible," he said.

"This *is* important, isn't it?"

"You'll test it for fingerprints, won't you, sir?"

"Of course," said Craddock.

Stoddart-West gave a deep sigh.

"Smashing luck for us, wasn't it?" he said. "On our last day, too."

"Last day?"

"Yes," said Alexander. "I'm going to Stodders' place to-morrow for the last few days of the holidays. Stodders' people have got a smashing house—Queen Anne, isn't it?"

"William and Mary," said Stoddart-West.

"I thought your mother said——"

"Mum's French. She doesn't really know about English architecture."

"But your father said it was built——"

Craddock was examining the envelope.

Clever of Lucy Eyelesbarrow. How had she managed to fake the post mark? He peered closely, but the light was too feeble. Great fun for the boys, of course, but rather awkward for him. Lucy, drat her, hadn't considered that angle. If this were genuine, it would enforce a course of action. There . . .

Beside him a learned architectural argument was being hotly pursued. He was deaf to it.

"Come on, boys," he said, "we'll go into the house. You've been very helpful."

CHAPTER XVIII

CRADDOCK WAS escorted by the boys through the back door into the house. This was, it seemed, their common mode of entrance. The kitchen was bright and cheerful. Lucy, in a large white apron, was rolling out pastry. Leaning against the dresser, watching her with a kind of dog-like attention, was Bryan Eastley. With one hand he tugged at his large fair moustache.

"Hallo, Dad," said Alexander kindly. "You out here again?"

"I like it out here," said Bryan, and added: "Miss Eyelesbarrow doesn't mind."

"Oh, I don't mind," said Lucy. "Good evening, Inspector Craddock."

"Coming to detect in the kitchen?" asked Bryan with interest.

"Not exactly. Mr. Cedric Crackenthorpe is still here, isn't he?"

"Oh, yes, Cedric's here. Do you want him?"

"I'd like a word with him—yes, please."

"I'll go and see if he's in," said Bryan. "He may have gone round to the local."

He unpropped himself from the dresser.

"Thank you so much," said Lucy to him. "My hands are all over flour or I'd go."

"What are you making?" asked Stoddart-West anxiously.

"Peach flan."

"Good-oh," said Stoddart-West.

"Is it nearly supper-time?" asked Alexander.

"No."

"Gosh! I'm terribly hungry."

"There's the end of the ginger cake in the larder."

The boys made a concerted rush and collided in the door.

"They're just like locusts," said Lucy.

"My congratulations to you," said Craddock.

"What on—exactly?"

"Your ingenuity—over this!"

"Over what?"

Craddock indicated the folder containing the letter.

"Very nicely done," he said.

"What *are* you talking about?"

"This, my dear girl—this." He half-drew it out.

She stared at him uncomprehendingly.

Craddock felt suddenly dizzy.

"Didn't you fake this clue—and put it in the boiler room for the boys to find? Quick—tell me."

"I haven't the faintest idea what you're talking about," said Lucy. "Do you mean that——?"

Craddock slipped the folder quickly back in his pocket as Bryan returned.

"Cedric's in the library," he said. "Go on in."

He resumed his place on the dresser. Inspector Craddock went to the library.

II

Cedric Crackenthorpe seemed delighted to see the inspector.

"Doing a spot more sleuthing down here?" he asked. "Got any further?"

"I think I can say we are a little further on, Mr. Crackenthorpe."

"Found out who the corpse was?"

"We've not got a definite identification, but we have a fairly shrewd idea."

"Good for you."

"Arising out of our latest information, we want to get a few statements. I'm starting with you, Mr. Crackenthorpe, as you're on the spot."

"I shan't be much longer. I'm going back to Iviza in a day or two."

"Then I seem to be just in time."

"Go ahead."

"I should like a detailed account, please, of exactly where you were and what you were doing on Friday, 20th December."

Cedric shot a quick glance at him. Then he leaned back, yawned, assumed an air of great nonchalance, and appeared to be lost in the effort of remembrance.

"Well, as I've already told you, I was in Iviza. Trouble is, one day there is so like another. Painting in the morning, siesta from three p.m. to five. Perhaps a spot of sketching if the light's suitable. Then an apéritif, sometimes with the Mayor, sometimes with the doctor, at the café in the Piazza. After that some kind of a scratch meal. Most of the evening in Scotty's Bar with some of my lower-class friends. Will that do you?"

"I'd rather have the truth, Mr. Crackenthorpe."

Cedric sat up.

"That's a most offensive remark, Inspector."

"Do you think so? You told me, Mr. Crackenthorpe, that you left Iviza on 21st December and arrived in England that same day?"

"So I did. Em! Hi, Em?"

Emma Crackenthorpe came through the adjoining door from the small morning-room. She looked inquiringly from Cedric to the inspector.

"Look here, Em. I arrived here for Christmas on the Saturday before, didn't I? Came straight from the airport?"

"Yes," said Emma wonderingly. "You got here about lunch time."

"There you are," said Cedric to the inspector.

"You must think us very foolish, Mr. Crackenthorpe," said Craddock pleasantly. "We can check on these things, you know. I think, if you'll show me your passport——"

He paused expectantly.

"Can't find the damned thing," said Cedric. "Was looking for it this morning. Wanted to send it to Cook's."

"I think you could find it, Mr. Crackenthorpe. But it's not really necessary. The records show that you actually entered this country on the evening of 19th December. Perhaps you will now account to me for your movements between that time until lunch-time on 21st December when you arrived here."

Cedric looked very cross indeed.

"That's the hell of life nowadays," he said angrily. "All this red tape and form-filling. That's what comes of a bureaucratic state. Can't go where you like and do as you please any more! Somebody's always asking questions. What's all this fuss about the 20th, anyway? What's special about the 20th?"

"It happens to be the day we believe the murder was committed. You can refuse to answer, of course, but——"

"Who says I refuse to answer? Give a chap time. And you were vague enough about the date of the murder at the inquest. What's turned up new since then?"

Craddock did not reply.

Cedric said, with a sidelong glance at Emma:

"Shall we go into the other room?"

Emma said quickly: "I'll leave you." At the door, she paused and turned.

"This is serious, you know, Cedric. If the 20th *was* the day of the murder, then you must tell Inspector Craddock exactly what you were doing."

She went through into the next room and closed the door behind her.

"Good old Em," said Cedric. "Well, here goes. Yes, I left Iviza on the 19th all right. Planned to break the journey in Paris, and spend a couple of days routing up some old friends on the Left Bank. But, as a matter of fact, there was a very attractive woman on the plane. . . . Quite a dish. To put it plainly, she and I got off together. She was on her way to the States, had to spend a couple of of nights in London to see about some business or other. We got to London on the 19th. We stayed at the Kingsway Palace in case your spies haven't found that out yet! Called myself John Brown—never does to use your own name on these occasions."

"And on the 20th?"

Cedric made a grimace.

"Morning pretty well occupied by a terrific hangover."

"And the afternoon. From three o'clock onwards?"

"Let me see. Well, I mooned about, as you might say.

Went into the National Gallery—that's respectable enough. Saw a film. *Rowenna of the Range.* I've always had a passion for Westerns. This was a corker. . . . Then a drink or two in the bar and a bit of a sleep in my room, and out about ten o'clock with the girl-friend and a round of various hot spots—can't even remember most of their names—Jumping Frog was one, I think. She knew 'em all. Got pretty well plastered and, to tell you the truth, don't remember much more till I woke up the next morning—with an even worse hangover. Girl-friend hopped off to catch her plane and I poured cold water over my head, got a chemist to give me a devil's brew, and then started off for this place, pretending I'd just arrived at Heathrow. No need to upset Emma, I thought. You know what women are—always hurt if you don't come straight home. I had to borrow money from her to pay the taxi. I was completely cleaned out. No use asking the old man. He'd never cough up. Mean old brute. Well, Inspector, satisfied?"

"Can any of this be substantiated, Mr. Crackenthorpe? Say, between 3 p.m. and 7 p.m."

"Most unlikely, I should think," said Cedric cheerfully. "National Gallery where the attendants look at you with lack-lustre eyes and a crowded picture house. No, not likely."

Emma re-entered. She held a small engagement book in her hand.

"You want to know what everyone was doing on 20th December, is that right, Inspector Craddock?"

"Well—er—yes, Miss Crackenthorpe."

"I have just been looking in my engagement book. On the 20th I went into Brackhampton to attend a meeting of the Church Restoration Fund. That finished about a quarter to one and I lunched with Lady Adington and

Miss Bartlett who were also on the Committee, at the Cadena Café. After lunch I did some shopping, stores for Christmas, and also Christmas presents. I went to Greenford's and Lyall and Swift's, Boots', and probably several other shops. I had tea about a quarter to five in the Shamrock Tea Rooms and then went to the station to meet Bryan who was coming by train. I got home about six o'clock and found my father in a very bad temper. I had left lunch ready for him, but Mrs. Hart who was to come in in the afternoon and give him his tea had not arrived. He was so angry that he had shut himself in his room and would not let me in or speak to me. He does not like my going out in the afternoon, but I make a point of doing so now and then."

"You're probably wise. Thank you, Miss Crackenthorpe."

He could hardly tell her that as she was a woman, height five foot seven, her movements that afternoon were of no great importance. Instead he said:

"Your other two brothers came down later, I understand?"

"Alfred came down late on Saturday evening. He tells me he tried to ring me on the telephone the afternoon I was out—but my father, if he is upset, will never answer the telephone. My brother Harold did not come down until Christmas Eve."

"Thank you, Miss Crackenthorpe."

"I suppose I mustn't ask "—she hesitated—"what has come up new that prompts these inquiries?"

Craddock took the folder from his pocket. Using the tips of his fingers, he extracted the envelope.

"Don't touch it, please, but do you recognise this?"

"But . . ." Emma stared at him, bewildered. "That's my handwriting. That's the letter I wrote to Martine."

"I thought it might be."

"But how did you get it? Did she——? Have you found her?"

"It would seem possible that we have—found her. This empty envelope was found *here*."

"In the house?"

"In the grounds."

"Then—she *did* come here! She . . . You mean—it was Martine there—in the sarcophagus?"

"It would seem very likely, Miss Crackenthorpe," said Craddock gently.

It seemed even more likely when he got back to town. A message was awaiting him from Armand Dessin.

"*One of the girl-friends has had a postcard from Anna Stravinska. Apparently the cruise story was true! She has reached Jamaica and is having, in your phrase, a wonderful time!*"

Craddock crumpled up the message and threw it into the wastepaper basket.

III

"I must say," said Alexander, sitting up in bed, thoughtfully consuming a chocolate bar, "that this has been the most smashing day ever. Actually finding a real *clue*!"

His voice was awed.

"In fact the whole holidays have been smashing," he added happily. "I don't suppose such a thing will ever happen again."

"I hope it won't happen again to me," said Lucy who was on her knees packing Alexander's clothes into a suit-case. "Do you want *all* this space fiction with you?"

"Not those two top ones. I've read them. The football and my football boots, and the gum-boots can go separately."

"What difficult things you boys do travel with."

"It won't matter. They're sending the Rolls for us. They've got a smashing Rolls. They've got one of the new Mercedes-Benzes too."

"They must be rich."

"Rolling! Jolly nice, too. All the same, I rather wish we weren't leaving here. Another body might turn up."

"I sincerely hope not."

"Well, it often does in books. I mean somebody who's seen something or heard something gets done in, too. It might be you," he added, unrolling a second chocolate bar.

"Thank you!"

"I don't want it to be you," Alexander assured her. "I like you very much and so does Stodders. We think you're out of this world as a cook. Absolutely lovely grub. You're very sensible, too."

This last was clearly an expression of high approval. Lucy took it as such, and said: "Thank you. But I don't intend to get killed just to please you."

"Well, you'd better be careful, then," Alexander told her.

He paused to consume more nourishment and then said in a slightly offhand voice:

"If Dad turns up from time to time, you'll look after him, won't you?"

"Yes, of course," said Lucy, a little surprised.

"The trouble with Dad is," Alexander informed her, "that London life doesn't suit him. He gets in, you know, with quite the wrong type of women." He shook his head in a worried manner.

"I'm very fond of him," he added; "but he needs someone to look after him. He drifts about and gets in with the wrong people. It's a great pity Mum died when she did. Bryan needs a proper home life."

He looked solemnly at Lucy and reached out for another chocolate bar.

"Not a fourth one, Alexander," Lucy pleaded. "You'll be sick."

"Oh, I don't think so. I ate six running once and I wasn't. I'm not the bilious type." He paused and then said:

"Bryan likes you, you know."

"That's very nice of him."

"He's a bit of an ass in some ways," said Bryan's son; "but he was a jolly good fighter pilot. He's awfully brave. And he's awfully good-natured."

He paused. Then, averting his eyes to the ceiling, he said rather self-consciously:

"I think, really, you know, it would be a good thing if he married again. . . . Somebody decent. . . . I shouldn't, myself, mind at all having a stepmother . . . not, I mean, if she was a decent sort. . . ."

With a sense of shock Lucy realised that there was a definite point in Alexander's conversation.

"All this stepmother bosh," went on Alexander, still addressing the ceiling, "is really quite out of date. Lots of chaps Stodders and I know have stepmothers—divorce and all that—and they get on quite well together. Depends on the stepmother, of course. And, of course, it does make a bit of confusion taking you out and on Sports Day, and all that. I mean if there are two sets of parents. Though again it helps if you want to cash in!" He paused, confronted with the problems of modern life. "It's nicest to have your own home and your own parents—but if your mother's dead—well, you see what I mean? If she's a decent sort," said Alexander for the third time.

Lucy felt touched.

"I think *you're* very sensible, Alexander," she said. "We must try and find a nice wife for your father."

"Yes," said Alexander noncommittally.

He added in an offhand manner:

"I thought I'd just mention it. Bryan likes you very much. He told me so. . . ."

"Really," thought Lucy to herself. "There's too much match-making round here. First Miss Marple and now Alexander!"

For some reason or other, pigsties came into her mind. She stood up.

"Good night, Alexander. There will be only your washing things and pyjamas to put in in the morning. Good night."

"Good night," said Alexander. He slid down in bed, laid his head on the pillow, closed his eyes, giving a perfect picture of a sleeping angel; and was immediately asleep.

CHAPTER XIX

"Not what you'd call conclusive," said Sergeant Wetherall with his usual gloom.

Craddock was reading through the report on Harold Crackenthorpe's alibi for 20th December.

He had been noticed at Sotheby's about three-thirty, but was thought to have left shortly after that. His photograph had not been recognised at Russell's teashop, but as they did a busy trade there at teatime, and he was not an *habitué*, that was hardly surprising. His man-servant confirmed that he had returned to Cardigan Gardens to dress for his dinner-party at a quarter to seven —rather late, since the dinner was at seven-thirty, and Mr. Crackenthorpe had been somewhat irritable in consequence. Did not remember hearing him come in that evening, but, as it was some time ago, could not remember accurately and, in any case, he frequently did not hear Mr. Crackenthorpe come in. He and his wife liked to retire early whenever they could. The garage in the mews where Harold kept his car was a private lock-up that he rented and there was no one to notice who came or went or any reason to remember one evening in particular.

"All negative," said Craddock, with a sigh.

"He was at the Caterers' Dinner all right, but left rather early before the end of the speeches."

"What about the railway stations?"

But there was nothing there, either at Brackhampton or at Paddington. It was nearly four weeks ago, and it was highly unlikely that anything would have been remembered.

Craddock sighed, and stretched out his hand for the data on Cedric. That again was negative, though a taxi-driver had made a doubtful recognition of having taken a fare to Paddington that day some time in the afternoon "what looked something like that bloke. Dirty trousers and a shock of hair. Cussed and swore a bit because fares had gone up since he was last in England." He identified the day because a horse called Crawler had won the two-thirty and he'd had a tidy bit on. Just after dropping the gent, he'd heard it on the radio in his cab and had gone home forthwith to celebrate.

"Thank God for racing!" said Craddock, and put the report aside.

"And here's Alfred," said Sergeant Wetherall.

Some nuance in his voice made Craddock look up sharply. Wetherall had the pleased appearance of a man who has kept a titbit until the end.

In the main the check was unsatisfactory. Alfred lived alone in his flat and came and went at unspecified times. His neighbours were not the inquisitive kind and were in any case office workers who were out all day. But towards the end of the report, Wetherall's large finger indicated the final paragraph.

Sergeant Leakie, assigned to a case of thefts from lorries, had been at the Load of Bricks, a lorry pull-up on the Waddington-Brackhampton Road, keeping certain lorry drivers under observation. He had noticed at an adjoining table, Chick Evans, one of the Dicky Rogers mob. With him had been Alfred Crackenthorpe whom he knew by sight, having seen him give evidence in the Dicky Rogers case. He'd wondered what they were cooking up together. Time, 9-30 p.m., Friday, 20th December. Alfred Cracken-thorpe had boarded a bus a few minutes later, going in the direction of Brackhampton. William Baker, ticket collector at Brackhampton station, had clipped ticket of gentleman whom he recognised by sight as one of Miss Crackenthorpe's brothers, just before departure of eleven-fifty-five train for Paddington. Remembers day as there had been story of some batty old lady who swore she had seen somebody murdered in a train that afternoon.

"Alfred?" said Craddock as he laid the report down. "Alfred? I wonder."

"Puts him right on the spot, there," Wetherall pointed out.

Craddock nodded. Yes, Alfred could have travelled down by the 4.33 to Brackhampton committing murder on the way. Then he could have gone out by bus to the

Load of Bricks. He could have left there at nine-thirty and would have had plenty of time to go to Rutherford Hall, move the body from the embankment to the sarcophagus, and get into Brackhampton in time to catch the 11.55 back to London. One of the Dicky Rogers gang might even have helped him move the body, though Craddock doubted this. An unpleasant lot, but not killers.

"Alfred?" he repeated speculatively.

II

At Rutherford Hall there had been a gathering of the Crackenthorpe family. Harold and Alfred had come down from London and very soon voices were raised and tempers were running high.

On her own initiative, Lucy mixed cocktails in a jug with ice and took them towards the library. The voices sounded clearly in the hall, and indicated that a good deal of acrimony was being directed towards Emma.

"Entirely *your* fault, Emma." Harold's deep bass voice rang out angrily. "How you could be so short-sighted and foolish beats me. If you hadn't taken that letter to Scotland Yard—and started all this——"

Alfred's higher-pitched voice said: "You must have been out of your senses!"

"Now don't bully her," said Cedric. "What's done is done. Much more fishy if they'd identified the woman as the missing Martine and we'd all kept mum about having heard from her."

"It's all very well for you, Cedric," said Harold angrily. "You were out of the country on the 20th which seems to be the day they are inquiring about. But it's very embarrassing for Alfred and myself. Fortunately, *I* can remember where I was that afternoon and what I was doing."

"I bet you can," said Alfred. "If you'd arranged a murder, Harold, you'd arrange your alibi very carefully, I'm sure."

"I gather you are not so fortunate," said Harold coldly.

"That depends," said Alfred. "Anything's better than presenting a cast-iron alibi to the police if it isn't really cast iron. They're so clever at breaking these things down."

"If you are insinuating that I killed the woman——"

"Oh, do stop, all of you," cried Emma. "Of course none of you killed the woman."

"And just for your information, I *wasn't* out of England on the 20th," said Cedric. "*And* the police are wise to it! So we're all under suspicion."

"If it hadn't been for Emma——"

"Oh, don't begin again, Harold," cried Emma.

Dr. Quimper came out of the study where he had been closeted with old Mr. Crackenthorpe. His eye fell on the jug in Lucy's hand.

"What's this? A celebration?"

"More in the nature of oil on troubled waters. They're at it hammer and tongs in there."

"Recriminations?"

"Mostly abusing Emma."

Dr. Quimper's eyebrows rose.

"Indeed?" He took the jug from Lucy's hand, opened the library door and went in.

"Good evening."

"Ah, Dr. Quimper, I should like a word with you." It was Harold's voice, raised and irritable. "I should like to know what you meant by interfering in a private and family matter, and telling my sister to go to Scotland Yard about it."

Dr. Quimper said calmly:

"Miss Crackenthorpe asked my advice. I gave it to her. In my opinion, she did perfectly right."

"You dare to say——"

"Girl!"

It was old Mr. Crackenthorpe's familiar salutation. He was peering out of the study door just behind Lucy.

Lucy turned rather reluctantly.

"Yes, Mr. Crackenthorpe?"

"What are you giving us for dinner to-night? I want curry. You make a very good curry. It's ages since we've had curry."

"The boys don't care much for curry, you see."

"The boys—the boys. What do the boys matter? I'm the one who matters. And, anyway, the boys have gone —good riddance. I want a nice hot curry, do you hear?"

"All right, Mr. Crackenthorpe, you shall have it."

"That's right. You're a good girl, Lucy. You look after me, and I'll look after you."

Lucy went back to the kitchen. Abandoning the fricassée of chicken which she had planned, she began to assemble the preparations for curry. The front door banged and from the window she saw Dr. Quimper stride angrily from the house to his car and drive away.

Lucy sighed. She missed the boys. And in a way she missed Bryan, too.

Oh, well. She sat down and began to peel mushrooms.

At any rate, she'd give the family a rattling good dinner.

Feed the brutes!

III

It was 3 a.m. when Dr. Quimper drove his car into the garage, closed the doors and came in pulling the front door behind him rather wearily. Well, Mrs. Josh Simpkins had a fine healthy pair of twins to add to her present family of eight. Mr. Simpkins had expressed no elation over the arrival. "Twins," he had said gloomily. "What's the good of they? Quads now, they're good for something. All sorts of things you get sent, and the Press comes round and there's pictures in the paper, and they do say as Her Majesty sends you a telegram. But what's twins except two mouths to feed instead of one? Never been twins in our family, nor in the missus's either. Don't seem fair, somehow."

Dr. Quimper walked upstairs to his bedroom and started throwing off his clothes. He glanced at his watch. Five minutes past three. It had proved an unexpectedly tricky business bringing those twins into the world, but all had gone well. He yawned. He was tired—very tired. He looked appreciatively at his bed.

Then the telephone rang.

Dr. Quimper swore, and picked up the receiver.

"Dr. Quimper?"

"Speaking."

"This is Lucy Eyelesbarrow from Rutherford Hall. I think you'd better come over. Everybody seems to have been taken ill."

"Taken ill? How? What symptoms?"

Lucy detailed them.

"I'll be over straight away. In the meantime . . ." He gave her short sharp instructions.

Then he quickly resumed his clothes, flung a few extra

things into his emergency bag, and hurried down to his car.

IV

It was some three hours later when the doctor and Lucy, both of them somewhat exhausted, sat down by the kitchen table to drink large cups of black coffee.

"Ha," Dr. Quimper drained his cup, set it down with a clatter on the saucer. "I needed that. Now, Miss Eyelesbarrow, let's get down to brass tacks."

Lucy looked at him. The lines of fatigue showed clearly on his face making him look older than his forty-four years, the dark hair on his temples was flecked with grey, and there were lines under his eyes.

"As far as I can judge," said the doctor, "they'll be all right now. But how come? That's what I want to know. Who cooked the dinner?"

"I did," said Lucy.

"And what was it? In detail."

"Mushroom soup. Curried chicken and rice. Syllabubs. A savoury of chicken livers in bacon."

"*Canapés Diane*," said Dr. Quimper unexpectedly.

Lucy smiled faintly.

"Yes, *Canapés Diane*."

"All right—let's go through it. Mushroom soup—out of a tin, I suppose?"

"Certainly not. I made it."

"You made it. Out of what?"

"Half a pound of mushrooms, chicken stock, milk, a roux of butter and flour, and lemon juice."

"Ah. And one's supposed to say ' It must have been the mushrooms.' "

"It wasn't the mushrooms. I had some of the soup myself and I'm quite all right."

"Yes, *you*'re quite all right. I hadn't forgotten that."

Lucy flushed.

"If you mean——"

"I don't mean. You're a highly intelligent girl. You'd be groaning upstairs, too, if I'd meant what you thought I meant. Anyway, I know all about you. I've taken the trouble to find out."

"Why on earth did you do that?"

Dr. Quimper's lips were set in a grim line.

"Because I'm making it my business to find out about the people who come here and settle themselves in. You're a *bona fide* young woman who does this particular job for a livelihood, *and* you seem never to have had any contact with the Crackenthorpe family previous to coming here. So you're not a girl-friend of either Cedric, Harold, or Alfred—helping them to do a bit of dirty work."

"Do you really think——?"

"I think quite a lot of things," said Quimper. "But I have to be careful. That's the worst of being a doctor. Now let's get on. Curried chicken. Did you have some of that?"

"No. When you've cooked a curry, you've dined off the smell, I find. I tasted it, of course. I had soup and some syllabub."

"How did you serve the syllabub?"

"In individual glasses."

"Now, then, how much of all this is cleared up?"

"If you mean washing up, everything was washed up and put away."

Dr. Quimper groaned.

"There's such a thing as being over-zealous," he said.

"Yes, I can see that, as things have turned out, but there it is, I'm afraid."

"What *do* you have still?"

"There's some of the curry left—in a bowl in the larder. I was planning to use it as a basis for mulligatawny soup this evening. There's some mushroom soup left, too. No syllabub and none of the savoury."

"I'll take the curry and the soup. What about chutney? Did they have chutney with it?"

"Yes. In one of those stone jars."

"I'll have some of that, too."

He rose. "I'll go up and have a look at them again. After that, can you hold the fort until morning? Keep an eye on them all? I can have a nurse round, with full instructions, by eight o'clock."

"I wish you'd tell me straight out. Do you think it's food poisoning—or—or—well, poisoning."

"I've told you already. Doctors can't think—they have to be sure. If there's a positive result from these food specimens I can go ahead. Otherwise——"

"Otherwise?" Lucy repeated.

Dr. Quimper laid a hand on her shoulder.

"Look after two people in particular," he said. "Look after Emma. I'm not going to have anything happen to Emma. . . ."

There was emotion in his voice that could not be disguised. "She's not even begun to live yet," he said. "And you know, people like Emma Crackenthorpe are the salt of the earth. . . . Emma—well, Emma means a lot to me. I've never told her so, but I shall. Look after Emma."

"You bet I will," said Lucy.

"And look after the old man. I can't say that he's ever been my favourite patient, but he *is* my patient, and I'm damned if I'm going to let him be hustled out of the world because one or other of his unpleasant sons—or all three of them, maybe—want him out of the way so that they can handle his money."

He threw her a sudden quizzical glance.

"There," he said. "I've opened my mouth too wide. But keep your eyes skinned, there's a good girl, and, incidentally, keep your mouth shut."

V

Inspector Bacon was looking upset.

"Arsenic?" he said. "Arsenic?"

"Yes. It was in the curry. Here's the rest of the curry —for your fellow to have a go at. I've only done a very rough test on a little of it, but the result was quite definite."

"So there's a poisoner at work?"

"It would seem so," said Dr. Quimper dryly.

"And they're all affected, you say—except that Miss Eyelesbarrow."

"Except Miss Eyelesbarrow."

"Looks a bit fishy for her. . . ."

"What motive could she possibly have?"

"Might be barmy," suggested Bacon. "Seem all right, they do, sometimes, and yet all the time they're right off their rocker, so to speak."

"Miss Eyelesbarrow isn't off her rocker. Speaking as a medical man, Miss Eyelesbarrow is as sane as you or I are. If Miss Eyelesbarrow is feeding the family arsenic in their curry, she's doing it for a reason. Moreover, being a highly intelligent young woman, she'd be careful *not* to be the only one unaffected. What she'd do, what any intelligent poisoner would do, would be to eat a very little of the poisoned curry, and then exaggerate the symptoms."

"And then you wouldn't be able to tell?"

"That she'd had less than the others? Probably not. People don't all react alike to poisons anyway—the same amount will upset some people more than others. Of course," added Dr. Quimper cheerfully, "once the patient's dead, you can estimate fairly closely how much was taken."

"Then it might be . . ." Inspector Bacon paused to consolidate his ideas. "It might be that there's one of the family now who's making more fuss than he need— someone who you might say is mucking in with the rest so as to avoid arousing suspicion? How's that?"

"The idea has already occurred to me. That's why I'm reporting to you. It's in your hands now. I've got a nurse on the job that I can trust, but she can't be every- where at once. In my opinion, nobody's had enough to cause death."

"Made a mistake, the poisoner did?"

"No. It seems to me more likely that the idea was to put enough in the curry to cause signs of food poisoning —for which probably the mushrooms would be blamed. People are always obsessed with the idea of mushroom- poisoning. Then one person would probably take a turn for the worse and die."

"Because he'd been given a second dose?"

The doctor nodded.

"That's why I'm reporting to you at once, and why I've put a special nurse on the job."

"She knows about the arsenic?"

"Of course. She knows and so does Miss Eyelesbarrow. You know your own job best, of course, but if I were you, I'd get out there and make it quite clear to them all that they're suffering from arsenic poisoning. That will probably put the fear of the Lord into our murderer and he won't dare to carry out his plan. He's probably been banking on the food-poisoning theory."

The telephone rang on the inspector's desk. He picked it up and said:

"O.K. Put her through." He said to Quimper, "It's your nurse on the phone. Yes, hallo—speaking. . . . What's that? Serious relapse. . . . Yes. . . . Dr. Quimper's with me now. . . . If you'd like a word with him . . ."

He handed the receiver to the doctor.

"Quimper speaking . . . I see. . . . Yes. . . . Quite right. . . . Yes, carry on with that. We'll be along."

He put the receiver down and turned to Bacon.

"Who is it?"

"It's Alfred," said Dr. Quimper. "And he's dead."

CHAPTER XX

OVER THE telephone, Craddock's voice came in sharp disbelief.

"Alfred?" he said. "*Alfred?*"

Inspector Bacon, shifting the telephone receiver a little, said: "You didn't expect that?"

"No, indeed. As a matter of fact, I'd just got him taped for the murderer!"

"I heard about him being spotted by the ticket collector. Looked bad for him all right. Yes, looked as though we'd got our man."

"Well," said Craddock flatly, "we were wrong."

There was a moment's silence. Then Craddock asked:

"There was a nurse in charge. How did she come to slip up?"

"Can't blame her. Miss Eyelesbarrow was all in and went to get a bit of sleep. The nurse had got five patients on her hands, the old man, Emma, Cedric, Harold and Alfred. She couldn't be everywhere at once. It seems old Mr. Crackenthorpe started creating in a big way. Said he was dying. She went in, got him soothed down, came back again and took Alfred in some tea with glucose. He drank it and that was that."

"Arsenic again?"

"Seems so. Of course it could have been a relapse, but Quimper doesn't think so and Johnson agrees."

"I suppose," said Craddock, doubtfully, "that Alfred was *meant* to be the victim?"

Bacon sounded interested. "You mean that whereas Alfred's death wouldn't do anyone a penn'orth of good, the old man's death would benefit the lot of them? I suppose it *might* have been a mistake—somebody *might* have thought the tea was intended for the old man."

"Are they sure that that's the way the stuff was administered?"

"No, of course they aren't sure. The nurse, like a good nurse, washed up the whole contraption. Cups, spoons, teapot—everything. But it seems the only feasible method."

"Meaning," said Craddock thoughtfully, "that one of the patients wasn't as ill as the others? Saw his chance and doped the cup?"

"Well, there won't be any more funny business," said Inspector Bacon grimly. "We've got two nurses on the job now, to say nothing of Miss Eyelesbarrow, and I've got a couple of men there too. You coming down?"

"As fast as I can make it!"

II

Lucy Eyelesbarrow came across the hall to meet Inspector Craddock. She looked pale and drawn.

"You've been having a bad time of it," said Craddock.

"It's been like one long ghastly nightmare," said Lucy. "I really thought last night that they were *all* dying."

"About this curry——"

"It was the curry?"

"Yes, very nicely laced with arsenic—quite the Borgia touch."

"If that's true," said Lucy. "It must—it's got to be—one of the family."

"No other possibility?"

"No, you see I only started making that damned curry quite late—after six o'clock—because Mr. Crackenthorpe specially asked for curry. And I had to open a new tin of curry powder—so *that* couldn't have been tampered with. I suppose curry would disguise the taste?"

"Arsenic hasn't any taste," said Craddock absently. "Now, opportunity. Which of them had the chance to tamper with the curry while it was cooking?"

Lucy considered.

"Actually," she said, "anyone could have sneaked into the kitchen whilst I was laying the table in the dining-room."

"I see. Now, who was there in the house? Old Mr. Crackenthorpe, Emma, Cedric——"

"Harold and Alfred. They'd come down from London in the afternoon. Oh, and Bryan—Bryan Eastley. But he left just before dinner. He had to meet a man in Brackhampton."

Craddock said thoughtfully, "It ties up with the old man's illness at Christmas. Quimper suspected that that was arsenic. Did they all seem equally ill last night?"

Lucy considered. "I think old Mr. Crackenthorpe seemed the worst. Dr. Quimper had to work like a maniac on him. He's a jolly good doctor, I will say. Cedric made by far the most fuss. Of course, strong healthy people always do."

"What about Emma?"

"She has been pretty bad."

"Why Alfred, I wonder?" said Craddock.

"I know," said Lucy. "I suppose it was *meant* to be Alfred?"

"Funny—I asked that too!"

"It seems, somehow, so pointless."

"If I could only get at the motive for all this business," said Craddock. "It doesn't seem to tie up. The strangled woman in the sarcophagus was Edmund Crackenthorpe's widow, Martine. Let's assume that. It's pretty well proved by now. There *must* be a connection between that and the deliberate poisoning of Alfred. It's all here, in the family somewhere. Even saying one of them's mad doesn't help."

"Not really," Lucy agreed.

"Well, look after yourself," said Craddock warningly. "There's a poisoner in this house, remember, and one of your patients upstairs probably isn't as ill as he pretends to be."

Lucy went upstairs again slowly after Craddock's departure. An imperious voice, somewhat weakened by illness, called to her as she passed old Mr. Crackenthorpe's room.

"Girl—girl—is that you? Come here."

Lucy entered the room. Mr. Crackenthorpe was lying

in bed well propped up with pillows. For a sick man he was looking, Lucy thought, remarkably cheerful.

"The house is full of damned hospital nurses," complained Mr. Crackenthorpe. "Rustling about, making themselves important, taking my temperature, not giving me what I want to eat—a pretty penny all that must be costing. Tell Emma to send 'em away. You could look after me quite well."

"Everybody's been taken ill, Mr. Crackenthorpe," said Lucy. "I can't look after everybody, you know."

"Mushrooms," said Mr. Crackenthorpe. "Damned dangerous things, mushrooms. It was that soup we had last night. You made it," he added accusingly.

"The mushrooms were quite all right, Mr. Crackenthorpe."

"I'm not blaming you, girl, I'm not blaming you. It's happened before. One blasted fungus slips in and does it. Nobody can tell. I know you're a good girl. You wouldn't do it on purpose. How's Emma?"

"Feeling rather better this afternoon."

"Ah. And Harold?"

"He's better too."

"What's this about Alfred having kicked the bucket?"

"Nobody's supposed to have told you that, Mr. Crackenthorpe."

Mr. Crackenthorpe laughed, a high, whinnying laugh of intense amusement. "I hear things," he said. "Can't keep things from the old man. They try to. So Alfred's dead, is he? *He* won't sponge on me any more, and he won't get any of the money either. They've all been waiting for *me* to die, you know—Alfred in particular. Now *he's* dead. I call that rather a good joke."

"That's not very kind of you, Mr. Crackenthorpe," said Lucy severely.

Mr. Crackenthorpe laughed again. "I'll outlive them all," he crowed. "You see if I don't, my girl. You see if I don't."

Lucy went to her room, she took out her dictionary and looked up the word "tontine." She closed the book thoughtfully and stared ahead of her.

III

"Don't see why you want to come to me," said Dr. Morris, irritably.

"You've known the Crackenthorpe family a long time," said Inspector Craddock.

"Yes, yes, I knew all the Crackenthorpes. I remember old Josiah Crackenthorpe. He was a hard nut—shrewd man, though. Made a lot of money." He shifted his aged form in his chair and peered under busy eyebrows at Inspector Craddock. "So you've been listening to that young fool, Quimper," he said. "These zealous young doctors! Always getting ideas in their heads. Got it into *his* head that somebody was trying to poison Luther Crackenthorpe. Nonsense! Melodrama! Of course, he had gastric attacks. I treated him for them. Didn't happen very often—nothing peculiar about them."

"Dr. Quimper," said Craddock, "seemed to think there was."

"Doesn't do for a doctor to go thinking. After all, I should hope I could recognise arsenical poisoning when I saw it."

"Quite a lot of well-known doctors haven't noticed it," Craddock pointed out. "There was "—he drew upon his memory—"the Greenbarrow case, Mrs. Reney, Charles Leeds, three people in the Westbury family, all buried nicely and tidily without the doctors who attended them having the least suspicion. Those doctors were all good, reputable men."

"All right, all right," said Doctor Morris, "you're saying that I could have made a mistake. Well, *I* don't think I did." He paused a minute and then said, "Who did Quimper think was doing it—if it was being done?"

"He didn't know," said Craddock. "He was worried. After all, you know," he added, "there's a great deal of money there."

"Yes, yes, I know, which they'll get when Luther Crackenthorpe dies. And they want it pretty badly. That is true enough, but it doesn't follow that they'd kill the old man to get it."

"Not necessarily," agreed Inspector Craddock.

"Anyway," said Dr. Morris, "my principle is not to go about suspecting things without due cause. Due cause," he repeated. "I'll admit that what you've just told me has shaken me up a bit. Arsenic on a big scale, apparently —but I still don't see why you come to *me*. All I can tell you is that *I* didn't suspect it. Maybe I should have. Maybe I should have taken those gastric attacks of Luther Crackenthorpe's much more seriously. But you've got a long way beyond that now."

Craddock agreed. "What I really need," he said, "is to know a little more about the Crackenthorpe family. Is there any queer mental strain in them—a kink of any kind?"

The eyes under the bushy eyebrows looked at him sharply. "Yes, I can see your thoughts might run that way. Well, old Josiah was sane enough. Hard as nails, very much all there. His wife was neurotic, had a tendency to melancholia. Came of an inbred family. She died soon after her second son was born. I'd say, you know, that

Luther inherited a certain—well, instability, from her. He was commonplace enough as a young man, but he was always at loggerheads with his father. His father was disappointed in him and I think he resented that and brooded on it, and in the end got a kind of obsession about it. He carried that on into his own married life. You'll notice, if you talk to him at all, that he's got a hearty dislike for all his own sons. His daughters he was fond of. Both Emma and Edie—the one who died."

"Why does he dislike the sons so much?" asked Craddock.

"You'll have to go to one of these new-fashioned psychiatrists to find that out. I'd just say that Luther has never felt very adequate as a man himself, and that he bitterly resents his financial position. He has possession of an income but no power of appointment of capital. If he had the power to disinherit his sons he probably wouldn't dislike them as much. Being powerless in that respect gives him a feeling of humiliation."

"That's why he's so pleased at the idea of outliving them all?" said Inspector Craddock.

"Possibly. It is the root, too, of his parsimony, I think. I should say that he's managed to save a considerable sum out of his large income—mostly, of course, before taxation rose to its present giddy heights."

A new idea struck Inspector Craddock. "I suppose he's left his savings by will to someone? That he *can* do."

"Oh, yes, though God knows who he has left it to. Maybe to Emma, but I should rather doubt it. She'll get her share of the old man's money. Maybe to Alexander, the grandson."

"He's fond of him, is he?" said Craddock.

"Used to be. Of course he was his daughter's child, not a son's child. That may have made a difference. And he had quite an affection for Bryan Eastley, Edie's husband. Of course I don't know Bryan well, it's some years since I've seen any of the family. But it struck me that he was going to be very much at a loose end after the war. He's got those qualities that you need in wartime; courage, dash, and a tendency to let the future take care of itself. But I don't think he's got any *stability*. He'll probably turn into a drifter."

"As far as you know there's no peculiar kink in any of the younger generation?"

"Cedric's an eccentric type, one of those natural rebels. I wouldn't say he was perfectly normal, but you might say, who is? Harold's fairly orthodox, not what I call a very pleasant character, cold-hearted, eye to the main chance. Alfred's got a touch of the delinquent about him. He's a wrong 'un, always was. Saw him taking money out of a missionary box once that they used to keep in the hall. That type of thing. Ah, well, the poor fellow's dead, I suppose I shouldn't be talking against him."

"What about..." Craddock hesitated. "Emma Crackenthorpe?"

"Nice girl, quiet, one doesn't always know what she's thinking. Has her own plans and her own ideas, but she keeps them to herself. She's more character than you might think from her general manner and appearance."

"You knew Edmund, I suppose, the son who was killed in France?"

"Yes. He was the best of the bunch I'd say. Good-hearted, gay, a nice boy."

"Did you ever hear that he was going to marry, or had married, a French girl just before he was killed?"

Dr. Morris frowned. "It seems as though I remember something about it," he said, "but it's a long time ago."

"Quite early on in the war, wasn't it?"

"Yes. Ah, well, I dare say he'd have lived to regret it if he had married a foreign wife."

"There's some reason to believe that he did do just that," said Craddock.

In a few brief sentences he gave an account of recent happenings.

"I remember seeing something in the papers about a woman found in a sarcophagus. So it was at Rutherford Hall."

"And there's reason to believe that the woman was Edmund Crackenthorpe's widow."

"Well, well, that seems extraordinary. More like a novel than real life. But who'd want to kill the poor thing—I mean, how does it tie up with arsenical poisoning in the Crackenthorpe family?"

"In one of two ways," said Craddock; "but they are both very far-fetched. Somebody perhaps is greedy and wants the whole of Josiah Crackenthorpe's fortune."

"Damn fool if he does," said Dr. Morris. "He'll only have to pay the most stupendous taxes on the income from it."

CHAPTER XXI

"NASTY THINGS, mushrooms," said Mrs. Kidder.

Mrs. Kidder had made the same remark about ten times in the last few days. Lucy did not reply.

"Never touch 'em myself," said Mrs. Kidder, "much too dangerous. It's a merciful Providence as there's only been one death. The whole lot might have gone, and you, too, miss. A wonderful escape, you've had."

"It wasn't the mushrooms," said Lucy. "They were perfectly all right."

"Don't you believe it," said Mrs. Kidder. "Dangerous they are, mushrooms. One toadstool in among the lot and you've had it.

"Funny," went on Mrs. Kidder, among the rattle of plates and dishes in the sink, "how things seem to come all together, as it were. My sister's eldest had measles and our Ernie fell down and broke 'is arm, and my 'usband came out all over with boils. All in the same week! You'd hardly believe it, would you? It's been the same thing here," went on Mrs. Kidder, "first that nasty murder and now Mr. Alfred dead with mushroom-poisoning. Who'll be the next, I'd like to show?"

Lucy felt rather uncomfortably that she would like to know too.

"My husband, he doesn't like me coming here now," said Mrs. Kidder, "thinks it's unlucky, but what I say is

I've known Miss Crackenthorpe a long time now and she's a nice lady and she depends on me. And I couldn't leave poor Miss Eyelesbarrow, I said, not to do everything herself in the house. Pretty hard it is on you, miss, all these trays."

Lucy was forced to agree that life did seem to consist very largely of trays at the moment. She was at the moment arranging trays to take to the various invalids.

"As for them nurses, they never do a hand's turn," said Mrs. Kidder. "All they want is pots and pots of tea made strong. And meals prepared. Wore out, that's what I am." She spoke in a tone of great satisfaction, though actually she had done very little more than her normal morning's work.

Lucy said solemnly, "You never spare yourself, Mrs. Kidder."

Mrs. Kidder looked pleased. Lucy picked up the first of the trays and started off up the stairs.

"What's *this*?" said Mr. Crackenthorpe disapprovingly.

"Beef tea and baked custard," said Lucy.

"Take it away," said Mr. Crackenthorpe. "I won't touch that sort of stuff. I told that nurse I wanted a beef steak."

"Dr. Quimper thinks you ought not to have beef steak just yet," said Lucy.

Mr. Crackenthorpe snorted. "I'm practically well again. I'm getting up to-morrow. How are the others?"

"Mr. Harold's much better," said Lucy. "He's going back to London to-morrow."

"Good riddance," said Mr. Crackenthorpe. "What about Cedric—any hope that he's going back to his island to-morrow?"

"He won't be going just yet."

"Pity. What's Emma doing? Why doesn't she come and see me?"

"She's still in bed, Mr. Crackenthorpe."

"Women always coddle themselves," said Mr. Crackenthorpe. "But you're a good strong girl," he added approvingly. "Run about all day, don't you?"

"I get plenty of exercise," said Lucy.

Old Mr. Crackenthorpe nodded his head approvingly. "You're a good strong girl," he said, "and don't think I've forgotten what I talked to you about before. One of these days you'll see what you'll see. Emma isn't always going to have things her own way. And don't listen to the others when they tell you I'm a mean old man. I'm careful of my money. I've got a nice little packet put by and I know who I'm going to spend it on when the time comes." He leered at her affectionately.

Lucy went rather quickly out of the room, avoiding his clutching hand.

The next tray was taken in to Emma.

"Oh, thank you, Lucy. I'm really feeling quite myself again by now. I'm hungry, and that's a good sign, isn't it? My dear," went on Emma as Lucy settled the tray on her knees, "I'm really feeling very upset about your aunt. You haven't had any time to go and see her, I suppose?"

"No, I haven't, as a matter of fact."

"I'm afraid she must be missing you."

"Oh, don't worry, Miss Crackenthorpe. She understands what a terrible time we've been through."

"Have you rung her up?"

"No, I haven't just lately."

"Well, do. Ring her up every day. It makes such a difference to old people to get news."

"You're very kind," said Lucy. Her conscience smote her a little as she went down to fetch the next tray. The complications of illness in a house had kept her thoroughly absorbed and she had had no time to think of anything else. She decided that she would ring Miss Marple up as soon as she had taken Cedric his meal.

There was only one nurse in the house now and she passed Lucy on the landing, exchanging greetings.

Cedric, looking incredibly tidied up and neat, was sitting up in bed writing busily on sheets of paper.

"Hallo, Lucy," he said, "what hell brew have you got for me to-day? I wish you'd get rid of that god-awful nurse, she's simply too arch for words. Calls me ' we ' for some reason. ' And how are we this morning? Have we slept well? Oh, dear, we're very naughty, throwing off the bedclothes like that.' " He imitated the refined accents of the nurse in a high falsetto voice.

"You seem very cheerful," said Lucy. "What are you busy with?"

"Plans," said Cedric. "Plans for what to do with this place when the old man pops off. It's a jolly good bit of land here, you know. I can't make up my mind whether I'd like to develop some of it myself, or whether I'll sell it in lots all in one go. Very valuable for industrial purposes. The house will do for a nursing home or a school. I'm not sure I shan't sell half the land and use the money to do something rather outrageous with the other half. What do you think?"

"You haven't got it yet," said Lucy, dryly.

"I shall have it, though," said Cedric. "It's not divided up like the other stuff. *I* get it outright. And if I sell it for a good fat price the money will be capital, not income, so I shan't have to pay taxes on it. Money to burn. Think of it."

"I always understood you rather despised money," said Lucy.

"Of course I despise money when I haven't got any," said Cedric. "It's the only dignified thing to do. What a lovely girl you are, Lucy, or do I just think so because I haven't seen any good-looking women for a long time?"

"I expect that's it," said Lucy.

"Still busy tidying everyone and everything up?"

"Somebody seems to have been tidying you up," said Lucy, looking at him.

"That's that damned nurse," said Cedric with feeling. "Have they had the inquest on Alfred yet? What happened?"

"It was adjourned," said Lucy.

"Police being cagey. This mass poisoning does give one a bit of a turn, doesn't it? Mentally, I mean. I'm not referring to more obvious aspects." He added : "Better look after yourself, my girl."

"I do," said Lucy.

"Has young Alexander gone back to school yet?"

"I think he's still with the Stoddart-Wests. I think it's the day after to-morrow that school begins."

Before getting her own lunch Lucy went to the telephone and rang up Miss Marple.

"I'm so terribly sorry I haven't been able to come over, but I've really been very busy."

"Of course, my dear, of course. Besides, there's nothing that can be done just now. We just have to wait."

"Yes, but what are we waiting for?"

"Elspeth McGillicuddy ought to be home very soon now," said Miss Marple. "I wrote to her to fly home at once. I said it was her duty. So don't worry too much, my dear." Her voice was kindly and reassuring.

"You don't think . . ." Lucy began, but stopped.

"That there will be any more deaths? Oh, I hope not, my dear. But one never knows, does one? When anyone is really wicked, I mean. And I think there is great wickedness here."

"Or madness," said Lucy.

"Of course I know that is the modern way of looking at things. I don't agree myself."

Lucy rang off, went into the kitchen and picked up her tray of lunch. Mrs. Kidder had divested herself of her apron and was about to leave.

"You'll be all right, miss, I hope?" she asked solicitously.

"Of course I shall be all right," snapped Lucy.

She took her tray not into the big, gloomy dining-room but into the small study. She was just finishing the meal when the door opened and Bryan Eastley came in.

"Hallo," said Lucy, "this is very unexpected."

"I suppose it is," said Bryan. "How is everybody?"

"Oh, much better. Harold's going back to London to-morrow."

"What do you think about it all? Was it really arsenic?"

"It was arsenic all right," said Lucy.

"It hasn't been in the papers yet."

"No, I think the police are keeping it up their sleeves for the moment."

"Somebody must have a pretty good down on the family," said Bryan. "Who's likely to have sneaked in and tampered with the food?"

"I suppose I'm the most likely person really," said Lucy.

Bryan looked at her anxiously. "But you didn't, did you?" he asked. He sounded slightly shocked.

"No. I didn't," said Lucy.

Nobody could have tampered with the curry. She had made it—alone in the kitchen, and brought it to table, and the only person who could have tampered with it was one of the five people who sat down to the meal.

"I mean—why should you?" said Bryan. "They're nothing to you, are they? I say," he added, "I hope you don't mind my coming back here like this?"

"No, no, of course I don't. Have you come to stay?"

"Well, I'd like to, if it wouldn't be an awful bore to you."

"No. No, we can manage."

"You see, I'm out of a job at the moment and I—well, I get rather fed up. Are you really sure you don't mind?"

"Oh, I'm not the person to mind, anyway. It's Emma."

"Oh, Emma's all right," said Bryan. "Emma's always been very nice to me. In her own way, you know. She keeps things to herself a lot, in fact, she's rather a dark horse, old Emma. This living here and looking after the old man would get most people down. Pity she never married. Too late now, I suppose."

"I don't think it's too late at all," said Lucy.

"Well . . ." Bryan considered. "A clergyman perhaps," he said hopefully. "She'd be useful in the parish and tactful with the Mothers' Union. I do mean the Mothers' Union, don't I? Not that I know what it really is, but you come across it sometimes in books. And she'd wear a hat in church on Sundays," he added.

"Doesn't sound much of a prospect to me," said Lucy, rising and picking up the tray.

"I'll do that," said Bryan, taking the tray from her. They went into the kitchen together. "Shall I help you wash up? I do like this kitchen," he added. "In fact, I know it isn't the sort of thing that people do like nowadays, but I like this whole house. Shocking taste, I suppose, but there it is. You could land a plane quite easily in the park," he added with enthusiasm.

He picked up a glass-cloth and began to wipe the spoons and forks.

"Seems a waste, its coming to Cedric," he remarked. "First thing he'll do is to sell the whole thing and go beaking off abroad again. Can't see, myself, why England isn't good enough for anybody. Harold wouldn't want this house either, and of course it's much too big for Emma. Now, if only it came to Alexander, he and I would be as happy together here as a couple of sand boys. Of course it would be nice to have a woman about the house." He looked thoughtfully at Lucy. "Oh, well, what's the good of talking? If Alexander were to get this place it would mean the whole lot of them would have to die first, and that's not really likely, is it? Though from what I've seen of the old boy he might easily live to be a hundred, just to annoy them all. I don't suppose he was much cut up by Alfred's death, was he?"

Lucy said shortly, "No, he wasn't."

"Cantankerous old devil," said Bryan Eastley cheerfully.

CHAPTER XXII

"Dreadful, the things people go about saying," said Mrs. Kidder. "I don't listen, mind you, more than I can help. But you'd hardly believe it." She waited hopefully.

"Yes, I suppose so," said Lucy.

"About that body that was found in the Long Barn," went on Mrs. Kidder, moving crablike backwards on her hands and knees, as she scrubbed the kitchen floor, "saying as how she'd been Mr. Edmund's fancy piece during the war, and how she come over here and a jealous husband followed her, and did her in. It is a likely thing as a foreigner would do, but it wouldn't be likely after all these years, would it?"

"It sounds most unlikely to me."

"But there's worse things than that, they say," said Mrs. Kidder. "Say anything, people will. You'd be surprised. There's those that say Mr. Harold married somewhere abroad and that she come over and found out he'd committed bigamy with that Lady Alice, and that she was going to bring 'im to court and that he met her down here and did her in, and hid her body in the sarcoffus. Did you ever!"

"Shocking," said Lucy vaguely, her mind elsewhere.

"Of course I don't listen," said Mrs. Kidder virtuously, "I wouldn't put no stock in such tales myself. It beats me how people think up such things, let alone say them. All

I hope is none of it gets to Miss Emma's ears. It might upset her and I shouldn't like that. She's a very nice lady, Miss Emma is, and I've not heard a word against her, not a word. And of course Mr. Alfred being dead nobody says anything against him now. Not even that it's a judgment, which they well might do. But it's awful, miss, isn't it, the wicked talk there is."

Mrs. Kidder spoke with immense enjoyment.

"It must be quite painful for you to listen to it," said Lucy.

"Oh, it is," said Mrs. Kidder. "It is indeed. I says to my husband, I says, however can they?"

The bell rang.

"There's the doctor, miss. Will you let 'im in, or shall I?"

"I'll go," said Lucy.

But it was not the doctor. On the doorstep stood a tall, elegant woman in a mink coat. Drawn up to the gravel sweep was a purring Rolls with a chauffeur at the wheel.

"Can I see Miss Emma Crackenthorpe, please?"

It was an attractive voice, the R's slightly blurred. The woman was attractive too. About thirty-five, with dark hair and expensively and beautifully made up.

"I'm sorry," said Lucy, "Miss Crackenthorpe is ill in bed and can't see anyone."

"I know she has been ill, yes; but it is very important that I should see her."

"I'm afraid," Lucy began.

The visitor interrupted her. "I think you are Miss Eyelesbarrow, are you not?" She smiled, an attractive smile. "My son has spoken of you, so I know. I am Lady Stoddart-West and Alexander is staying with me now."

"Oh, I see," said Lucy.

"And it is really important that I should see Miss Crackenthorpe," continued the other. "I know all about her illness and I assure you this is not just a social call. It is because of something that the boys have said to me —that my son has said to me. It is, I think, a matter of grave importance and I would like to speak to Miss Crackenthorpe about it. Please, will you ask her?"

"Come in." Lucy ushered her visitor into the hall and into the drawing-room. Then she said, "I'll go up and ask Miss Crackenthorpe."

She went upstairs, knocked on Emma's door and entered.

"Lady Stoddart-West is here," she said. "She wants to see you very particularly."

"Lady Stoddart-West?" Emma looked surprised. A look of alarm came into her face. "There's nothing wrong, is there, with the boys—with Alexander?"

"No, no," Lucy reassured her. "I'm sure the boys are all right. It seems to be something the boys have told her or said to her."

"Oh. Well . . ." Emma hesitated. "Perhaps I ought to see her. Do I look all right, Lucy?"

"You look very nice," said Lucy.

Emma was sitting up in bed, a soft pink shawl was round her shoulders and brought out the faint rose-pink of her cheeks. Her dark hair had been neatly brushed and combed by Nurse. Lucy had placed a bowl of autumn leaves on the dressing-table the day before. Her room looked attractive and quite unlike a sick room.

"I'm really quite well enough to get up," said Emma. "Dr. Quimper said I could to-morrow."

"You look really quite yourself again," said Lucy. "Shall I bring Lady Stoddart-West up?"

"Yes, do."

Lucy went downstairs again. "Will you come up to Miss Crackenthorpe's room?"

She escorted the visitor upstairs, opened the door for her to pass in and then shut it. Lady Stoddart-West approached the bed with outstretched hand.

"Miss Crackenthorpe? I really do apologise for breaking in on you like this. I have seen you, I think, at the sports at the school."

"Yes," said Emma, "I remember you quite well. Do sit down."

In the chair conveniently placed by the bed Lady Stoddart-West sat down. She said in a quiet low voice:

"You must think it very strange of me coming here like this, but I have a reason. I think it is an important reason. You see, the boys have been telling me things. You can understand that they were very excited about the murder that happened here. I confess I did not like it at the time. I was nervous. I wanted to bring James home at once. But my husband laughed. He said that obviously it was a murder that had nothing to do with the house and the family, and he said that from what he remembered from his boyhood, and from James's letters, both he and Alexander were enjoying themselves so wildly that it would be sheer cruelty to bring them back. So I gave in and agreed that they should stay on until the time arranged for James to bring Alexander back with him."

Emma said: "You think we ought to have sent your son home earlier?"

"No, no, that is not what I mean at all. Oh, it is difficult for me, this! But what I have to say must be said. You see, they have picked up a good deal, the boys. They told me that this woman—the murdered woman—that the police have an idea that she may be a French girl

221

whom your eldest brother—who was killed in the war—knew in France. That is so?"

"It is a possibility," said Emma, her voice breaking slightly, "that we are forced to consider. It may have been so."

"There is some reason for believing that the body is that of this girl, this Martine?"

"I have told you, it is a possibility."

"But why—why should they think that she was this Martine? Did she have letters on her—papers?"

"No. Nothing of that kind. But you see, I had had a letter, from this Martine."

"You had had a letter—from *Martine*?"

"Yes. A letter telling me she was in England and would like to come and see me. I invited her down here, but got a telegram saying she was going back to France. Perhaps she did go back to France. We do not know. But since then an envelope was found here addressed to her. That seems to show that she had come down here. But I really don't see . . ." She broke off.

Lady Stoddart-West broke in quickly:

"You really do not see what concern it is of mine? That is very true. I should not in your place. But when I heard this—or rather, a garbled account of this—I had to come to make sure it was really so because, if it is——"

"Yes?" said Emma.

"Then I must tell you something that I had never intended to tell you. You see, *I am Martine Dubois*."

Emma stared at her guest as though she could hardly take in the sense of her words.

"You!" she said. "You are Martine?"

The other nodded vigorously. "But, yes. It surprises you, I am sure, but it is true. I met your brother Edmund in the first days of the war. He was indeed billeted at our house. Well, you know the rest. We fell in love. We intended to be married, and then there was the retreat to Dunkirk, Edmund was reported missing. Later he was reported killed. I will not speak to you of that time. It was long ago and it is over. But I will say to you that I loved your brother very much. . . .

"Then came the grim realities of war. The Germans occupied France. I became a worker for the Resistance. I was one of those who was assigned to pass Englishmen through France to England. It was in that way that I met my present husband. He was an Air Force officer, parachuted into France to do special work. When the war ended we were married. I considered once or twice whether I should write to you or come and see you, but I decided against it. It could do no good, I thought, to rake up old memories. I had a new life and I had no wish to recall the old." She paused and then said: "But it gave me, I will tell you, a strange pleasure when I found that my son James's greatest friend at his school was a boy whom I found to be Edmund's nephew. Alexander, I may say, is very like Edmund, as I dare say you yourself appreciate. It seemed to me a very happy state of affairs that James and Alexander should be such friends."

She leaned forward and placed her hand on Emma's arm. "But you see, dear Emma, do you not, that when I heard this story about the murder, about this dead woman being suspected to be the Martine that Edmund had known, that I had to come and tell you the truth. Either you or I must inform the police of the fact. Whoever the dead woman is, she is not Martine."

"I can hardly take it in," said Emma, "that you, *you* should be the Martine that dear Edmund wrote to me about." She sighed, shaking her head, then she frowned perplexedly. "But I don't understand. Was it you, then, who wrote to me?"

Lady Stoddart-West shook a vigorous head. "No, no, of course I did not write to you."

"Then . . ." Emma stopped.

"Then there was someone pretending to be Martine who wanted perhaps to get money out of you? That is what it must have been. But who can it be?"

Emma said slowly: "I suppose there were people at the time, who knew?"

The other shrugged her shoulders. "Probably, yes. But there was no one intimate with me, no one very close to me. I have never spoken of it since I came to England. And why wait all this time? It is curious, very curious."

Emma said: "I don't understand it. We will have to see what Inspector Craddock has to say." She looked with suddenly softened eyes at her visitor. "I'm so glad to know you at last, my dear."

"And I you. . . . Edmund spoke of you very often. He was very fond of you. I am happy in my new life, but all the same, I do not quite forget."

Emma leaned back and heaved a deep sigh. "It's a terrible relief," she said. "As long as we feared that the dead woman might be Martine—it seemed to be tied up with the family. But now—oh, it's an absolute load off my back. I don't know who the poor soul was but she can't have had anything to do with *us!*"

CHAPTER XXIII

THE STREAMLINED secretary brought Harold Crackenthorpe his usual afternoon cup of tea.

"Thanks, Miss Ellis, I shall be going home early to-day."

"I'm sure you ought really not to have come at all, Mr. Crackenthorpe," said Miss Ellis. "You look quite pulled down still."

"I'm all right," said Harold Crackenthorpe, but he did feel pulled down. No doubt about it, he'd had a very nasty turn. Ah, well, that was over.

Extraordinary, he thought broodingly, that Alfred should have succumbed and the old man should have come through. After all, what was he—seventy-three—seventy-four? Been an invalid for years. If there was one person you'd have thought would have been taken off, it would have been the old man. But no. It had to be Alfred. Alfred who, as far as Harold knew, was a healthy wiry sort of chap. Nothing much the matter with him.

He leaned back in his chair sighing. That girl was right. He didn't feel up to things yet, but he had wanted to come down to the office. Wanted to get the hang of how affairs were going. Touch and go, that's what it was! Touch and go. All this—he looked round him—the richly appointed office, the pale gleaming wood, the expensive modern chairs, it all looked prosperous enough, and a good thing too! That's where Alfred had always gone wrong. If you looked prosperous, people thought you were prosperous. There were no rumours going around as yet about his financial stability. All the same, the crash couldn't be delayed very long. Now, if only his father had passed out instead of Alfred, as surely, surely he ought to have done. Practically seemed to thrive on arsenic! Yes, if his father had succumbed—well, there wouldn't have been anything to worry about.

Still, the great thing was not to seem worried. A prosperous appearance. Not like poor old Alfred who always looked seedy and shiftless, who looked in fact exactly what he was. One of those small-time speculators, never going all out boldly for the big money. In with a shady crowd here, doing a doubtful deal there, never quite rendering himself liable to prosecution but going very near the edge. And where had it got him? Short periods of affluence and then back to seediness and shabbiness once more. No broad outlook about Alfred. Taken all in all, you couldn't say Alfred was much loss. He'd never been particularly fond of Alfred and with Alfred out of the way the money that was coming to him from that old curmudgeon, his grandfather, would be sensibly increased, divided not into five shares but into four shares. Very much better.

Harold's face brightened a little. He rose, took his hat and coat and left the office. Better take it easy for a day or two. He wasn't feeling too strong yet. His car was waiting below and very soon he was weaving through the London traffic to his house.

Darwin, his manservant, opened the door.

"Her ladyship has just arrived, sir," he said.

For a moment Harold stared at him. Alice! Good

heavens, was it to-day that Alice was coming home? He'd forgotten all about it. Good thing Darwin had warned him. It wouldn't have looked so good if he'd gone upstairs and looked too astonished at seeing her. Not that it really mattered, he supposed. Neither Alice nor he had many illusions about the feeling they had for each other. Perhaps Alice was fond of him—he didn't know.

All in all, Alice was a great disappointment to him. He hadn't been in love with her, of course, but though a plain woman she was quite a pleasant one. And her family and connections had undoubtedly been useful. Not perhaps as useful as they might have been, because in marrying Alice he had been considering the position of hypothetical children. Nice relations for his boys to have. But there hadn't been any boys, or girls either, and all that had remained had been he and Alice growing older together without much to say to each other and with no particular pleasure in each other's company.

She stayed away a good deal with relations and usually went to the Riviera in the winter. It suited her and it didn't worry him.

He went upstairs now into the drawing-room and greeted her punctiliously.

"So you're back, my dear. Sorry I couldn't meet you, but I was held up in the City. I got back as early as I could. How was San Raphael?"

Alice told him how San Raphael was. She was a thin woman with sandy-coloured hair, a well-arched nose and vague, hazel eyes. She talked in a well-bred, monotonous and rather depressing voice. It had been a good journey back, the Channel a little rough. The Customs, as usual, very trying at Dover.

"You should come by air," said Harold, as he always did. "So much simpler."

"I dare say, but I don't really like air travel. I never have. Makes me nervous."

"Saves a lot of time," said Harold.

Lady Alice Crackenthorpe did not answer. It was possible that her problem in life was not to save time but to occupy it. She inquired politely after her husband's health.

"Emma's telegram quite alarmed me," she said. "You were all taken ill, I understand."

"Yes, yes," said Harold.

"I read in the paper the other day," said Alice, "of forty people in a hotel going down with food poisoning at the same time. All this refrigeration is dangerous, I think. People keep things too long in them."

"Possibly," said Harold. Should he, or should he not mention arsenic? Somehow, looking at Alice, he felt himself quite unable to do so. In Alice's world, he felt, there was no place for poisoning by arsenic. It was a thing you read about in the papers. It didn't happen to you or your own family. But it had happened in the Crackenthorpe family. . . .

He went up to his room and lay down for an hour or two before dressing for dinner. At dinner, tête-à-tête with his wife, the conversation ran on much the same lines. Desultory, polite. The mention of acquaintances and friends at San Raphael.

"There's a parcel for you on the hall table, a small one," Alice said.

"Is there? I didn't notice it."

"It's an extraordinary thing but somebody was telling me about a murdered woman having been found in a barn, or something like that. She said it was at Rutherford Hall. I suppose it must be some other Rutherford Hall."

228

"No," said Harold, "no, it isn't. It was in our barn, as a matter of fact."

"Really, Harold! A murdered woman in the barn at Rutherford Hall—and you never told me anything about it."

"Well, there hasn't been much time, really," said Harold, "and it was all rather unpleasant. Nothing to do with us, of course. The Press milled round a good deal. Of course we had to deal with the police and all that sort of thing."

"Very unpleasant," said Alice. "Did they find out who did it?" she added, with rather perfunctory interest.

"Not yet," said Harold.

"What sort of a woman was she?"

"Nobody knows. French apparently."

"Oh, *French*," said Alice, and allowing for the difference in class, her tone was not unlike that of Inspector Bacon. "Very annoying for you all," she agreed.

They went out from the dining-room and crossed into the small study where they usually sat when they were alone. Harold was feeling quite exhausted by now. "I'll go up to bed early," he thought.

He picked up the small parcel from the hall table, about which his wife had spoken to him. It was a small neatly waxed parcel, done up with meticulous exactness. Harold ripped it open as he came to sit down in his usual chair by the fire.

Inside was a small tablet box bearing the label, "Two to be taken nightly." With it was a small piece of paper with the chemist's heading in Brackhampton, "Sent by request of Doctor Quimper," was written on it.

Harold Crackenthorpe frowned. He opened the box and looked at the tablets. Yes, they seemed to be the same tablets he had been having. But surely, surely Quimper had said that he needn't take any more? "You won't want them now." That's what Quimper had said.

"What is it, dear?" said Alice. "You look worried."

"Oh, it's just—some tablets. I've been taking them at night. But I rather thought the doctor said don't take any more."

His wife said placidly: "He probably said don't forget to take them."

"He may have done, I suppose," said Harold doubtfully.

He looked across at her. She was watching him. Just for a moment or two he wondered—he didn't often wonder about Alice—exactly what she was thinking. That mild gaze of hers told him nothing. Her eyes were like windows in an empty house. What did Alice think about him, feel about him? Had she been in love with him once? He supposed she had. Or did she marry him because she thought he was doing well in the City, and she was tired of her own impecunious existence? Well, on the whole, she'd done quite well out of it. She'd got a car and a house in London, she could travel abroad when she felt like it and get herself expensive clothes, though goodness knows they never looked like anything on Alice. Yes, on the whole she'd done pretty well. He wondered if she thought so. She wasn't really fond of him, of course, but then he wasn't really fond of her. They had nothing in common, nothing to talk about, no memories to share. If there had been children—but there hadn't been any children—odd that there were no children in the family except young Edie's boy. Young Edie. She'd been a silly girl, making that foolish, hasty war-time marriage. Well, he'd given her good advice.

He'd said: "It's all very well, these dashing young pilots, glamour, courage, all that, but he'll be no good in peace-time, you know. Probably be barely able to support you."

And Edie had said, what did it matter? She loved Bryan and Bryan loved her, and he'd probably be killed quite soon. Why shouldn't they have some happiness? What was the good of looking to the future when they might all be bombed any minute. And after all, Edie had said, the future doesn't really matter because some day there'll be all grandfather's money.

Harold squirmed uneasily in his chair. Really, that will of his grandfather's had been iniquitous! Keeping them all dangling on a string. The will hadn't pleased anybody. It didn't please the grandchildren and it made their father quite livid. The old boy was absolutely determined not to die. That's what made him take so much care of himself. But he'd have to die soon. Surely, surely he'd have to die soon. Otherwise—all Harold's worries swept over him once more making him feel sick and tired and giddy.

Alice was still watching him, he noticed. Those pale, thoughtful eyes, they made him uneasy somehow.

"I think I shall go to bed," he said. "It's been my first day out in the City."

"Yes," said Alice, "I think that's a good idea. I'm sure the doctor told you to take things easily at first."

"Doctors always tell you that," said Harold.

"And don't forget to take your tablets, dear," said Alice. She picked up the box and handed it to him.

He said good night and went upstairs. Yes, he needed the tablets. It would have been a mistake to leave them off too soon. He took two of them and swallowed them with a glass of water.

CHAPTER XXIV

"NOBODY COULD have made more of a muck of it than I seem to have done," said Dermot Craddock gloomily.

He sat, his long legs stretched out, looking somehow incongruous in faithful Florence's somewhat over-furnished parlour. He was thoroughly tired, upset and dispirited.

Miss Marple made soft, soothing noises of dissent. "No, no, you've done very good work, my dear boy. Very good work indeed."

"I've done very good work, have I? I've let a whole family be poisoned, Alfred Crackenthorpe's dead and now Harold's dead too. What the hell's going on there? That's what I should like to know."

"Poisoned tablets," said Miss Marple thoughtfully.

"Yes. Devilishly cunning, really. They looked just like the tablets that he'd been having. There was a printed slip sent in with them ' by Doctor Quimper's instructions.' Well, Quimper never ordered them. There were chemist's labels used. The chemist knew nothing about it, either. No. That box of tablets came from Rutherford Hall."

"Do you actually *know* it came from Rutherford Hall?"

"Yes. We've had a thorough check up. Actually, it's the box that held the sedative tablets prescribed for Emma."

"Oh, I see. For Emma. . . ."

"Yes. It's got her fingerprints on it and the fingerprints of both the nurses and the fingerprint of the chemist who made it up. Nobody else's, naturally. The person who sent them was careful."

"And the sedative tablets were removed and something else substituted?"

"Yes. That of course is the devil with tablets. One tablet looks exactly like another."

"You are so right," agreed Miss Marple. "I remember so very well in my young days, the *black* mixture and the *brown* mixture (the cough mixture that was) and the white mixture, and Doctor So-and-So's *pink* mixture. People didn't mix those up nearly as much. In fact, you know, in my village of St. Mary Mead we still like that kind of medicine. It's a bottle they always want, not tablets. What were the tablets?" she asked.

"Aconite. They were the kind of tablets that are usually kept in a poison bottle, diluted one in a hundred for outside application."

"And so Harold took them, and died," Miss Marple said thoughtfully. Dermot Craddock uttered something like a groan.

"You mustn't mind my letting off steam to you," he said. "Tell it all to Aunt Jane; that's how I feel!"

"That's very, very nice of you," said Miss Marple, "and I do appreciate it. I feel towards you, as Sir Henry's godson, quite differently from the way I should feel to any ordinary detective-inspector."

Dermot Craddock gave her a fleeting grin. "But the fact remains that I've made the most ghastly mess of things all along the line," he said. "The Chief Constable down here calls in Scotland Yard, and what do they get? They get me making a prize ass of myself!"

"No, no," said Miss Marple.

"Yes, yes. I don't know who poisoned Alfred, I don't know who poisoned Harold, and, to cap it all, I haven't the least idea now who the original murdered woman was! This Martine business seemed a perfectly safe bet. The whole thing seemed to tie up. And now what happens? The real Martine shows up and turns out, most improbably, to be the wife of Sir Robert Stoddart-West. So who's the woman in the barn now? Goodness knows. First I go all out on the idea she's Anna Stravinska, and then *she's* out of it——"

He was arrested by Miss Marple giving one of her small peculiarly significant coughs.

"But is she?" she murmured.

Craddock stared at her. "Well, that postcard from Jamaica——"

"Yes," said Miss Marple; "but that isn't really evidence, is it? I mean, anyone can get a postcard sent from almost anywhere, I suppose. I remember Mrs. Brierly, such a very bad nervous breakdown. Finally, they said she ought to go to the mental hospital for observation, and she was so worried about the children knowing about it and so she wrote about fourteen postcards and arranged that they should be posted from different places abroad, and told them that Mummy was going abroad on a holiday." She added, looking at Dermot Craddock, "You see what I mean."

"Yes, of course," said Craddock, staring at her. "Naturally we'd have checked that postcard if it hadn't been for the Martine business fitting the bill so well."

"So convenient," murmured Miss Marple.

"It tied up," said Craddock. "After all, there's the letter Emma received signed Martine Crackenthorpe. Lady Stoddart-West didn't send that, but *somebody* did. Somebody who was going to pretend to be Martine, and who was going to cash in, if possible, on being Martine. You can't deny *that*."

"No, no."

"And then, the envelope of the letter Emma wrote to her with the London address on it. Found at Rutherford Hall, showing she'd actually been there."

"But the murdered woman *hadn't* been there!" Miss Marple pointed out. "Not in the sense *you* mean. *She* only came to Rutherford Hall *after she was dead*. Pushed out of a train on to the railway embankment."

"Oh, yes."

"What the envelope really proves is that the *murderer* was there. Presumably he took that envelope off her with her other papers and things, and then dropped it by mistake—or—I wonder now, was it a mistake? Surely Inspector Bacon, and your men too, made a thorough search of the place, didn't they, and didn't find it. It only turned up later in the boiler house."

"That's understandable," said Craddock. "The old gardener chap used to spear up any odd stuff that was blowing about and shove it in there."

"Where it was very convenient for the boys to find," said Miss Marple thoughtfully.

"You think we were meant to find it?"

"Well, I just wonder. After all, it would be fairly easy to know where the boys were going to look next, or even to suggest to them. . . . Yes, I do wonder. It stopped you thinking about Anna Stravinska any more, didn't it?"

Craddock said: "And you think it really may be her all the time?"

"I think *someone* may have got alarmed when you started making inquiries about her, that's all. . . . I think somebody didn't want those inquiries made."

"Let's hold on to the basic fact that someone was going

to impersonate Martine," said Craddock. "And then for some reason—didn't. Why?"

"That's a very interesting question," said Miss Marple.

"Somebody sent a wire saying Martine was going back to France, then arranged to travel down with the girl and kill her on the way. You agree so far?"

"Not exactly," said Miss Marple. "I don't think, really, you're making it simple enough."

"Simple!" exclaimed Craddock. "You're mixing me up," he complained.

Miss Marple said in a distressed voice that she wouldn't think of doing anything like *that*.

"Come, tell me," said Craddock, "do you or do you not think you know who the murdered woman was?"

Miss Marple sighed. "It's so difficult," she said, "to put it the right way. I mean, I don't know *who* she was, but at the same time I'm fairly sure who she *was*, if you know what I mean."

Craddock threw up his head. "Know what you mean? I haven't the faintest idea." He looked out through the window. "There's your Lucy Eyelesbarrow coming to see you," he said. "Well, I'll be off. My *amour propre* is very low this afternoon and having a young woman coming in, radiant with efficiency and success, is more than I can bear."

CHAPTER XXV

"I LOOKED up tontine in the dictionary," said Lucy.

The first greetings were over and now Lucy was wandering rather aimlessly round the room, touching a china dog here, an antimacassar there, the plastic workbox in the window.

"I thought you probably would," said Miss Marple equably.

Lucy spoke slowly, quoting the words. "Lorenzo Tonti, Italian banker, originator, 1653, of a form of annuity in which the shares of subscribers who die are added to the profit shares of the survivors." She paused. "That's it, isn't it? That fits well enough, and you were thinking of it even *then* before the last two deaths."

She took up once more her restless, almost aimless prowl round the room. Miss Marple sat watching her. This was a very different Lucy Eyelesbarrow from the one she knew.

"I suppose it was asking for it really," said Lucy. "A will of that kind, ending so that if there was only one survivor left he'd get the lot. And yet—there was quite a lot of money, wasn't there? You'd think it would be enough shared out . . ." She paused, the words tailing off.

"The trouble is," said Miss Marple, "that people are greedy. Some people. That's so often, you know, how things start. You don't start with murder, with wanting

237

to do murder, or even thinking of it. You just start by being greedy, by wanting more than you're going to have." She laid her knitting down on her knee and stared ahead of her into space. "That's how I came across Inspector Craddock first, you know. A case in the country. Near Medenham Spa. That began the same way, just a weak amiable character who wanted a great deal of money. Money that that person wasn't entitled to, but there seemed an easy way to get it. Not murder then. Just something so easy and simple that it hardly seemed wrong. That's how things begin. . . . But it ended with three murders."

"Just like this," said Lucy. "We've had three murders now. The woman who impersonated Martine and who would have been able to claim a share for her son, and then Alfred, and then Harold. And now it only leaves two, doesn't it?"

"You mean," said Miss Marple, "there are only Cedric and Emma left?"

"Not Emma. Emma isn't a tall dark man. No. I mean Cedric and Bryan Eastley. I never thought of Bryan because he's fair. He's got a fair moustache and blue eyes, but you see—the other day . . ." She paused.

"Yes, go on," said Miss Marple. "Tell me. Something has upset you very badly, hasn't it?"

"It was when Lady Stoddart-West was going away. She had said good-bye and then suddenly turned to me just as she was getting into the car and asked: 'Who was that tall dark man who was standing on the terrace as I came in?'

"I couldn't imagine who she meant at first, because Cedric was still laid up. So I said, rather puzzled, 'You don't mean Bryan Eastley?' and she said, 'Of course, that's who it was, Squadron Leader Eastley. He was hidden in our loft once in France during the Resistance. I remembered the way he stood, and the set of his shoulders,' and she said, 'I should like to meet him again,' but we couldn't find him."

Miss Marple said nothing, just waited.

"And then," said Lucy, "later I looked at him. . . . He was standing with his back to me and I saw what I ought to have seen before. That even when a man's fair his hair looks dark because he plasters it down with stuff. Bryan's hair is a sort of medium brown, I suppose, but it can *look* dark. So you see, it might have been *Bryan* that your friend saw in the train. It might . . ."

"Yes," said Miss Marple. "I had thought of that."

"I suppose you think of everything!" said Lucy bitterly.

"Well, dear, one has to really."

"But I can't see what Bryan would get out of it. I mean the money would come to Alexander, not to him. I suppose it would make an easier life, they could have a bit more luxury, but he wouldn't be able to tap the capital for his schemes, or anything like that."

"But if anything happened to Alexander before he was twenty-one, then Bryan would get the money as his father and next of kin," Miss Marple pointed out.

Lucy cast a look of horror at her.

"He'd never do *that*. No father would ever do that just —just to get the money."

Miss Marple sighed. "People do, my dear. It's very sad and very terrible, but they do.

"People do very terrible things," went on Miss Marple. "I know a woman who poisoned three of her children just for a little bit of insurance money. And then there was an old woman, quite a nice old woman apparently, who poisoned her son when he came home on leave. Then there was that old Mrs. Stanwich. That case was in the papers. I dare say you read about it. Her daughter died and her son, and then she said she was poisoned herself. There *was* poison in some gruel, but it came out, you know, that she'd put it there herself. She was just planning to poison the last daughter. That wasn't exactly for money. She was jealous of them for being younger than she was and alive, and she was afraid—it's a terrible thing to say but it's true—they would enjoy themselves after she was gone. She'd always kept a very tight hold on the purse strings. Yes, of course she was a little peculiar, as they say, but I never see myself that *that*'s any real excuse. I mean you can be a little peculiar in so many different ways. Sometimes you just go about giving all your possessions away and writing cheques on bank accounts that don't exist, just so as to benefit people. It shows, you see, that behind being peculiar you have quite a nice disposition. But of course if you're peculiar and behind it you have a bad disposition—well, there you are. Now, does that help you at all, my dear Lucy?"

"Does what help me?" asked Lucy bewildered.

"What I've been telling you," said Miss Marple. She added gently, "You mustn't worry, you know. You really mustn't worry. Elspeth McGillicuddy will be here any day now."

"I don't see what that has to do with it."

"No, dear, perhaps not. But *I* think it's important myself."

"I can't help worrying," said Lucy. "You see I've got interested in the family."

"I know, dear, it's very difficult for you because you are quite strongly attracted to both of them, aren't you, in very different ways."

"What do you mean?" said Lucy. Her tone was sharp.

"I was talking about the two sons of the house," said Miss Marple. "Or rather the son and the son-in-law. It's unfortunate that the two more unpleasant members of the family have died and the two more attractive ones are left. I can see that Cedric Crackenthorpe *is* very attractive. He is inclined to make himself out worse than he is and has a provocative way with him."

"He makes me fighting mad sometimes," said Lucy.

"Yes," said Miss Marple, "and you enjoy that, don't you? You're a girl with a lot of spirit and you enjoy a battle. Yes, I can see where that attraction lies. And then Mr. Eastley is a rather plaintive type, rather like an unhappy little boy. That, of course, is attractive, too."

"And one of them's a murderer," said Lucy bitterly, "and it may be either of them. There's nothing to choose between them really. There's Cedric, not caring a bit about his brother Alfred's death or about Harold's. He just sits back looking thoroughly pleased making plans for what he'll do with Rutherford Hall, and he keeps saying that it'll need a lot of money to develop it in the way he wants to do. Of course I know he's the sort of person who exaggerates his own callousness and all that. But that could be a cover, too. I mean everyone says that you're more callous than you really are. But you mightn't be. You might be even more callous than you seem!"

"Dear, dear Lucy, I'm so sorry about all this."

"And then Bryan," went on Lucy. "It's extraordinary, but Bryan really seems to want to live there. He thinks he and Alexander would find it awfully jolly and he's full of schemes."

"He's always full of schemes of one kind or another, isn't he?"

"Yes, I think he is. They all *sound* rather wonderful—

241

but I've got an uneasy feeling that they'd never really work. I mean, they're not practical. The *idea* sounds all right—but I don't think he ever considers the actual working difficulties."

"They are up in the air, so to speak?"

"Yes, in more ways than one. I mean they are usually literally up in the air. They are all air schemes. Perhaps a really good fighter pilot never does quite come down to earth again. . . ."

She added: "And he likes Rutherford Hall so much because it reminds him of the big rambling Victorian house he lived in when he was a child."

"I see," said Miss Marple thoughtfully. "Yes, I see . . ."

Then, with a quick sideways glance at Lucy, she said with a kind of verbal pounce, "But that isn't all of it, is it, dear? There's something else."

"Oh, yes, there's something else. Just something that I didn't realise until just a couple of days ago. Bryan could actually have been on that train."

"On the 4.33 from Paddington?"

"Yes. You see Emma thought she was required to account for *her* movements on 20th December and she went over it all very carefully—a committee meeting in the morning, and then shopping in the afternoon and tea at the Green Shamrock, and then, she said, *she went to meet Bryan at the station*. The train she met was the 4.50 from Paddington, but he could have been on the earlier train and pretended to come by the later one. He told me quite casually that his car had had a biff and was being repaired and so he had to come down by train—an awful bore, he said, he hates trains. He seemed quite natural about it all. . . . It may be quite all right—but I wish, somehow, he hadn't came down by train."

"Actually on the train," said Miss Marple thoughtfully.

"It doesn't really prove anything. The awful thing is all this suspicion. Not to *know*. And perhaps we never shall know!"

"Of course we shall know, dear," said Miss Marple briskly. "I mean—all this isn't going to stop just at this point. The one thing I *do* know about murderers is that they can never let well alone. Or perhaps one should say —ill alone. At any rate," said Miss Marple with finality, "they can't once they've done a second murder. Now don't get too upset, Lucy. The police are doing all they can, and looking after everybody—and the great thing is that Elspeth McGillicuddy will be here very soon now!"

CHAPTER XXVI

"Now, ELSPETH, you're quite clear as to what I want you to do?"

"I'm clear enough," said Mrs. McGillicuddy, "but what I say to you is, Jane, that it seems very *odd*."

"It's not odd at all," said Miss Marple.

"Well, I think so. To arrive at the house and to ask almost immediately whether I can—er—go upstairs."

"It's very cold weather," Miss Marple pointed out, "and after all, you might have eaten something that disagreed with you and—er—have to ask to go upstairs. I mean, these things happen. I remember poor Louisa Felby came to see me once and she had to ask to go upstairs five times during one little half-hour. That," added Miss Marple parenthetically, "was a bad Cornish pasty."

"If you'd just tell me what you're driving at, Jane," said Mrs. McGillicuddy.

"That's just what I don't want to do," said Miss Marple.

"How irritating you are, Jane. First you make me come all the way back to England before I need——"

"I'm sorry about that," said Miss Marple; "but I couldn't do anything else. Someone, you see, may be killed at any moment. Oh, I know they're all on their guard and the police are taking all the precautions they can, but there's always the outside chance that the murderer might be too clever for them. So you see, Elspeth, it was your duty to come back. After all, you and I were brought up to do our duty, weren't we?"

"We certainly were," said Mrs. McGillicuddy, "no laxness in our young days."

"So that's quite all right," said Miss Marple, "and that's the taxi now," she added, as a faint hoot was heard outside the house.

Mrs. McGillicuddy donned her heavy pepper-and-salt coat and Miss Marple wrapped herself up with a good many shawls and scarves. Then the two ladies got into the taxi and were driven to Rutherford Hall.

II

"Who can this be driving up?" Emma asked, looking out of the window, as the taxi swept past it. "I do believe it's Lucy's old aunt."

"What a bore," said Cedric.

He was lying back in a long chair looking at *Country Life* with his feet reposing on the side of the mantelpiece.

"Tell her you're not at home."

"When you say tell her I'm not at home, do you mean that I should go out and *say* so? Or that I should tell Lucy to tell her aunt so?"

"Hadn't thought of that," said Cedric. "I suppose I was thinking of our butler and footman days, if we ever had them. I seem to remember a footman before the war. He had an affair with the kitchen maid and there was a terrific rumpus about it. Isn't there one of those old hags about the place cleaning?"

But at that moment the door was opened by Mrs. Hart, whose afternoon it was for cleaning the brasses, and Miss Marple came in, very fluttery, in a whirl of shawls and scarves, with a tall uncompromising figure behind her.

"I do hope," said Miss Marple, taking Emma's hand, "that we are not intruding. But you see, I'm going home the day after to-morrow, and I couldn't bear not to come over and see you and say good-bye, and thank you again for your goodness to Lucy. Oh, I forgot. May I introduce my friend, Mrs. McGillicuddy, who is staying with me?"

"How d'you do," said Mrs. McGillicuddy, looking at Emma with complete attention and then shifting her gaze to Cedric, who had now risen to his feet. Lucy entered the room at this moment.

"Aunt Jane, I had no idea . . ."

"I had to come and say good-bye to Miss Cracken-thorpe," said Miss Marple, turning to her, "who has been so very, very kind to you, Lucy."

"It's Lucy who's been very kind to us," said Emma.

"Yes, indeed," said Cedric. "We've worked her like a galley slave. Waiting on the sick room, running up and down the stairs, cooking little invalid messes. . . ."

Miss Marple broke in. "I was so very, very sorry to hear of your illness. I do hope you're quite recovered now, Miss Crackenthorpe?"

"Oh, we're quite well again now," said Emma.

"Lucy told me you were all very ill. So dangerous, isn't it, food poisoning? Mushrooms, I understand."

"The cause remains rather mysterious," said Emma.

"Don't you believe it," said Cedric. "I bet you've heard the rumours that are flying round, Miss—er——"

"Marple," said Miss Marple.

"Well, as I say, I bet you've heard the rumours that are flying round. Nothing like arsenic for raising a little flutter in the neighbourhood."

"Cedric," said Emma, "I wish you wouldn't. You know Inspector Craddock said . . ."

"Bah," said Cedric, "everybody knows. Even you've heard something, haven't you?" He turned to Miss Marple and Mrs. McGillicuddy.

"I myself," said Mrs. McGillicuddy, "have only just returned from abroad, the day before yesterday," she added.

"Ah, well, you're not up in our local scandal then," said Cedric. "Arsenic in the curry, that's what it was. Lucy's aunt knows all about it, I bet."

"Well," said Miss Marple, "I did just hear—I mean, it was just a *hint*, but of course I didn't want to embarrass you in any way, Miss Crackenthorpe."

"You must pay no attention to my brother," said Emma. "He just likes making people uncomfortable." She gave him an affectionate smile as she spoke.

The door opened and Mr. Crackenthorpe came in, tapping angrily with his stick.

"Where's tea?" he said, "why isn't tea ready? You! Girl!" he addressed Lucy, "why haven't you brought tea in?"

"It's just ready, Mr. Crackenthorpe. I'm bringing it in now. I was just setting the table ready."

Lucy went out of the room again and Mr. Crackenthorpe was introduced to Miss Marple and Mrs. McGillicuddy.

"Like my meals on time," said Mr. Crackenthorpe. "Punctuality and economy. Those are my watchwords."

"Very necessary, I'm sure," said Miss Marple, "especially in these times with taxation and everything."

Mr. Crackenthorpe snorted. "Taxation! Don't talk to me of those robbers. A miserable pauper—that's what I am. And it's going to get worse, not better. You wait, my boy," he addressed Cedric, "when you get this place ten to one the Socialists will have it off you and turn it into a Welfare Centre or something. *And* take all your income to keep it up with!"

Lucy reappeared with a tea tray, Bryan Eastley followed her carrying a tray of sandwiches, bread and butter and cake.

"What's this? What's this?" Mr. Crackenthorpe inspected the tray. "Frosted cake? We having a party to-day? Nobody told me about it."

A faint flush came into Emma's face.

"Dr. Quimper's coming to tea, Father. It's his birthday to-day and——"

"Birthday?" snorted the old man, "what's he doing with a birthday? Birthdays are only for children. I never count my birthdays and I won't let anyone else celebrate them either."

"Much cheaper," agreed Cedric. "You save the price of candles on your cake."

"That's enough from you, boy," said Mr. Crackenthorpe.

Miss Marple was shaking hands with Bryan Eastley. "I've heard about you, of course," she said, "from Lucy. Dear me, you remind me *so* much of someone I used to know at St. Mary Mead. That's the village where I've lived for so many years, you know. Ronnie Wells, the solicitor's son. Couldn't seem to settle somehow when he

247

went into his father's business. He went out to East Africa and started a series of cargo boats on the lakes out there. Victoria Nyanza, or is it Albert, I mean? Anyway, I'm sorry to say that it wasn't a success, and he lost *all* his capital. Most unfortunate! Not any relation of yours, I suppose? The likeness is so great."

"No," said Bryan, "I don't think I've any relations called Wells."

"He was engaged to a very nice girl," said Miss Marple. "Very sensible. She tried to dissuade him, but he wouldn't listen to her. He was wrong of course. Women have a lot of sense, you know, when it comes to money matters. Not high finance, of course. No woman can hope to understand *that*, my dear father said. But everyday L s.d. —that sort of thing. What a delightful view you have from this window," she added, making her way across and looking out.

Emma joined her.

"Such an expanse of parkland! How picturesque the cattle look against the trees. One would never dream that one was in the middle of a town."

"We're rather an anachronism, I think," said Emma. "If the windows were open now you'd hear far off the noise of the traffic."

"Oh, of course," said Miss Marple, "there's noise everywhere, isn't there? Even in St. Mary Mead. We're now quite close to an airfield, you know, and really the way those jet planes fly over! Most frightening. Two panes in my little greenhouse broken the other day. Going through the sound barrier, or so I understand, though what it means I never have known."

"It's quite simple, really," said Bryan, approaching amiably. "You see, it's like this."

Miss Marple dropped her handbag and Bryan politely

picked it up. At the same moment Mrs. McGillicuddy approached Emma and murmured, in an anguished voice —the anguish was quite genuine since Mrs. McGillicuddy deeply disliked the task which she was now performing:

"I wonder—could I go upstairs for a moment?"

"Of course," said Emma.

"I'll take you," said Lucy.

Lucy and Mrs. McGillicuddy left the room together.

"Very cold, driving to-day," said Miss Marple in a vaguely explanatory manner.

"About the sound barrier," said Bryan, "you see, it's like this . . . Oh, hallo, there's Quimper."

The doctor drove up in his car. He came in rubbing his hands and looking very cold.

"Going to snow," he said, "that's my guess. Hallo, Emma, how are you? Good lord, what's all this?"

"We made you a birthday cake," said Emma. "D'you remember? You told me to-day was your birthday."

"I didn't expect all this," said Quimper. "You know it's years—why, it must be—yes, sixteen years since anyone's remembered my birthday." He looked almost uncomfortably touched.

"Do you know Miss Marple?" Emma introduced him.

"Oh, yes," said Miss Marple, "I met Dr. Quimper here before and he came and saw me when I had a very nasty chill the other day and he was most kind."

"All right again now, I hope?" said the doctor.

Miss Marple assured him that she was quite all right now.

"You haven't been to see *me* lately, Quimper," said Mr. Crackenthorpe. "I might be dying for all the notice you take of me!"

"I don't see you dying yet awhile," said Dr. Quimper.

"I don't mean to," said Mr. Crackenthorpe. "Come on, let's have tea. What're we waiting for?"

"Oh, please," said Miss Marple, "don't wait for my friend. She would be most upset if you did."

They sat down and started tea. Miss Marple accepted a piece of bread and butter first, and then went on to a sandwich.

"Are they——?" She hesitated.

"Fish," said Bryan. "I helped make 'em."

Mr. Crackenthorpe gave a cackle of laughter.

"Poisoned fishpaste," he said. "That's what they are. Eat 'em at your peril."

"Please, Father!"

"You've got to be careful what you eat in this house," said Mr. Crackenthorpe to Miss Marple. "Two of my sons have been murdered like flies. Who's doing it—that's what I want to know."

"Don't let him put you off," said Cedric, handing the plate once more to Miss Marple. "A touch of arsenic improves the complexion, they say, so long as you don't have too much."

"Eat one yourself, boy," said old Mr. Crackenthorpe.

"Want me to be official taster?" said Cedric. "Here goes."

He took a sandwich and put it whole into his mouth. Miss Marple gave a gentle, ladylike little laugh and took a sandwich. She took a bite, and said:

"I do think it's so brave of you all to make these jokes. Yes, really, I think it's very brave indeed. I do admire bravery so much."

She gave a sudden gasp and began to choke. "A fish bone," she gasped out, "in my throat."

Quimper rose quickly. He went across to her, moved her backwards towards the window and told her to open her mouth. He pulled out a case from his pocket, selecting some forceps from it. With quick professional skill he peered down the old lady's throat. At that moment the door opened and Mrs. McGillicuddy followed by Lucy, came in. Mrs. McGillicuddy gave a sudden gasp as her eyes fell on the tableau in front of her, Miss Marple leaning back and the doctor holding her throat and tilting up her head.

"But that's *him*," cried Mrs. McGillicuddy. "That's the man in the train. . . ."

With incredible swiftness Miss Marple slipped from the doctor's grasp and came towards her friend.

"I *thought* you'd recognise him, Elspeth!" she said. "No. Don't say another word." She turned triumphantly round to Dr. Quimper. "You didn't know, did you, Doctor, when you strangled that woman in the train, that somebody *actually saw you do it*? It was my friend here. Mrs. McGillicuddy. She *saw* you. Do you understand? *Saw you with her own eyes*. She was in another train that was running parallel with yours."

"What the hell?" Dr. Quimper made a quick step towards Mrs. McGillicuddy but again, swiftly, Miss Marple was between him and her.

"Yes," said Miss Marple. "She saw you, and *she recognises you*, and she'll swear to it in court. It's not often, I believe," went on Miss Marple in her gentle plaintive voice, "that anyone actually sees a murder committed. It's usually circumstantial evidence of course. But in this case the conditions were very unusual. There was actually *an eye witness to murder*."

"You devilish old hag," said Dr. Quimper. He lunged forward at Miss Marple but this time it was Cedric who caught him by the shoulder.

"So *you*'re the murdering devil, are you?" said Cedric

as he swung him round. "I never liked you and I always thought you were a wrong 'un, but lord knows, I never suspected you."

Bryan Eastley came quickly to Cedric's assistance. Inspector Craddock and Inspector Bacon entered the room from the farther door.

"Dr. Quimper," said Bacon, "I must caution you that . . ."

"You can take your caution to hell," said Dr. Quimper. "Do you think anyone's going to believe what a couple of batty old women say? Who's ever heard of all this rigmarole about a train!"

Miss Marple said: "Elspeth McGillicuddy reported the murder to the police at once on the 20th of December and gave a description of the man."

Dr. Quimper gave a sudden heave of the shoulders. "If ever a man had the devil's own luck," said Dr. Quimper.

"But——" said Mrs. McGillicuddy.

"Be quiet, Elspeth," said Miss Marple.

"Why should I want to murder a perfectly strange woman?" said Dr. Quimper.

"She wasn't a strange woman," said Inspector Craddock. "*She was your wife.*"

CHAPTER XXVII

"So you see," said Miss Marple, "it really turned out to be, as I began to suspect, very, very simple. The simplest kind of crime. So many men seem to murder their wives."

Mrs. McGillicuddy looked at Miss Marple and Inspector Craddock. "I'd be obliged," she said, "if you'd put me a little more up to date."

"He saw a chance, you see," said Miss Marple, "of marrying a rich wife, Emma Crackenthorpe. Only he couldn't marry her because he had a wife already. They'd been separated for years but she wouldn't divorce him. That fitted in very well with what Inspector Craddock told me of this girl who called herself Anna Stravinska. *She* had an English husband, so she told one of her friends, and it was also said she was a very devout Catholic. Dr. Quimper couldn't risk marrying Emma bigamously, so he decided, being a very ruthless and cold-blooded man, that he would get rid of his wife. The idea of murdering her in the train and later putting her body in the sarcophagus in the barn was really rather a clever one. He meant it to tie up, you see, with the Crackenthorpe family. Before that he'd written a letter to Emma which purported to be from the girl Martine whom Edmund Crackenthorpe had talked of marrying. Emma had told Dr. Quimper all about her brother, you see. Then, when the moment arose he encouraged her to go to the police with the story.

He wanted the dead woman identified as Martine. I think he may have heard that inquiries were being made by the Paris police about Anna Stravinska, and so he arranged to have a postcard come from her from Jamaica.

"It was easy for him to arrange to meet his wife in London, to tell her that he hoped to be reconciled with her and that he would like her to come down and 'meet his family.' We won't talk about the next part of it, which is very unpleasant to think about. Of course he was a greedy man. When he thought about taxation, and how much it cuts into income, he began thinking that it would be nice to have a good deal more capital. Perhaps he'd already thought of that before he decided to murder his wife. Anyway, he started spreading rumours that someone was trying to poison old Mr. Crackenthorpe so as to get the ground prepared, and then he ended by administering arsenic to the family. Not too much, of course, for he didn't want old Mr. Crackenthorpe to die."

"But I still don't see how he managed," said Craddock. "He wasn't in the house when the curry was being prepared."

"Oh, but there wasn't any arsenic in the curry *then*," said Miss Marple. "He added it to the curry afterwards when he took it away to be tested. He probably put the arsenic in the cocktail jug earlier. Then, of course, it was quite easy for him, in his role of medical attendant, to poison off Alfred Crackenthorpe and also to send the tablets to Harold in London, having safeguarded himself by telling Harold that he wouldn't need any more tablets. Everything he did was bold and audacious and cruel and greedy, and I am really very, very sorry," finished Miss Marple, looking as fierce as a fluffy old lady can look, "that they have abolished capital punishment because

I do feel that if there is anyone who ought to hang, it's Dr. Quimper."

"Hear, hear," said Inspector Craddock.

"It occurred to me, you know," continued Miss Marple, "that even if you only see anybody from the back view, so to speak, nevertheless a back view *is* characteristic. I thought that if Elspeth were to see Dr. Quimper in exactly the same position as she'd seen the man in the train in, that is, with his back to her, bent over a woman whom he was holding by the throat, then I was almost sure she would recognise him, or would make some kind of startled exclamation. That is why I had to lay my little plan with Lucy's kind assistance."

"I must say," said Mrs. McGillicuddy, "it gave me quite a turn. I said, ' That's him ' before I could stop myself. And yet, you know, I hadn't actually seen the man's face and——"

"I was terribly afraid that you were going to say so, Elspeth," said Miss Marple.

"I was," said Mrs. McGillicuddy. "I was going to say that of course I hadn't seen his *face*."

"That," said Miss Marple, "would have been *quite fatal!* You see, dear, he thought you really *did* recognise him. I mean, *he* couldn't know that you hadn't seen his face."

"A good thing I held my tongue then," said Mrs. McGillicuddy.

"I wasn't going to let you say another word," said Miss Marple.

Craddock laughed suddenly. "You two!" he said. "You're a marvellous pair. What next, Miss Marple? What's the happy ending? What happens to poor Emma Crackenthorpe, for instance?"

"She'll get over the doctor, of course," said Miss Marple, "and I dare say if her father were to die—and I don't think he's quite so robust as he thinks he is—that she'd go on a cruise or perhaps to stay abroad like Geraldine Webb, and I dare say something might come of it. A *nicer* man than Dr. Quimper, I hope."

"What about Lucy Eyelesbarrow? Wedding bells there too?"

"Perhaps," said Miss Marple, "I shouldn't wonder."

"Which of 'em is she going to choose?" said Dermot Craddock.

"Don't you know?" said Miss Marple.

"No, I don't," said Craddock. "Do you?"

"Oh, yes, I think so," said Miss Marple.

And she twinkled at him.

THE END